Sarah Rose

A Novel

Cateenna Davis

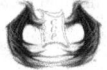

Cat's Corner Publications, LLC
http://www.catscornerpublications.com

Sarah Rose from the mind of Cateenna Davis.

Published by Arrived, an imprint of Cat's Corner Publications
Fort Lauderdale, Florida
Copyright © 2011 by Cateenna Davis
Cover Design by Cat's Corner Publications
Illustrations by Elton Davis
All Rights Reserved

Note: This is work of fiction. Names, characters, places, and incidents either are the product of the author's imagination or are used fictitiously, and any resemblance to actual persons, living or dead, business establishments, events, or locales is entirely coincidental.

ISBN: (10) 0-615-53644-1
ISBN Print: (13) 978-0-615-53644-6
Manufactured in the USA

Dedications

To my husband, Elton Davis Sr.,
To my sons and daughter, Roosevelt Hood Jr.,
Elton Davis Jr., and Denise Davis,
I love you all.

Acknowledgements

Gratias ad virum, Elton Davis, eius ideas et fortitude.
Thanks to my husband, Elton Davis, for his ideas and fortitude.

Introduction

I had eaten, drank, danced, and married the devil. I never knew life could be so complicated and full of strife. I lost my mama and soon after, I would lose Papa—not to mention myself....

So that you understand, let me start from the beginning....

Sarah Rose

Event 001.00

Pa was tall and slender, he had deep-set brown eyes, and jet-black hair with skin to match. His temperament was even and calm, that is before Ma died. There were great days before then. Papa would take us into town for a movie and ice cream sodas.

We would drive into town on a Friday—it was always the busiest night of the week. Folks would come from out of town to find side work. Most of the people around were sharecroppers; at least what was left of us and at harvesting time would need help before winter set in.

"All right, tonight we do the movie house and then the soda shop. That last crop gave us a bit of extra cash," Papa said, as he pulled his coat from the rack.

The ice cream soda was my favorite part of the night. I remember I would get to have candy sprinkles in mine. Papa and Mama would sip from the same glass racing to the last drop—funny how Mama would always win. Papa blamed his loss on the ice cream giving him brain freeze and at the end, he would suddenly forget how to sip a straw. I thought it was corny, but Mama loved it, and if it made her happy, then Papa was happy too.

"Let's go to the picture show first, Pa!" I yelled, pulling from Mama and running over to see if he would agree.

"Sarah Lambert, I ain't done yet, come back here gal!" Ma was standing in the middle of the hall with her hands on her hips waiting for me to return.

"Sorry Mama," I said with my head down and a mischievous grin on my face. I had altogether forgotten she was combing my hair.

"Sarah, don't go gettin' yo' ma upset tonight," Papa was behind us tickling her waist. "That way she can deal with the likes of me all weekend."

We lived on a small farm in Wauwatosa, Wisconsin. We didn't own any livestock, except for a few chickens and a pig I begged Papa for when I was a little girl. When he grew larger than me, Pa said I had to make a pen to keep it in. After a while, I would only go out to feed him and nothing more. One-winter, things were tough harvesting time didn't do well— needless-to-say...we had to eat.

Our house was nothing fancy, Papa and Mama had put there all into it. It only had two small bedrooms, a living area, and a small kitchen area. My bedroom over looked the backyard. That way I could look out and see the forest. Papa and Mama's room was across the hall—it overlooked the fields. Papa said it gave him reason to step outside on those cold fall and winter days. Mama liked the fact she could watch the sun setting when she did the ironing in the evening. Plus, it eased her mind when Papa was out there on really cold days trying to save the winter crops.

Mama was the product of a long line of Great-Grand-Mothers ancestry being, "belly warmers"—as they called them—for the slave master. She was a short slim woman, smooth light brown skin, light brown wavy hair, in which she always kept cut short. Her eyes were as wide as the blue skies—on a count of they were blue—and boyy a black woman with blue eyes, that sure was a sight to see. The other women in town hated her for it. They would always throw themselves at Papa to get under her skin. Of course, Papa threw back.

I was like Mama, slim, but tall like Papa, with the color of my skin being somewhere in between. My eyes aren't blue or brown, but a deep pitch black and wide like Mamas.

I recall some folks in town telling Ma it was un-natural for a child to have eyes like coal and that I would be nothing but trouble. She never paid any mind to them or replied to the comments they made about me.

"Sarah," she would say. *"When people say things they know nothing about or are afraid of, they tend*

to say mean and nasty things. You pay them no mind and keep right on walking."

Mama was like that, always trying to keep the peace. Papa hated when she allowed people walk over her like that. Again, I came somewhere in between.

I would stick my tongue out at the old bitches when they had something stupid to say. If Mama wasn't around, I'd like to pretend I was putting spells on them by throwing dirt in their paths. Once, while tossing dirt, I hadn't realized I'd wished aloud for ol' Miss Bea to drop dead.

Funny how things have a way of working out, later that afternoon I heard she'd died in the market— no one ever found out what killed her. After that, I stopped wishing when I threw dirt.

Mama had been murdered one winter night, when our old rust bucket of a car broke down. A white man told her he would take her into town to get help— she never made it. The sheriff would soon after find the man that had taken her into the forest and left her there to die. He had beaten and raped her. No one knows why he carved the words, *nigga bitch reject,* into her back.

To this day, no one can say if he meant blacks rejected her or what—we know how whites felt about her. They felt the same way about all the blacks—at least the ones that didn't work for them.

Most of them hated us and wished we weren't there. However, the number of those that hated us was dying fast, as times were changing and so was the number of blacks moving into the small town.

The day Pa received the news about Ma's killing he went crazy. He ran through town cussing, screaming, and damning everyone in his path. It took the entire sheriff's department to get him to calm down. He was never the same after that.

On the day of Mama's funeral, he was dirty and reeking of booze, he hadn't bathed since hearing of Mama's death. He sat quiet at the back of the church. Family tried to comfort him, but he'd just pushed them away with groans, grunts, and sinister looks.

"What's wrong wit'em," a fat woman asked, speaking in a low whisper and dabbing sweat from her upper lip. "What's to happen to the girl?"

"His wife been killed in an ungodly way and you askin' such a fool headed question! Her pa will see after her, they be all right I 'spose. 'Sides, I wouldn't want the likes of that gal 'round me. You evea see a child with eyes as black as coal? I hear she had somethin' to do with old lady Bea dyin' and all. Goin' around throwin' dirt at folk's feet. It ain't right." The lesser fat woman said, watching Sarah as family and friends passed by giving their condolences.

What could I do about their whispers and gossip? Nothing, but remember what Mama told me about people talking about what they know nothing about. Since Papa wasn't paying any attention to anything or anyone around him, I gave the old farts the finger.

Pa left the church with the rest of the procession

leading the way to the burial site, but he was gone before they put Mama's body in the ground.

After the last guest had left, I went to see how Pa was doing. He was in his room drinking another bottle of the moonshine he had purchased on the day of the news. He refused to spend time with family and friends that had shown up to pay their respects. Most had stopped by to drop off food—those that had chosen to stay were only there to eat.

"Papa," I called out, walking down the hall and peeking into his room. I could see him sitting on the edge of the bed with his head down and barely holding the liquor bottle. He didn't answer when I first called. On the third call, he answered with a sound of disgust.

"What the hell ya calling me fo', gal? I wanna be alone," he shouted, throwing his empty bottle in my direction.

Startled, I jumped back and slowly closed the door. There I was left standing abandoned with thousands of feelings and thoughts running fast through my mind.

What will I do now? I was alone.

Event 002.00

One morning unexpected Papa called me out of bed—he sounded mad. In a daze with my heart pounding louder and faster than I can ever remember, I grabbed my housecoat and ran to see what he wanted.

"Yes sir," I replied, clearing my eyes and trying to keep my body from shaking.

"Sarah, come here and sit on my lap," Papa had a distant look in his eyes. I was glad to see him out of his room. However, as I would soon find out, I would have been happier if he had died in his sleep.

I walked slowly over to him and sat on his lap. His breath smelled of old stale booze. He was sweating as if someone had poured a bucket of water on him. There was a change in his voice, it was slow and distant, as if he was thinking out loud and not talking to anyone directly. Plenty about him had changed since Ma died, and it was making me feel very nervous.

I tried calming my own anxieties by asking him if he were ill. He just sat there...watching me—it felt more as if he was looking through me. I tried comforting him by putting my arms around him—really, it was more to comfort myself. That's when he pushed me off his lap, with full force. I fell to the floor in shock. My eyes began to fill with tears. It was then I realized with the look in his eyes and the forceful push from his lap, that my life was about to change. I just had no idea how.

Quickly getting up, I ran to my room slamming the door behind me.

What's happening to him? What's going to happen to me? I thought leaning against the door terrified and listening to him yell my name.

"Sarah," he screamed. "Sarah, come back here… Come here right now!" He was angry and yelling like a mad man. I heard him barreling down the corridor. That's when I ran into my closet to hide. Then, I heard the sound of my bedroom door being kicked in. I held my breath, placed my hands over my mouth to stifle my screams, and closed my eyes as tightly as I could. All the while my heart was pounding for a way out of my now uncontrollable quivering body.

"Come here Sarah!"

This wasn't the man I knew or wanted to. I opened my eyes and took a few deep breaths. Then, getting up from my corner and still trembling, I stepped out. Before I had the chance to set my bearings, he grabbed me by the hair and pulled me to the bed.

As he stood over me I watched him. I had never seen such hate in his eyes—his face didn't even look the same. He appeared old, tattered, and more wrinkled than I remembered. He was unshaven and reeking of stale liquor and must—the stench leaking from every pore of his being reminded me of the dead fish in the creek after it dried up.

He watched me for a moment and then suddenly, I knew.

I tried rolling over to get away, but he was fast. He grabbed me, punching me in the face and stomach. Between his punches, I yelled for him to stop, but he just kept going. Then, there was a hard punch to my face—which prompted me to give up my struggle. He pulled my housecoat and gown off climbing on top of me.

"Papa, please don't...whatcha doin'? Please...no." Tears ran down my face—like rain from stormy skies. I found the strength to fight again.

As I yelled for him to stop, I was kicking and biting, hitting and scratching at every part of his body my limbs could reach. At one point I scratched him in his face so hard I could see the blood dripping down his cheek. It must have hurt because for a moment he stopped. He watched me, holding his face.

Then, with his hand high he punched me once again—this time in the nose. It felt like he had taken a knife and stabbed me in the face. Feeling the warm fluid running down my cheek, I once more stopped fighting. I laid there crying—with no sound—waiting for the whole thing to be over.

He watched me for a moment, maybe waiting to see if I'd finished fighting.

"Why ya doin' this?" I asked in tears, my voice trembling. Saying nothing he pulled me to him, ripping off my panties. He licked his fingers before sticking them inside me. I fought, wiggling and twisting trying to break free, but he was too strong.

Papa kissed my breast and stomach, moving up to kiss me on the mouth. The smell of stale booze, cigarettes, old sweat, and mustiness made me want to vomit. I found myself thinking of my mama.

Is this what you felt when Hawkins beat and raped you?

I pleaded again with him to stop—I was his daughter—but he heard nothing. My cries went unanswered and my pleas echoed— fading into the night.

That's when it happened. Papa did the unthinkable. He plunged his manhood into me fast, hard, and deep. The pain was more than I could bear—I yelled out in agony—but he just kept going. The taste of whiskey on his lips made me turn my head. I yelled out to him. "Pa you're hurtin' me," he paid no mine and continued.

For what seemed like hours I lay there crying hoping he would stop. He pounded me hard and fast never stopping. I yelled out as loudly as I could for my mama. "MOMMYY," and at that moment, he stopped. And, for a swift second, I thought I had seen my pa again. That's when he rolled off.

I quickly moved to the edge of the bed and curled up at the corner. Finally, he was done and so was I.

Feeling life leaving my body and my sole quickly behind it, I swore no man would ever do this to me again, unless I had say over it.

Afraid and outraged and through gritted teeth I swore, *all men would pay for what this one man has done.*

Laying there on the bed in silence I made a deal with the devil. *Make me strong and I will do whatever it takes to stay alive*— My devout petition would be cut short.

"Now that yo' fool Mama gone and got herself killed, you gonna do what she use to. Ya hear what I say gal? And if'n ya evea tell anyone, you'll join her," he said, with his back to me, "Now, get your ass up and fix my supper!" He continued, turning to kicked me from the corner of the bed.

When he left my room I got up from the floor, gathered some things to dress with, and went into the bathroom to shower and change. I wasn't able to cry at that point, my body numbed—frozen by what he had done. The water was scolding hot, but it didn't burn.

The wallpaper Mama and I put up had faded to a dirty brownish yellow, it was tethered and peeling away from the wall. I stood watching it and longing for the days when things were good.

With that thought, I wanted to kill him, but I was weak. I was bleeding and in the worst pain.

After sitting for what may have been hours, I stepped out of the tub and watched myself in the mirror. I could see myself growing dark, harsh, and forbidding—I was growing cold inside. I could feel the room spinning out of control, but I remained motionless. The lighting turned a crimson red.

As the room continued to spin, I could see an image in the mirror other than my own. I tried to focus on it, but I was unable to make it out. Then, I heard a voice whisper to me, "I have heard you child, wait for me," I closed my eyes, lifted my head towards the ceiling, and took a deep breath. The room was warm and for a moment, I felt as if my mama was holding me tightly in her arms.

When I opened them, all was back to normal. I stood there for a moment waiting to see what would happen next—nothing did.

Finally, I dressed and went into the room where Pa was. Giving the matter of the bathroom no more thought and not feeling scared about the whole thing.

I tried to walk past him with as little noise as possible, but he opened his eyes and grabbed my wrist. I gasped in fear, shacking so hard he must have thought I was trying to break free, because his grip tightened.

"Don't chu fo'get gal, if'n ya evea mention this to anyone you'll join yo' fool mama. Ya hear me gal?" He spoke in a low tone, head down, and eyes pointed upward.

"Yes sir," I replied, pulling away with little effort. I walked quickly to the kitchen. I had to get his supper. I was good at making chicken stew, so I hurried as fast as I could to get it ready—leaving out a few items.

When I was finished, I went into the living room where Pa was laying. He was there on the couch sound asleep. I stood there for a moment with the tray in hand, not very sure of what to do with it. I thought to wake him, but that was the last thing I wanted to do.

I saw a rat run across the floor and thought of the rat poison, but it didn't work on the rats. I figured it wouldn't work on the biggest rat of them all. I left the tray on the table and covered it. I went back into the kitchen to get it cleaned up.

There I stood looking around, thinking how happy Ma was here. Remembering the day the men came with her new stove and fridge.

"Mama, there's men at the door. They come in a big truck," I yelled.

"Let them in, Sarah, it's the men from the appliance store with my new things, let them in chil'," Mama yelled back to me from the kitchen.

She was so happy because she was able to talk the storeowner into giving her the stuff on a credit.

They only did those kinds of things for white folks. Mama had to pay more than the whites did as well. Pa didn't like the idea and thought we shouldn't get it. Mama convinced him to say yes anyway.

"All this yelling back and forth these people goin' think somethin' is wrong wit' us." Pa yelled coming out of the bedroom.

The men worked fast to get the kitchen together. Ma offered them to a glass of water. They drank quickly and headed out.

Ma was so happy. I remember she couldn't wait to get it set up properly. She and Papa went to work right away with the painting and hanging of the flower printed wallpaper. They worked long into the night getting it finished.

The next morning, the paint and glue had dried

enough for Ma to hang the laced curtains her aunt in Mississippi had sent for her birthday. The space was bright and beautiful when she was done.

My thought was interrupted when Pa woke up, yelling for me to come warm his plate. I was so scared. I moved as fast as I could trying not to upset him.

When I entered the front room, he was staring out the window holding a booze bottle in one hand and a glass in the other. I quickly picked up the tray I had brought him about an hour before and went into the kitchen.

As I waited for the food to warm, I thought I would look out to see if Pa was still there. He wasn't. That's when I caught a glimpse of his shadow and knew he had moved out to the front porch.

When the food had finished cooking, I put it on the tray and rushed to the porch with it. I hadn't noticed him coming back in. I ran into him spilling food all over his shirt. My heart raced and I could feel the sweat pooling up on my forehead, as I slowly lifted my head to look into his eyes.

"I'm...I'm sorry...I didn't see ya. I'll clean it up and get ya somethin' else right away." I trembled with every word.

"Damn girl, what the hell is wrong wit' chu? Watch where the fuck ya goin'...I'll bet ya was hopin' to burn me...or maybe ya was tryna do with food whatchu been out there doin' wit' dirt. Well it's gon' take mo' den some hot food or dirt to do the trick. Ya don't think I knew what folks sayin' 'bout cha...? I hear people talkin' 'bout chu goin' around throwin' dirt at their feet." he yelled.

I wanted so badly to tell him. *You bet your fucking ass I do. I want chu dead more than anythin' in this livin' world!* But, I knew a bit of hot food wasn't going to do the trick.

While I was cleaning the mess and trying not to look up. Pa reached down and grabbed me up by the hair. Pulling me into the kitchen and yelling for me to fix him something else.

As he walked back into the other room, he was yelling and cursing how much trouble I was since Ma was gone.

Right then, I needed her badly and I wondered if she could really hear my cries. Then, I figured there was no way she could, because she wouldn't stand for this.

When the food finished I went to serve him. He sat and ate in peace, while I scrubbed the floor from the plate of stew I dropped earlier.

While on my knees, I lifted my head to look outside. The farm was nothing like it had been when Ma was alive. I found myself nostalgic for the moment's Ma and I shared. Wishing for her to be here to explain to me why Pa suddenly hated me. Did he blame me for her death?

The man I once knew as my pa was gone—seems he died when Mama died—and with all that, it would be that I had too.

Sarah Rose

Event 003.00

One year after Mama was found dead, Pa decided to threw out all the stuff that belonged to her. He said it was too much for him to bear. I was able to save a few things. A silver hand mirror, a few photos, a string of beads she had handmade—knowing Pa would remember them and take them from me. I often wore them when I was alone.

I stood in my window holding the mirror and wearing the beads. Gazing out over the field where I use to play and would come home muddy from playing in the creek—that at that time was slowly drying up. It was different looking. The world was different. I was different.

As I was changing for bed, I heard Pa speaking in the other room. I pulled my pants back up and stepped out to see if I could see anyone. It was the man from the bank. He had been coming around quite often lately to see if Pa had the money he owed them. Pa always told him the same thing, 'next week.' This time, they were not willing to wait.

A truck was outside ready to take whatever would equal the debt owed.

Suddenly, I heard the door slam and Pa went to cursing and throwing things. I decided to slip out my bedroom window before he came after me. I wasn't sure of where I was going and I didn't care—just as long as I got away from there.

Ma had told me to start saving my money, so one day I would be able to get something nice for myself. But, Pa found most of it. I still had a few cents left in the floor of my closet. Just enough for an ice cream soda.

The road that led into town was long and it hadn't been rocked over yet. The dirt was hard under my feet and I could hear night animals rustling in the woods.

As I made my way to the soda shop, I saw the sons of the man that had been accused of killing my mama. I wasn't sure if I should run or just stand my ground. I hadn't seen hide nor hair of them since Mama's death—almost four years ago. There I stood, watching them as they walked closer, seeming not to realize who I was in the shadows. But, when they reached me simultaneously they all paused—as if someone had flipped a switch to turn them off. They stood staring at me, as if they had seen my ma's very own ghost.

"It's her," one of the boys said in an audible whisper, while pointing at me. We all stood there not saying a word—just staring at each other. At that moment, I couldn't help but notice all the lightning bugs dancing around them. It was as if they were trying to light up their faces so I could get a good look...and I did.

"Yesss child, remember all that have wronged you. Never forget...," said the echoing voice, as the glow of the flies turned a crimson red.

"I won't forget...I'll never forget," I replied silently to no one.

I waited for them to say something. Then suddenly, the echoing voice, the lightning bugs red glow, and my anger were interrupted by the voice of a woman coming towards us.

"You boys move from here, gon' with your business," she said as she stepped between us, then she turned to me. "You all right girly, they hurt chu?"

It was the woman who owned the store that didn't have anything in the windows—just big red velvet curtains. Mama said I was never allowed in there and that I was to never speak to the women working there.

As I remember it, people were always coming and going, men mostly. It seemed all the women had bright red lips, sheer rosy cheeks, fancy dresses, and high heels. There would be cigarettes hanging from their lips and they would smell of the finest perfumes.

"Girl, I asked you a question, you deaf or somethin'?" She asked, taking a puff of her cigarette.

"No...No Ma'am, I ain't hurt." I said still consumed by her beauty. She had come closer and leaned her head to the side as if to get a better look at me, then she said.

"You're the Lamberts girl ain't chu? Sorry to hear about your mama."

"Yes Ma'am," I replied holding my head down.

"You know," she said turning me by the shoulders and leading me to the place with nothing in the windows, but big red velvet curtains and opening the door for me to go inside. "Your mama was a good woman to me and my family. She was the only woman in town that would sale her baked goods to me. I see your Pa around from time to time, he don't stop here though—at least not anymore. I s'pose it's to be expected after what has happened and all. How old Grady doin' anyway, he all right?" she asked, as she pulled off her shawl and laid it on a table next to the door.

"Yes Ma'am…he all right I guess," I replied, with the corner of my mouth turned up. I wanted to say. *"Hell naw he ain't all right! He done gone and lost his fucking mind! He fucking and beating me. Open yo' eyes heffa, take a look at my face."* Instead, I just said, *"he was all right."*

My heart sank after that. Trying to change the subject, I blurted out. "My mama always told me to never speak to you or come inside this place." It was a desperate attempt to ignore the fact she had even allowed Papa cross my mind. I'm not sure if she noticed the spite in my tone and the curl on my upper lip. Then again, she may have because she leaned her head to the side and gave me a half grin.

"You hongry? I got some cookies upstairs—I hide them for special guests. You wait right here and I'll be right back," she went up a flight of stairs and disappeared around the corner.

I was still standing at the front door so, I moved in to have a look around. The place had lots of couches, tables, and chairs. Not at all what I expected. The first room was spacious—nothing fancy though—a large chandelier hung from the ceiling with low lighting. There were a few pictures on the walls, the staircase started in the middle of the room—it narrowed in as it reached the top landing. Thick heavy red velvet curtains divided some of the rooms into private areas. There were lots of half empty glasses everywhere and used cigarettes in the ashtrays.

I could hear laughter coming from behind one of the drapes—which separated me from the noise. Without any thought, I pulled back the curtain to see what was so funny.

"Holy shit gal, what the hell ya think ya doin'?" Yelled the woman, sitting in the lap of a man, who lost his smile when he noticed me.

The woman was in nothing but her underwear and the man had his pants around his ankles. When I realized what I was witnessing I gasped and pulled the curtain back shut. I could feel my face turn as red as a beet.

"Ohh, sorry." I said, as my heart filled my throat, and my blood pumped fast.

"Savannah! Savannah? What's this young gal doing in here wandering around like she owns the joint," the woman yelled pulling back the curtain and almost knocking me over to pass. "She walked right in on Busta and me. What's she doing in here anyway? When you start lettin' kids in here to run about as they please?"

The woman was yelling as she was going up the stairs, pulling up her clothes, and watching me at the same time. I just stood in the corner waiting to see what would happen next.

"Lucinda, why in hell are ya yelling like that? The child meant no harm. Did ya honey?" Savannah asked looking at me and giving me a wink from the top of the stairs.

"No Ma'am. I said I was sorry. It won't happen again. I was just having a look around. I didn't mean to hurt nobody," I replied, watching the woman who seemed like she had on too much make up. Her dress seemed two sizes too small, but that didn't stop her from squeezing herself into it.

All the while she was watching me, I was watching her as Savannah led me into the kitchen.

The walls were old with chipped paint. There were two wood planks holding up the oven door. The fridge seemed to be the only decent thing there. The cupboards were old and falling off their hinges, things were neat though. The table had a mix match of chairs around it. In the middle of the table sat a candle still smoking—it appeared as though the flame may have just gone out.

"Oh chil', don't chu mind ol' Lue. She full of hot air, but she do mean well," Savannah said and sat in a seat next to me, taking herself a cookie, and then passed one to me. I looked up to see the mad woman leaning against the doorway with her hand on her hip and a cigar hanging from her lips.

"This nappy headed little bitch gonna pay my tricks

bill? He done run out ya know," she asked eyeing me.

At the thought of her calling me a bitch, I squinted my eyes in disgust.

"Lue, I'll pay ya later and there ain't no need to be calling this gal no bitch, now gon' and leave us be. He'll be back anyway. You know Butsa always lookin' for a reason to get back to ya. Now gon' and leave us be." Savannah said laughing at the thought of a half-naked man running from her place. She turned back to Sarah with a bright smile. "Now that ya seem to know my name, I don't think I know yours. Your mama told me she had a little girl, might 'a told me ya name, but I can't seem to recall."

"Sarah," I said, as I took a big bite from the cookie. It reminded me of the cookies Mama used to bake. I hadn't realized how hungry I was, I ate fast and grabbed more from the plate.

"Well, Sarah, I'm Savannah, Savannah Fulsome. Most folks 'round here call me Vann, you might as well too."

I couldn't stop thinking about how pretty she was. She had a hole in her face when she smiled. When she walked, she seemed to be dancing, and her dress was her partner. Her dark cocoa brown skin blanketed her voluptuous curves, her eyes were a light shade of brown, and her hair was long and jet-black with spiral curls that hung past her shoulders.

"I like Savannah better then Vann...did you know my mama long?" I asked, shoveling cookies in my mouth as fast as I could and noticing how they muffled my voice.

"No. She use to come in from time to time to sale me

her baked goods. Then she'd be on her way. I think she came in mostly to see if yo' daddy was here. You finish ya cookies and get on back home, it's too dark for such a young gal to be roaming the streets like you doin'. Business should be starting up for this ol' gal soon. Those boys should be long gone by now. You come back and see me now," she said, as she led me to the first door on the side of the kitchen. It wasn't the way I'd come in.

"Okay, thanks for the cookies. I'll see ya 'round," as I was leaving, a man came in the door. He wasn't very good looking, a bit on the fat side, with nappy uncombed hair, and a beard that hadn't filled in on all sides. His eyes were dark and deep-set, the whites' were blood shot—like he'd been awake for days. Actually, the old man was downright ugly.

"Why hello, Sam, long time no see and why you comin' in this door," she took him by the arm and spoke to me as she led him to the staircase. "You run along home now, Sarah. Savannahs got work to do," She gave me a wink and turned to the short, round, somewhat fat man standing before her.

"You gettin'em kind of young, Vann ain't chu?" He asked laughing as they both ascended the stairs, then she turned to me for one last look before disappearing around the corner.

"You ol' fool, Sam, she don't work here. Her mama saw to that…too bad though, she would have been a spicy one."

Looking on for a moment at the empty staircase, Savannah wondered what happened to Sarah's face and thinking about what she had said. Her heart saddened. Then, she closed the door behind them.

"Bye Savannah, thanks again," I yelled, and then pulled the door closed behind me.

I gave the area a once over before stepping off the stoop. Those boys may have still been around, but I didn't want to stand around and find out. I ran over to the soda shop to get my ice cream soda. I took a seat at one of the window tables and watched folks walk by. I watched the other kids in the shop slurp and suck their sodas.

I could hear some of them asking one another what happened to me. Some gave their own version of what they thought happened and others just shrugged their shoulders.

My attention was totally taken over by a boy standing near the counter. I guessed he was trying to figure out what soda he wanted. He was medium build, very tall, black hair, his skin a sort of walnut color, and he had dark brown eyes. I hadn't remembered seeing him around before. I was so taken in by him, I didn't realize I was pouring soda into my lap. When I did feel the cold liquid dripping down my leg, I jumped up so fast I hit the table—over it went, then into the couple sitting at the table in front of me. The glass I was holding fell to the floor—shattering. I stood there in the middle of it all—feeling my face turn as red as a beet.

While I was bending over to pick up the mess, I could hear the storekeeper yelling. "Look at what you have done to my store, gal! Are you crazy or something?" He was coming towards me with his arms flailing wildly above his head and a pale in one hand. I had a flashback of Papa doing the same thing. I stood to my feet for a moment and then ran out the door.

As I ran down the street, I could hear him yelling for me to return and clean up my mess. What an idiot I must have seemed like to the boy standing at the counter. And, what an idiot I felt like to myself. Besides, it didn't matter much anyway. I'm sure I must have looked awful—Pa saw to that.

Event 004.00

Arriving back home it was later than I thought—the clock read half past nine. Papa was in the kitchen I could hear him pulling things out of the pantry. I tried to get to my room without him noticing me, but it was no use.

"Sarah, that you—you little shit—get in here. Where the hell ya been? I been calling you for hours," Papa was drunk and loud, as he had been for many months now. He was coming from the kitchen stumbling over himself. "I asked, where ya been ya little shit? You think you can come and go as ya please?"

"No sir," I replied, trying to think fast and keep from shaking out of my pants. "I was in my room sleepin' I...I didn't hear ya." I stood before him shaking and feeling weak in the knees. Papa had that sinister look in his eyes—one I had seen many times before. At that moment, I'd wished I'd drop dead. Then, with a mighty blast of his fist, he struck me in the head—I suppose it was for answering his question—I fell to the floor.

For a few seconds I'd lost my senses. There was nothing there—nothing at all. The room went black then came back again. I tried to stand, but my feeble legs would not allow it.

I tried focusing my eyes to see where Pa was and then I felt it again. Papa had hit me with the object he held in his hand. I couldn't see what it was—it all happened so fast. I fell back to the floor. I could feel the warm liquid running down the side of my face—it dripped to the floor—and for a split second, I felt misty for the touch of his warm hugs and not the backs of his hands.

Pa kicked me and my stomach felt as if it had been set ablaze. I rolled over to my side and tried to get under the table—He was yelling and cursing how he wished I were dead. Going on about how it was my fault Mama was dead and how I should join her—Pa pushed over the table and came towards me. He put his hand around my neck and began to squeeze. As I gasped for air, I grabbed hold of his arms and tried pulling them apart. Unable to do so, I reached for a pair of scissors that lay on the floor next to me. With all my might, I stabbed Papa in the arm. He jumped off yelling in pain.

He done it…he finally done it…I knew the day would come…but he failed. I thought to myself.

"We hear you child…Waait."

I tried to see who was speaking, but I was weak, tired, and breathless. All I could do was allow my body to give into its distress.

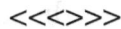

When I woke, I was still in the living room lying in

my own blood. For a moment, I had forgotten what happened and then bit by bit, it all came back like rewinding a bad flick.

Slowly I stood to my feet. The room was spinning and everything within eyesight needed work on making it clear.

Papa was in his chair passed out. I noticed his lame attempt to bandage his arm.

I wished I had stabbed him in that thing he called a heart.

The images of him trying to take my life kept playing over and over in my dizzy mind.

I sat on the floor watching him, building up the courage to go over and kill him where he sat. It was in me—I could feel it fueling like hot fire—and I wanted to do it, but I couldn't muster the strength.

Just then, as plain as the days are clear, I heard it again—while the room turned a crimson red. "Waait my child...his time is not near...Waait."

Just give me the strength. I pleaded silently, but the voice said nothing else.

Weak, exhausted, and in pain I rose up unsteadily and made my way to the bathroom and into the mirror. Some of the blood had dried up and stuck to my hair and face. I turned on the shower then closed the door. Not one moment wondering if Pa would be in—maybe at that moment not caring.

The water was hot and soothing to my aching and battered body. As I stood there with my head hanging down, I had hoped the running waters would take me with it wherever it went when it left here.

After several minutes of watching crimson waters

run from my body, the water began to clear. I pulled back the curtain and much to my surprise, Pa was standing there. I gasped while reaching for the bath towel. Pa grabbed me and pulled me into the bedroom pushing me to the bed. I was in no mood to fight with him this time. My body ached and my head pounded.

This time was different—I allowed him to do what he wanted to me. I was in too much pain to fight back and to numb to care.

Maybe it had much to do with the blows I took to my head—maybe I am getting use to him—perhaps I was enjoying it. No matter how I tried to analyze it, I just lay there. I had no more fight left in me that night.

I watched him—never taking my eyes off—often squinting to get a better look. I lay there still and stiff waiting for him to finish. I could see him eyeing me from time to time. I think he might have been wondering why I was no longer fighting or perhaps waiting for me to do something. Either way he didn't care, he just kept going.

My anger and disgust boiled silently within. And at one point, he stopped and watched me—and I watched him. I thought I had seen a glimpse of my pa again, but just as quickly as the image came, it was gone—he continued.

When he was finished, I got up and put on my clothes. Pa went to his room and closed the door. I then closed mine.

I walked over to the window; I could now see the moon. The night was clear—it seemed that all the stars were out.

The tears I had held filled the wells of my eyes, and then fell slowly down my cheek—almost motionless. My heart was now heavier than ever before. With the loneliness and the hate building every second, I thought again of Mama.

As I stood there gazing at the night sky, in my head I cried out to her hoping somehow she would hear me.

Ma, I need cha. I need cha so bad—I'm losing my mind—my childhood too. Mama what can I do to stop him? I'm not the same girl I was befo' you was killed. Mama can ya hear me? Ma can you see me? The more I spoke, the more my heart broke, the colder I grew.

Slowly I think I began to lose touch with reality. I was feeling like a marionette—and Pa—he was my manipulator...doing as he pleased.

Moving away from the window and drying my eyes. I curled up on my bed with the box of things that once belonged to Mama. Remembering how she used to brush my hair and put her favorite bows and clips in.

Something changed in me that night—I felt that shameful frightened little girl drift away—while hatred and anger took its rightful place.

The moonlight shining through my window glowed a crimson red, and then I heard it again. "Waait... you're not ready, his time will come. Build on this, his time will come. Build on this. Learn from it. Waait...his time will come child, waait...."

I slept with those words dancing in my head.

Sarah Rose

Event 005.00

The next morning I awoke in so much pain, every part of my being was aching. I listened to the still air, trying to hear any indication of Pa, but he was gone.

I found the strength to get started on cleaning up the mess from the night before. As I did so, every item I picked up or stood upright replayed that small moment in time and the reason for the objects obscurity.

My stomach was bruised where Pa decided to rear-range my insides. It hurt like hell when I bent over and my head throbbed with each heartbeat. I hated him; I hated him with all my soul.

"I hate chu, ya hear me ya rat bastard!? I hate you!" I cried aloud.

As my head pounded, I sat thinking of ways to get rid of him. Maybe a little poison in his drink. I could fix his brakes and hope the same thing would happen to him that happened to Mama. The longer I sat there—in the middle of the floor—the more sanity drained from my sweating skin. I could feel my blood start to boil. I wanted him dead. I wanted it done in the worst way imagined by man. At that moment, I didn't care how it happened.

Consumed with anger, I waited for him to come home. Would this anger stay with me until he was dead or would the very sight of him bring me cowering to my knees like a helpless child?

Tears flooded the wells of my eyes once more. Was all my anger in vain? I hadn't the heart to do what my brain and soul were telling me to do. So I gave up on the idea and decided to go for a walk, not sure of where I was going just as long as it wasn't here.

The ground was wet from the morning dew. I could see my breath in the wind as I breathed. The trees were losing their colorful leaves—winter was setting in.

I went into the woods to see if there was anything new that would interest me.

The old creek that ran down the middle of the woods was dried up. I could see all the garbage folks had thrown in over the years. As I reached the edge of the woods, I thought I had better start heading back.

Up ahead I could see a figure standing perfectly still behind a large tree. At first, I was afraid and thought I should turn around and go the long way. After all this is the place Hawkins brought my mama.

I stood hidden under the thicket of the forests canopy, at least until I could see the figure up close.

It was the boy from the soda shop. He had on a bright orange suit and a camouflaged hat. I ran fast to duck behind a closer tree and watch him. He was eyeing a deer nearby, he stood very quiet and as still as he possibly could. The woods were damp and the moss from the tree made me sneeze. The deer must have heard me because it ran off.

"Who's there?" The boy yelled trying to peer through the trees.

What was I going to do? I didn't want him to know I was there.

"Who's out there? Show yourself," I think he was more scared then I was. Slowly I stepped out from the spot that held me grounded.

"Sorry you lost ya deer. I tried not to sneeze," I said eyeing his rifle and not planning to take my eyes off it—simply because he had it pointed right at me. "Mind, yo' gun, you're still aiming it at me."

"Yeah right, my apologize," he pushed the weapon behind him as if he was trying to hide it.

"You know, ya ought not to point that thang at people, you could shoot someone's face off," I said. He was more gorgeous then I remembered him being in the soda shop the night before.

"Like I said Miss—my apologize—I'm Tobias George Scott, most people call me Toby. What's yours?" His voice was strong yet gentle, not what I was used to hearing. In this small town to hear a strong voice meant you had done something wrong and were about to pay.

"Sarah Lambert...you ain't from 'round here, are ya, Tobias?" The sound of his name on my lips felt like a kiss of wind on a crisp fall afternoon—and the way my lips puckered forming the perfect O—I was lost in him—and he noticed.

"You sho' you all right?" he asked with his eyebrows

twisted, probably wondering why I was looking so half-baked at him, he stood for a moment watching me. I wanted to melt into the woods with the rest of the dead foliage.

"Sho' I'm fine, 'sides you nevea answered me, you from 'round here?" I asked trying to take back control of my emotions.

"Nope...not really anyway, born here though. My real Ma sold me to some folks passin' through, or so I was told. I'm from New York," he was not like the other boys around here, not that I knew much about the other boys. I wanted to know about him though, as much as I could.

"I was born and raised here," I said, letting him know I was not a traveler like him. Then I realized I must look like death warmed over. I had forgotten about the bruises on my face. I shied away hiding my face before I knew it. "I...I have to go!" Without waiting for him to say another word, I ran into the tall trees, not taking the path. He called for me, but now I was ashamed. I ran until I was out of breath and sure he wasn't following me, only coming to rest at an opening where the forest meets the road.

Dropping to my knees, I held my head in my hands and cried. I was caught by surprise when a voice called out to me from the road.

"Sarah? That you girl, whatcha doin on the ground, are you cryin' child?" It was Savannah. I tried to dry my eyes as quickly as I could.

"No Ma'am I got some dirt in my eyes when I was picking wild berries," I walked over to where she had stopped her car and wondered what was with folks and all their questions.

"What in God's name happened to you," she jumped from her car and ran to me. Putting her shawl around my arms and guiding me into the car. Then she sprinted back to the driver's side. Shouting words that were inaudible to me until she opened the door. "What happened to you? Who did this to your face? I bet it was those Hawkins boys?"

"No," I said snappily and quick. "I…I…fell from the loft in the barn and landed on some piles of old wire and stuff!" I don't know if she believed me or not, but she could never know what really happened.

"Sarah you sure are one clumsy child. I suppose the bruises that were healing when we first met were from a fall as well," she said, rolling her eyes back to the road. "If you don't tell me what happened how can I help you?"

"Who says I need yo help? I ain't asked nobody for no help!" I was on the defense by then. She couldn't find out, she just couldn't. "It's almost noon I'm guessin'. Ya mind driving me home? I live just up the road a bit?"

"Sure," she said not at all convinced by what I had said. "I meant no harm chil', I suppose I was bein' a little too nosey." Savannah put the car in gear and drove slowly up the old dirt road that led to my house.

She hadn't said another word, but I could tell she wanted to. She had that same look on her face my ma used to when she had something to say and didn't want to make any one angry. Maybe all women had this look from time to time.

I didn't want Papa to see me with her, "stop here and I can walk the rest." I demanded.

"I can take you to the door and make sure you get in okay and all."

"No," I yelled. "I have to walk the rest of the way—look...I ain't supposed to be talkin' to you anyway! So just let me out here like I ask!" I pulled the door open, that's when Savannah grabbed me by the arm and slammed on the breaks.

"Gal, I understand how you must be feelin', but don't go jumpin' out no movin' car," she said stunned with eyes wide open. "Look-a-here, if you evea need anyone...and we all do...you come see me, my door will always be open." She smiled a sweet smile and rubbed my cheek. I pushed her hand away, got out of the car not making comment for her feelings of concern and walked quickly to the house.

Savannah sat for a moment watching Sarah walk quickly up the road, while flashbacks of her past ran through her mind. Savannah remembered her father beating her when she didn't bring home enough money to supply his habit of opium and moonshine.

She continued watching as Sarah walked into the house and wondered had old Grady been up to no good.

As Savannah sat—wondering—she pulled a long drag from her cigarette. She could feel Sarah's hurt in the pit of her stomach.

What in God's name is going on in that house?

Event 006.00

Pa was in the living room playing his records and drinking himself into a crazed stupor. He hadn't seen me come in or at least he pretended not to—at this point I was glad either way.

I went into the kitchen, fixed myself a sandwich, and went to my room. I stayed up all night thinking of the words that Savannah had said. Why the sudden interest in me? She had never said anything to me before the day the Hawkins boys cornered me in town. Why did Papa and Mama never want me to speak to her? She seemed kind enough, I was finding out I didn't know much about anything. I was growing up fast and all sorts of doors were opening. Some I wished would have stayed shut.

Morning came and I got up to see if Pa was still home. I really hoped he wasn't. However, he was, and still in the same spot I left him in last night. There were moonshine bottles all around him. As he slept, I fixed breakfast.

I had accidentally dropped the eggs on the floor—need I say...that getting them up was the hard part—what I did next took no effort at all. I decided since I was adding a little spice to his life, I may as well add more of me.

I lifted my dress, placed the pot of grits between my legs, and took a much needed morning piss in them. Then I thought, why stop there. I placed a few rat droppings in with the sausages, after all, you are what you eat—and Lord knows that man had become a shitty rat bastard.

Being careful not to awaken him, I stood over him with the tray in hand and wondered what he dreamt about—or if he dreamt at all. The person he has become, what could he be dreaming of? The more I stood there, the more I thought a man like him must have been dreaming of something evil. Even in his sleep, he appeared cold and hard.

This would have been the perfect time to kill him, pour moonshine on him, light a match, and set his evil ass ablaze, "burn mothafucka burn," I said silently to myself, as I pictured it with my head tilted sideways, and feeling a smile ran across my face.

I sat the tray down and decided that what I had done in the kitchen would have to be good enough—for now.

This morning I wasn't going to wait around for his malicious ass to wake from his drunken coma. I quickly dressed and thought I would go out to the edge of the woods.

It was a beautiful morning, the skies were as blue

as the ocean, and the clouds were huge like pillows. I took notice of wild berries growing on a vine—they seemed to summon for me to pick them, so I willing-ly obliged.

When I reached my destination, it seemed different from yesterday. The trees taller, the leaves greener, even the dead foliage seemed to be alive and I won-dered if it had anything to do with Tobias. I won-dered if he would be here today.

I had been out for some time, so I thought I would get ready to head back and start my chores before it got too late. Papa should be up and off to work by now, or gone to get more moonshine—the old fuck drank more than anything else now-a-days.

I was startled by the sound of a voice behind me.

"Hey, I thought I saw you. How are you?" It was Tobias. For a moment, I just stood there. I couldn't believe he was here.

"Holy Shit," I yelled, "what the hell ya doin' comin' up behind me like that? I damn near jumped outta my skin!"

"Sorry," he said smiling.

"You should be," I replied, trying to sound bold and unafraid.

"Whatcha doin' out here? You come out here often?" He asked.

"I just like to walk—and why you ask so many questions?

"I'm sorry it's not polite to ask someone you hard-ly know so many questions," his voice was kind and soft, his eyes just as caring.

"It's okay I s'pose. How come ya always out here

hunting...? Ain't hardly nothing left out here to hunt. I ain't even sure it's legal for you to be out here shooting at wild animals."

"It's about all there is to do in such a small town, besides coming from a big city this is something new for me and I like it—even if I don't catch anything."

"Seems like a waste of time to me if you ain't catchin' nothin'."

By this time, I allowed myself to relax and let the conversation flow, as not to scare him off. For a short time, we both just stood there, not saying anything to each other. He was looking one way and me the other.

I managed to swat a few bugs away from my face. While, he played with his riffle pretending to fix what wasn't broken. The situation was beginning to feel awkward. I had no idea what to say, but before I could think of anything.

"Sarah," he said.

"Yeah," I replied swinging myself around to get a better listen.

"You mind if I ask you a question? A personal question?"

My heart pounded. "No...I guess not." No one ever asked me a personal question before—not sure what that really meant either.

"What happened to your face?"

Shit...the one thing I hadn't thought about. What did he think happened to it? Why did he want to know? Was it that bad? What was I going to say? All these questions shot through my mind like pellets from a sawed-off shotgun shooting through the air, and I just stood there—frozen.

"Sarah…you okay?"

"Yeah…fine…what was it you asked me?" Knowing perfectly well what he had asked. Somewhat hoping he really hadn't asked me that.

"Your face, what happened to it?" He asked again, watching my bruises one by one.

"It's like I said befo'…you sho' ask loads of questions not to have known a person long…I gotta go." I replied and pushed past him.

I walked fast—a few paces short of trotting—to the path leading back to the road. Looking back only when I got to the end—halfheartedly hoping he had followed.

I couldn't tell him what happened. For a few minutes, I sat at the edge of the road where the path ended until I was able to catch my breath. I watched the clouds go by and the birds singing in the trees and I wondered what life was like for other girls my age.

After I'd rested, I got up and started home.

Event 007.00

Savannah you all right? You been mighty silent since ya come in last night." It was one of Savannah's girls in the kitchen when she walked in.

"I'm all right, just got somethin' on my mind is all. What you doin' down here? I thought you had a late night." She asked, lighting a cigarette and tossing the lighter on the table and watching it slide onto the floor.

"I just couldn't sleep, I got somethin' on my mind too...somethin' I been meanin' to talk to ya 'bout," the young girl picked up the lighter before sitting in the seat across from her. "I got somethin to tell ya, but I don't wantchu to get upset."

Savannah could see worry in her eyes and a slight shiver as the feathers on her gown moved on her shoulders. "Just come out and say it gal. It cain't be all that bad...less'n ya kill somebody." Savannah said winking at her and taking a long drag from her cigarette.

"No nothing like that...I'm...oh there ain't no easy way to say it is there?"

"I wouldn't know, you ain't said nothin' yet. Now on

with it chil' I got thangs to do."

"I'm…I'm with child," the young girl blurted out.

"WHAT!" Savannah said, choking on the smoke coming from her lips. "I thought I told you before you started working…," she said between smoke filled coughs. "…that I was not gonna allow any woman to stay here and raise a child…you a child yo' self. What the hell you supposin' I'm to do 'bout this?" Savannah put out the cigarette she had in her hand, went over to the cabinets, and pulled out a bottle of whisky and two glasses.

"I'm woman enough fo' ya to let me work here, now suddenly ya know my age. 'Sides it be only one man I laid wit' and not worry 'bout anythin' 'cause he say he cain't have babies." The young girl said with her head held high—as if trying to impress her.

"He say *he* can't *have* babies! He didn't say nothing 'bout he can't *make'em*, you foolish gal! I told chu to watch out for them slick talkers, they will tell you anything. Damn gal," she replied, while yelling at the teary-eyed young girl. "I told you ladies never let these men tell ya want they cain't do. Ya young, and these men see this and they'll tell you anything to get what they want. Why go and spoil everything for yourself by letting some man ruin your life. I toldcha to come to me when these men tell ya what you can and cain't do. I'm the only one to tell ya what you can and cain't do. This my place and ya work for me not them. Lawd have mercy chil'…what we gon' do now?" Savannah poured the whisky while the young girl held her face in her hands crying.

"I can't go home…, my ma find out she'll… Help me

Savannah. This why I come to ya." The young girl was on her knees begging for help.

Savannah watched her for a moment, then held out her hand and took the young girl's. "This be your last time, Eva. I stuck my neck out fo' ya when you come want'n work and not telling yo Ma then. This be the last time, it happin' again you on your own, ya hear?" Savannah took a swig of the whiskey from her glass. Remembering that she too was once young and in need of help and had no one to turn to.

"Clean ya face and have some whisky. First thangs first, we got to get chu to the docs, find out how far you are. You gotta get rid of it...if it ain't to late already. You cain't tell no one gal. I mean no one. You gotta take this wit'chu to the grave. People will look down on you—as if they don't already. They will drive you out of town. Not only are you a whore, but you will be a baby killer too. They don't understand people like us, you cain't 'spect them to eitha." Savannah was nervously rearranging the salt and pepper shakers on the tabletop. All the while thinking of her own experience.

Savannah listened, and watched the young girl as she talked, sipping on her whisky. She wondered how she could allow a young girl like this into a world of sex, booze, lies, and most of all loneliness.

"Savannah, you got a date!" It was Lucinda calling from the front room.

"I'll be right there. Take whoever it is into the parlor." She never took her eyes off the young girl. She pulled her from her seat and led her to the stairs.

"You go and rest now. Thangs be fine in the mornin'.

I'm giving you the rest of the day to ya' self. Gon' now." Savannah watched her as she walked slowly and despairingly out of sight.

"Savannah?" The man in the parlor called out. She turned slowly with her head held down and walked into the room.

The man was sitting in the shadows. She didn't like the sound in his voice, and all she could make out was his silhouette and the smell of his cheap cigar. She moved in closer to get a better look.

"Who are ya and why ya hidin'? Come out so's I can see ya. Ain't in no mood for guessin' games. Whatcha come here fo'? Come on out and let's get this over wit'." Savannah was turning to let herself out of the room when the man stepped out from the shadow.

"Hello old gal, been a long time since you and me seen each other ain't it?" Grady said, as he came from the shadows. Savannah turned back around apprehensive at the sound of his voice—her heart racing. She stood in shock for a moment, watching him. His eyes were dark and cold. His face had hardened and he had many more wrinkles then she had remembered. His hair was a dirty shade of salt and pepper.

Grady managed a smile, yet something was missing from it. "You still look beautiful old girl, just like you did twenty years ago." He said with a smile, as his cigar bounced up and down on his lips with every word.

"What in the hell you doin here? I told you to never

step foot in here again. Whatch'a doin here?" Her voice was hard and face curled as she took a few steps back.

"I come 'cause it be time to pay up," Grady said with a cold voice, while watching her with a sinister smile.

"Pay up? You gone and get outta here. I don't owe you nothin', Grady Lambert. I got nothin' you need or want," she was trying to think of a way to get him out without causing a scene. "Look, Grady, you got no business here, now please go." Her tone had a slight worry in it.

"Now look-a-here. You owe me and I come to collect." He took a step toward her. He moved so fast she thought for sure he was about to grab her. She could smell the old booze on his breath and it seemed to her he hadn't bathed in years.

"You cain't refuse me woman, you owe me and now it's time to pay!" He threw the glass he held in his hand to the ground. Savannah let out a small yell.

"Fine...damn it...fine I'll give ya whatchu think I owe, then you...gotta get the hell out!" She said with a tremble in her voice and remembering what it was he had helped her with so many years ago.

"It's Sarah," he said.

Savannahs eyes widened. She knew Grady was the girls' father, but what did she have to do with that. She pulled the parlor doors closed and pulled up a chair far away from the old man. She lit a cigarette, puffed long and hard, and then asked.

"What about her?"

"I know she been in here." He said with a spark of

deviance in his voice.

"She never step foot in here—"

"Don't lie whore! I've seen her leave here!" He shouted, although he hadn't seen anything, nor did he know for sure. At this point, all he could do was fish for something to use, and it worked.

"All right...she been here. Some boys were givin' her a hard time so I let her in until they left. That's all." She couldn't stop shaking.

"She know whatchu do here?" Grady sat back down and hid in the shadows again only his silhouette visible in the afternoon light.

"I don't know, Grady. She yo' gal. You ought to know that one."

"Did she see anythin' while she was here?" Savannah remembered her walking in on Lucinda and Busta.

"No...no one was here when she come. Whatchu gettin' at, Grady I got things to do?" Savannah's heart was beating so fast and hard she thought for sure old Grady could hear it.

Grady took a long pause before he found the words he was looking for, and just as cold as he looked, his words were more. "I want chu to take her. I sold the farm and got no use fo' her now. I'm gettin' outta this town and I don't got no plans on takin' her wit' me. I could just leave her in the streets. At least here, she can work and make her own way. I done showed her the way of life and she been fixed, so she good and ready fo' whatevea. She obeys as good as a well-trained field mule." Grady said, as he put out his cigar on the bottom of his shoe and took a cigarette from the holder in the middle of the table.

"Me! You want me to take her? What in the hell am I s'pose to do wit' her? This look like an orphanage to you? It ain't no halfway house either! This here is my business! I cain't take her, Grady! No...no ya gotta find someone else! And, whatchu mean you done fixed her? Them bruises in that chil's face..., it was you was'n it?" Savannah sat forward in her seat, "Grady, whatchu done gone and did to dat gal—"

"Look-a-here bitch, I'm doin all the talkin' right now and I ain't askin' ya I'm tellin' ya. You gone take her, you owe me or have you forgot?" He said interrupting her and leaning forward for her to get a better look at his face in the light.

"It has been so long now," she said reflecting back to the day he was referring to.

"A debt never too old to be paid back. When the white folks wanted to hang ya for havin' sto'keeps kid—a nigga with a white man's chil'. I was the one to hide ya—against what my dead wife wanted— ya know that really hurt her when I helped chu, a whore. I even helped ya sale ya boy to them folks that was passin' through, but that's what a man in-love do for a woman after all!"

"That may be true...and had I known yo' kinda love had a price. I would have nevea let ya do it." Savannah turned her head in shame, and let all the memories of that dreadful day come to surface.

"Hang that nigga whore and her baby!" An angry

white man yelled from the crowd. People from all over the town had come to see me hang that morning. I was accused of sleeping with the towns grocery store keep.

He told me when he'd come in one night that it would never get out he was coming to the house to see me.

Like so many of the white men in town did. He became a regular—every Friday and Saturday night. He wouldn't see any of the other girls.

He became more controlling as time went on, soon ordering me not to see any of the other men in town. Some of the men had been talking about us in the bars and this made him angry.

When I finally told him about the baby, he told me he would tell everyone, I just wanted to get back at him for not coming to the house and bring me any of the white business.

One night we fought—he beat me bad. Sam was here that night and heard the whole thing. He went after him and killed him. I figured if I told the sheriff I did it. I would get off easier than him. A black man killing a white man meant a hanging without a trial for sure. That's when Grady came in to help—but at a cost. I had to let Grady come to the house once a week and have any girl he wanted, but he always wanted me.

Grady had some kind of pull with the sheriff, so he went to talk with him and got me off. That's when I had to move the girls from the middle of town to the edge.

After the baby was born, Grady helped me sale him

to a couple passing through town. Last I heard, he was up north somewhere. I often wonder what happened to him and is he all right. What does he look like now? I have no regrets though this would have been no life for him.

"You hear me woman?" Grady was standing in front of her. "You hear what I'm sain' to you?"

Savannah was stunned at the fact he was standing in front of her. She had been so deep in thought she never saw him coming.

"Yeah…I hear ya, Grady. Why here though? This no place for her, ya know the kinds of men that come in here," Savannah reached around him to get herself a cigarette. Grady was taken aback for a moment, as her breast brushed lightly against the side of his leg.

"Well she gon' be yo' problem now. I didn't ask you how I was supposed to help you, did I? So now you figure out how ya gonna do it." Grady was standing inches from her face with a dead look in his eyes.

Savannahs heart raced and her legs shook, as she stood to her feet. "You're crazy, gon' now and get outta here!" Savannah tried to move out of his way, but he stood in front of her.

"You do like I say…or I'll help the past catch up to ya. You know what I mean don'tcha?"

"All right…all right…I'll do it. Now get the hell out of here and nevea comeback ya hear me, nevea comeback!" Grady watched her as she stood with her head down, and then turned placing his hat atop of his head and walked out.

With tears in her eyes, she slammed the door and went to her room without a word to anyone standing by.

Alone, she cried in silence. With anger consuming her every pore, she pushed her vanity to the floor.

Event 008.00

Papa was out late tonight, which was all right with me. I was putting out the trash when he pulled up. I tried to hide in the shadows hoping he wouldn't see me—but it failed. Papa had eyes like a hawk. I wondered if all evil people did.

I could see he was boozed up and I wondered for a moment if he had a woman with him. He hated when the women would see me.

"Get in here gal. I got somethin' to tell ya," The sound of his voice calling to me always made me jump and made my skin crawl. "Sarah, getcho ass in here, now!"

I walked into the house and saw him sitting in the chair next to the window—as he had done so many times before. This time was different though. I wasn't sure why, but I knew I wasn't going to like it.

"I'm leaving this place gal, ain't nothing here fo' me now since yo' mama gone. I done fixed it so you can go stay wit' the woman at the edge of town in the whorehouse. The bank done took the fuckin' farm and most of the farming equipment, I got nothin' left, I got to get out. I'm sho' I fixed ya good fo' ya to be able to support yo'self. This it gal I'm leaving on a train tonight."

All the while Pa spoke, all I could do was think of the one word I heard clearly—'whorehouse'—*Now I know I am not the brightest in the bunch, but I think this disgusting ass man just told me I was to be a whore for the rest of my life.*

"Whatcha talkin' 'bout?" I asked, afraid of him leaving, but more afraid of him staying.

"Don't be questionin' me 'bout what I do. If I say you goin', then ya goin'. If I say you ain't, you ain't, nothing else to be said 'bout it," Pa got up and walked to the kitchen to get a bottle of booze. "Get to ya room… I'm comin' in to give ya a good fair well."

Thinking to myself I said, *What the hell! This man a damn fool if he think I'm gonna just let him lay me down one last time.* "No!" I said aloud, without thinking of the forthcoming consequence of my outright defiance.

He turned to me and our eyes locked on each other.

"What was that? What was that I heard you say gal?" He asked, as he took a step towards me.

With my eyes wide open, I took a deep breath and allowed my shoulders to rise up, and I said it again. "No!" At that moment, I thought to myself as I was taking two steps back. *You think you gonna walk out and not give me my chance to kill ya.*

"Getcho skinny…little nappy headed ass in the room!" He yelled throwing his booze bottle at me.

"No!" I yelled, ducking from the bottle, as it shattered beside me.

Before I could finish my sentence, his fist came

down like a bolt of lightning. I fell to the floor grabbing my face. I crawled back up against the wall. He came barreling toward me. I tried to punch him, but missed—although one of my kicks landed in his groin. As he bent over in pain I turned to crawl away, but I wasn't fast enough. He pulled me by the hair and punched me in the face. I swung with all my might, but my punches would go out in vain—and I hit nothing but wind.

Blow after blow Papa beat me. With every blow I could feel my life slipping away.

I managed to break free. I ran to the kitchen and grabbed a knife from the table.

"Whatchu gon' do with that? Ya wanna kill me? Well come on ya little bitch try and get me!" Pa was laughing and edging me on.

I ran to him with the knife in my hand. I swung at him—but missed. He tripped me getting hold of the knife and holding it to my throat. "This whatchu thought you was gon' do to me? This whatcha wanna do? Well I'm gon' sho' ya, you little bitch getcho ass up," he dragged me into the bedroom by my hair kicking and screaming. He used the knife to cut off my clothes. Papa turned me over.

"Now ya done ask fo' it and I'ma give it to ya," He said in low snarling growl.

He managed to get his body between my legs as I twisted and squirmed to break free. I fought with him, but he was powerful and I wasn't able to wrangle him off.

He smashed my face into the mattress so hard I wasn't able to catch my breath. I must have passed out for a moment because when I came to, it was only to the sounds of my own screams as I felt him thrust his thing into my backside.

I screamed in pain—it felt as if he had taken the knife and ripped my backside open a new. He lay on my back thrusting his body in and out of me.

I was only able to take in small breaths through a tiny hole where I managed to get my hand between the mattress and my face.

I lay there as still and as stiff as I possibly could, I could feel the anger growing within me.

The pain I was feeling suddenly stopped—the room went crimson red. Through my tears I was able to see the figure I thought I had seen in the bathroom a few days before. I called out to it in a whisper. "Help me," the figure seemed to step out of the shadows with its arms out stretched. The room grew cold, suddenly Pa spoke.

"This what will happen to whores that think they can outsmart a man!"

I barely heard the words he said to me as I watched the figure come closer, then shoot right past us into the ceiling. Then I heard the voice say. "Wait...not yet...his time is near...Waait."

"Noo...," I yelled, with tears flowing fast and harder now. That's when I realized Pa was no longer on top of me, but standing bedside, pulling up his pants.

"You a real woman now," he said, and walked out.

Event 009.00

I wasn't sure if I was supposed to be relieved or scared. I heard the door slam when he left. I lay there bleeding and in pain.

I didn't have to worry about Papa coming to me in the middle of the night anymore.

I was angry, so many questions and not one answer—his last demoralizing act.

How could he do this to me? How could my ma have died and left me here to face a life of nothing but hurt and pain. I said I would always have the last laugh—I'm far from laughing.

I was pissed as hell and at the breaking point of insanity. More importantly thought, why had the figure not helped me, what was I waiting for?

Damn him. "You hear me Pa? Damn you! Damn you to the hell you belong in!" I shouted to the man that was no longer there.

He never taught me anything about living—showed me even less. Alone and scared of what was going to happen to me, I ran through the house pushing things over and pulling things from the walls. I stopped in front of a picture of the two of us at the lake when I was no more than about three years old. We were sitting on a blanket at the edge of the creek, surrounded by wild flowers. Mama must have been the one taking the picture, because she wasn't in this one. The sun was high in the sky and Papa smiled the biggest smile I ever remembered seeing. I was sitting in his lap with a cookie in my hand.

At the thought of how happy I must have been then, I ripped the picture from its frame throwing it into the fire burning in the fireplace. He had defeated me once again and now I felt I was going insane.

"Wait child...he'll get his," The voice I had been hearing for some time now said.

"What the hell am I waiting fo'? I waited...now the bastard is gone. What the hell am I waitin' fo'?" I yelled back to no one. Still there was no answer.

I sat in silence for a while longer and then I went to the cabinet where Papa kept his booze. There was one bottle left. I slowly removed it.

For the first time in my life, I wanted a taste and I wanted it badly. The wells of my eyes filled once more and all I wanted was for this life to be over.

My hands shook as I slowly removed the cap. I brought the bottle slow to my mouth, the smell of it made me gag—but I quickly got over it.

I choked on the first taste—it burned my throat and set my chest ablaze as it went down. The booze ran down the corner of my mouth and down my neck. The more I drank the harder and faster my tears came.

My second taste turned into my first gulp. It wasn't

so bad this time. Holding the bottle high, I slid down the wall to finish my taste and I drank until I was out of breath.

The room was spinning and with my head heavy I got up off the floor, I noticed I'd stopped crying—I can't remember when—I just knew that I had.

I could see the night sky from where I was standing. It was beautiful, more beautiful than I ever seen it before. I thought of Mama and how we would sit outside and count the stars and sometimes she would take me for walks up the road. "That's what I need, to go for a walk—a long walk up the road." I said aloud.

I put on my coat and collected the last bit of booze I could muster up. Not sure of which way to go, I stood in the middle of the road and spun myself around. Whatever direction I stopped, that would be the way I'd go.

"Looks like I go this way. Goood...I'll be needin' more of this whisky." I gathered myself and stumbled on—unaware the path I left behind shined a bright crimson.

Event 010.00

"Savannah? You okay in there what was that noise, open this doe and let me in?" Shouted Lue, with Eva racing close behind her. "Chil' go cross the way to the saloon and get Busta, he'll know what to do! Run now, hurry!"

"What I tell'em?" She yelled from the bottom of the stairs

"Just tell'em Savannah need'em. Gon' chil' hurry!" She yelled back, waving her arms for Eva to go on.

"Van, open this doe now! Van?"

The door slowly opened creakily and Lucinda pushed it the rest of the way to get a better look. All that illuminated the room was the light from the street post outside. Lucinda could see the vanity that was thrown to the floor. She could also make out Savannah's figure standing in the darkness.

"Van, you alone," Lue asked in a whisper.

"Naw," she replied sarcastically.

"Who else is here?" Lue asked, waiting for the person that wasn't there to answer.

"You are! Now get out and leave me be!"

"You the one open the doe fo' me, what's goin' on?" Lue asked, not daring to leave her friend alone.

"I opened the doe so's you could getcho eyes full and leave. Not for you to stand there like a scared chil' asking me questions. Now go." Savannah was frigid and annulled. Lucinda had never seen her like this before.

In the meantime Eva had her hands full trying to reach Busta.

"Busta Busta! Come quick, it's Savannah, she need you." Eva was pulling at his arm.

"Wait a minute now! What y'all do over yanda is y'alls doin'. I got nuttin' to do wit' what go on over there." He turned back to his whisky.

"But Lue send me to get—"

"Lue..., she all right?" Busta jumped from his seat like a fire was set beneath him. They both ran across the street to the whorehouse. Busta could see Lucinda standing outside Savannah's room.

"What's going on...you ladies all right?" Busta's concerns were only about one lady. He hadn't taken time to see what Lucinda was staring at.

"We fine, Busta. Sorry to bring ya over like this..., but we just fine now. Savannah just dropped something is all. The door was jammed and I thought she was in trouble. Sorry to bring ya here like this. Come on now let's leave her be. Seeing's you already here, how 'bouts me and you have us some fun?" Lucinda led him away from the room still looking back and trying not to sound worried.

"But that young gal said something was wrong!" Busta said, still trying to get some sort of understanding.

"She misunderstood. Ya know kid's always grabbin' thangs by the tail and runnin' wit' it. But I'm sho' happy to see ya." After one last look, Lue closed her bedroom door.

Looking at the mess and trying to bring herself to clean it up. Savannah heard someone outside her door and called to them

"Who's there?" hearing nothing on the first or second call, she walked over and pulled the door open, it was Eva.

"What's wrong wit' chu? Didn't you hear me callin'?"

"Yes Ma'am, I was afraid to answer, ya sounded so mad-n-all—then I was afraid to move." She replied, standing there with a small trimmer under her nightgown. Savannah stood watching her under the dim light and thought to herself how beautiful she is. Remembering when she gleamed as Eva does now.

"Girl, you thought anymore 'bout what I said to you in the kitchen earlier?"

"No Ma'am, cain't says I have—ain't had no time—I was asleep like you said. Then when I was awake, I was across the way gettin' Busta like Lue said. Ain't had no time for thinkin'." Eva replied.

"Good…'cause I changed my mind. You havin' that baby and I'm gonna help ya do thangs the right way. Maybe it get me in good wit' God. Gone back to ya room and I'll be there in the mornin' to letchu know what I come up with."

"Yes Ma'am," Before Eva could turn good, she stopped in her tracks. "Miss Van?"

"Chil'."

"Thank you," Savannah gave her a smile and a wink then watched as she disappeared into her room.

The night was long, Savannah had to figure out a way to help Eva keep her baby. Then she had the big one, Sarah.

What in the hell am I gonna to say to her. Savannah didn't know anything about the girl. Once more, she didn't know if Sarah would come to live with her—let alone work. "Anyone stay here got to work—no bones about that." She said aloud while picking up the mess she'd made and remembering when she herself was sold to the highest bidder.

My mother had run off with the butcher. Last, I heard the butcher had dropped her off on the side of the road, after some white men stopped him and shook him up pretty bad.

I was told at the next town, mother got out to use the toilet and the butcher drove off without her. No one knows what happened to her after that. My father never spoke of her again.

He soon after started putting me out to a few of his friends when times would get rough.

"Now Van, this only gonna help us pay for food and such." He said.

He would always say, he'd only sell me to his best

of friends and never let any harm come to me—that didn't last very long—he began taking me to the juke joints and selling me to any and everything that had money to pay, I can recall a few women too.

"Money is money it can't tell the difference between a man and a woman."

I took off on my own when I was twenty—turning tricks here and there for food and a place to sleep for the night.

I had slowly saved enough money to buy a small house of my own. I put out a sign to take in boarders, but it wasn't bringing in the money I was use to. Therefore, my sign went to **Male Boarders Only**. I didn't care what the people in town had to say. No one was taking care of me but me.

After three months, things were becoming more than I could handle. Up went another sign. **Care Takers Wanted** and right next to that one, **Women Only**.

I found three women I liked right away. After about a year, the place was too small so I moved to the middle of town in the large old court building. It had lots of room for everyone to have peace and privacy.

Savannah's thoughts of the past where interrupted by a knock on her door.

"Hey, sweet thang you in there?" A deep voice called to her from the hall.

"Sam that chu?" Savannah called with a halfhearted smile.

"Yeah, baby it's me," she let out a deep sigh, pinched her cheeks, and splashed on some smell goods before opening the door.

"Sam suga, you back fo' mo' already? Well...come on in." She pulled him into the room and led him to the bed. He could see the sadness in her eyes.

"Savannah, I know ya a private person and all. I don't mean to be meddlesome..., but what's wrong? You feelin' all right? What the hell happened in here?"

Savannah managed another fake smile. "I'm just fine suga...no need to worry this Van you lookin' at. Ain't nothin' gone get me down suga'. At least not so far down I cain't pick myself up. As for the mess, it's the only way I'll get myself a new vanity. Now you come here to talk or what...'cause tonight I ain't in no mood to talk—at least not 'bout me." She pulled a cigarette from the nightstand and lit it.

While he waited for her to have a few puffs of her freshly lit smoking stick, he removed the spread from the bed and placed the pillows in a pile on the middle of the bed.

He then returned to her placing his hand tenderly on the nape of her neck, pulling her to him. He kissed her lips delicately and stroked her long silky hair. Pulling up her evening gown, he exposed her creamy colored legs and thighs, up a little more to kiss her on the navel. He slowly laid her down allowing her head to rest on the mounds of pillows.

He climbed atop of her removing her panties to get to the sweets that God had blessed her with. He entered her and for one moment she remember what

it was like as a young girl whoring for the first time.
How can I bring another young life into this world of shame...?

Event 011.00

I had gone into town and was back home now. I was sitting in the barn at the entrance of the loft, remembering all the times I had to pull hay up on my own. Thinking and laughing to myself—at moments tearing up with feelings of happiness and joy—because the one thing that tormented me most was out of my life.

The pain from the last beating was dulled from all the booze I had consumed. I stood to my feet to sing a song to me meant freedom. Remembering I didn't have one, I made one up.

Nobody knows / the bullshit I've seen / Nobody knows my story. / Now I sing / because / ain't no more Papa. / To beat and hurt me. / Rape or abuse me. / Nobody knows / the bullshit I've seen. / Nobody knows / my story.

I sat back down to see if the bottle of moonshine I stole from an old man in the middle of town was still where I placed it. Picking it up to take another swig, I stopped short. I thought of the way Papa behaved when he was drunk. He would become violent, mean and surly—cursing me...beating me...raping me. "ROT IN HELL YOU DIRTY BASTARD...ROT IN HELL!" I shouted so loudly my voice echoed over and over—carried away by the night wind.

I fell to my knees and shoved my face into my hands—weeping.

My thoughts went searching for Mama wondering if she knew of all the turmoil and tribulation I was going through.

Still on my knees, I felt melancholy—longing for the days I know cheerfulness and contentment.

I was alarmed by a voice in the yard. Thinking it was Pa, I remained very still.

"Sarah, where are you?"

Could it be? I thought running to the ladder with my bottle in hand. "Tobias." I said in a relieved whisper.

"There you are, you all right? I was out on horseback and I thought I heard yelling coming from here," he called up with a bewildered look. "I couldn't tell what was being said, but I thought I would come and take a look."

It was him and he was beautiful in the high moonlight.

"Yeah, just fine. Had to let off some...some a... sweam...squeam...steam." I struggled to find my composure through my drunken stupor.

"You've been drinkin'," he asked with eyes wide open.

"Tobias," I shouted trying to pretend as though I didn't know who he really was. "That chu," I squinted my eyes, "you very sharp-eyed ain't cha?"

"Miss Sarah, get down from there...you...you too close to the edge." He was yelling up to me, as he dismounted his horse.

"Maannn...you got no idea just how close to the edge I really am. Whatchu want? I ain't invite you here." I was making my way down the rope, only to be met by his gentle hands trying to help.

"I heard shouting. So, I came to see if things were okay. The closer I came I knew I recognized the voice. Where did you get liquor?" He asked as he was reaching for the bottle and I was taking one-step back—trying not to fall over.

He seemed somewhat stupid to me at that moment—but beautifully stupid. "That's mighty bold of ya, comin' on folks land just 'cause ya hear shoutin'...," but the thought of him being concerned for me gave me a feeling of warmth, a feeling I hadn't felt in a long time. "Yeah noises do carry out here, damn wind need to mind its own," I said, thinking about the second half of his question. "And 'sides where ya been at boy, under a rock? This countryside, don't you know you can get moonshine anywhere. Hell everywhere." I said as I raised the bottle to my face too fast and hit myself hard in the mouth.

The sound echoed in my head from the clanging of the bottle on my teeth. Barely able to stand, I tried to look as if I had done nothing strange and went to sit on the porch.

"Come and sit, Toby, mind if I call ya, Toby, seems nicer then Tobias. Listen to it, *TOOOBBBYY*, just like a song." I rubbed my nose and turned my head to look at the horse snatching what little grass there was left from the lawn.

"Sarah, you all right?" Tobias asked with concern in his eyes. He wondered why he felt so much compassion for a girl he didn't know—and by the way things were looking, he wasn't sure if he wanted to know.

"Sho' suga'. My pa,that bastard, is gone and left me here to take care of myself. I can do it too—better than he ever could—that rat bastard," she stood to her feet to shout it again, *"YOU RAT MOTHA-FUCKA, YA HEAR ME, I CAN TAKE CARE OF ME JUST FINE!"*

"Well, Miss Sarah, looks to me like you goin' 'bout it the wrong way. Let us go inside and get you some coffee, let me have the bottle. What's this 'bout your father leaving?" He gave her a shoulder to lean on as they walked inside.

He watched her carefully as she stumbled into the kitchen, shaking his head and letting out a small giggle when she tripped over her own feet.

Sarah sat at the table, placing her elbows on the its top, resting her face in the palms of her hands, and watched Toby as he searched for the items needed to prepare the coffee and feeling a sense of amiability and contentment enter her every pore.

"Where is the coffee, you do have coffee don't chu?" He asked looking up from the bottom cupboard.

"Above ya head, on top of the shelf. It's gotta be old as shit cause ain't nobody had coffee since my mama died. That can has gotta be ova' four years old." I said, with a smile.

"You nevea told me whatchu meant outside, about your pa leavin'," Toby made it a point not to look at her.

"Just what I said, the rat bastard left me here to do fo' myself. He come home tonight and say, *'The bank took the farm, I'm outta here and you couldn't go.'* It's all good though…'cause me and Papa, we is two different kinds of folks see. I'm good…at least I like to think so. Papa he mean and nasty—a rat bastard—just like I said."

"Did he do them things to your face?" Toby was at the table now looking her straight in the eyes.

"Boy, you don't waste no time on askin' whatcha wanna know do ya," I replied looking around the room for my bottle.

"I just thought you might want to talk."

"I guess it would be nice. I'm just not use to all this is all." I replied, still looking for my bottle. The water was boiling in the old banged up pot Toby did manage to find.

He stood to get the coffee ready, but saw it was so old it was stuck inside the can like cement. He held the can upside down and together they laughed.

"Whisky it is then. Now where did my bottle get to?"

"Right here, look," Toby was pointing to the bottle on the edge of the counter next to him.

"Well give it to me. I don't wanna look at it, I know what it look like. Now hand it here." I demanded with my head to the side and hoping he caught a hint of playful sarcasm in it all.

"How about just plain hot water instead? The coffee

won't come out of the can," he said still holding the tin and poking a fork into it, seconds later trying the same thing with a knife.

"Hot water," I replied, wrinkling my nose and twisting my eyebrows at the thought, "how's 'bout *you* have hot water and *I'll* have whisky, 'sides I already told ya it ain't been used in four years."

I was standing so closely in front of him now looking him in the eyes—our bodies could have become one.

Toby hadn't realized just how beautiful Sarah really was. All he had seen was her bruised face and swelled lip. However, her big round raven colored eyes had a way of drawing him in—hypnotizing him. They also seemed to call out for help.

The ruby redness of her lips shown, as if she were wearing ruby red lipstick—and the only thing left was the faded pigment that stained them. Her raven eyes and her pecan skin glowed under the light of the lantern. Even the smell of liquor on her breath was seductively intoxicating. At that moment, he wanted nothing more but to take her in his arms and kiss her.

"My bottle," she asked interrupting his thought.

"Huh...oh yeah...here." He smiled with fires of shame in his cheeks and wondered if she'd knew what he'd been thinking.

"Thanks," I said with a glance at him from the corners of my eyes and a half grin that turned up the corner of my mouth.

Toby poured the two of us a cup of the hot water— now appearing to know that I knew what was on his mind—and went to sit at the table across from me.

"Sarah, I wanna ask ya something. Why won't you tell me what happened to your face? Was it your father?" He asked looking into his glass trying to avoid looking me in the eyes.

I gave him a long glance from over the top of the bottle I was sipping from and finally said. "No...! 'sides...why he the first person ya think of?" I was suddenly stricken with feelings of shame and guilt. Hoping his questions would somehow fade and not remind me of the terrible things my papa had done.

"Look, I know we don't know each other, but I'd like that to change. I wanna know ya Sarah.... When I saw you in the soda shop for the first time," Toby was looking her in the eyes, trying to get past the bottle she was hiding behind. "I thought you were the cutest girl I had seen in a long time. Some of the gang told me you don't go to school because your father didn't want chu to. They also said a few other things, but I want to hear from you. I mean I don't believe a person should just believe whatever other people say...," he was searching his mind for the right words to say when she spoke.

"You right. You *don't* know me...and I'd like it if ya found somethin' else to yap about. Ya sound like old lady Haggerdy up the road a spell, always goin' on about other folks business." Still, I thought it would be great to have someone know what life was really like for me. I wanted so bad to tell him everything, ever dirty little thing that bastard put me through, the beatings, the rape, the torcher. I wanted to tell it all, but the shame I felt when I was around him wouldn't allow it.

"Whatchua gonna do now he gone?" Toby asked reluctantly.

"What all folks do when they on they own fool. Survive. It's all I know how to do." I replied, turning my head trying to fight back the tears.

"You ever been on your own befo'? I hear it's pretty hard you know."

"Toby, you ain't very bright, ya ask so many questions, all ya gotta do is look and the answer is right there already. Did ya listen to the stories ya was told? There some bit of truth in them. Life can no longer throw nothin' at me I cain't handle—I've had it all already. 'Sides what chu know 'bout being alone, or grown for that matter. Hell by the way you look and dress you got folks that care for ya, a loving Ma and Pa. You make it sound like...I'm some helpless chil' right out of dippers." I was a little annoyed by his senselessness. I then figured it wasn't his fault, he was only trying to get at the truth.

Tears began to swell in my eyes. I turned from him hoping he hadn't seen them. The first tear fell down the corner of my nose and onto my lips. The next tear was close behind before I could stop it. It rolled down the center of my cheek. I hid my face in the palms of my hands. Tobias stood from his seat and came over to hold me. Shocked by his sudden movement I pulled away. After a brief moment he tried again, this time I allowed him to embrace me.

"I'm sorry Miss Sarah, I nevea meant fo' ya to cry or make ya feel bad. No more questions—at least for now."

He held her tight, but not too tight and he stroked the back of her head and down the center of her back. His embrace was genuine and tender, nothing like what she was use to with her Papa. She parted her legs to allow him in closer. He slid in and held her close. She could feel his heart beat against hers and the warmth of his body was soothing as well. For a brief moment, she felt safe and secure.

Tobias was pleased that she had allowed him to comfort her.

"Sarah, talk to me, I won't tell anyone. I promise." He said stroking her hair.

"I cain't, I cain't ever tell anyone. Ya hear no one... and you said no more questions." I pulled him closer hoping he would hold me tighter. He released himself from our tight embrace and gazed deep into my teary eyes. I reached up to dry the water from my face. He pulled my hands down and dried my cheeks himself.

"I don't know what it is, maybe the night air, but I feel like I have known you forever. My heart aches for your pain and your sadness. Let me help you." He pleaded.

"You cain't help me. All is done and nothing can hurt me now."

I wished he would leave it all alone, but deep down I knew if he did, I might never see him again.

Toby stood to his feet, pulled me up from the chair and took me in his arms once more. He held me close and I like a child melted in his strong embrace.

He kissed me gentle on the lips and I returned the kiss with a strong passionate one of my own and wanted him to keep going, but it was short and sweet. Then I thought that maybe it was the booze, because I never felt anything like this before. My knees were weak and my heart raced. My body shook with nervousness. Mama didn't have the chance to tell me about love. Was this it?

My own words, *'you cain't help me. All is done and nothing can hurt me now.'* echoed back in my mind.

I couldn't decide who I was trying to convince, myself or Tobias. Nevertheless, I had to believe it.

Then, there it was again. "It's time you knew, no man can ever love you the way you want. Let the boy go." The voice I'd been hearing said.

As I stood arm in arm with Toby, my heart stopped beating, I waited to hear the voice again. "No man can love you like you want."

I whispered back, "That cain't be true."

"What?" Toby asked still holding me.

"Nothin', I thought I heard ya say somethin', neveamind." I closed my eyes and held on to him tight.

Event 012.00

The next morning Savannah awoke to find Sam had left sometime during the night. He placed the money on the table as many men had done before. She took a cigarette from the nightstand and lit it with the small flame burning from the candle.

She got up from the bed and pulled back the curtains to allow the sun in to caress her face—and seeing the mess—she woefully searched for the strength to clean it up.

"What I'ma do, Lord," she asked, "I got one child with child and another that has to come work here. Lord, I know I toldcha I wouldn't have one more chil' in here. But, I feel like my hands are tied." At that moment, there was a knock at the door.

"Yes."

"Can I come in?"

"Yeah Lue," the door slowly opened and she peered in head first and slowly let the rest of her body follow.

"You all right this mornin'? What's goin' on witcha? Is there anythin' I can do for ya?" Lue asked, stepping forward with every word. Savannah moved from the window over to the mess on the floor. "Naw, ain't nothin' you can do. I gotta take care of this one on my own."

"Van, we been friends a mighty long time and we been through some thangs even married folk ain't gone through. I was your first girl. You know you can talk to me 'bout anythang. Something ain't right wit'cha and I think I have the right to know." Lue was helping her pick up things that weren't broken.

"Lue, you good people, now just 'cause we friends that don't mean you got the right to know what I don't want to tell ya. On the other hand I'ma tell ya what's goin' on. But, not 'cause ya think it's yo right. It's only 'cause I gotta tell somebody fo' I lose my mind behind it all." The women laughed and Van began to tell her the story from day one.

"So now ya gonna bring her here? This no place for that gal. I got a bad feeling 'bout havin' her here—and a bad feelin' 'bout her. You heard the stories ya know that chil' ain't right. 'Sides she know what go on here?" Lue said in a high voice and wide eyed.

"Lue, everyone knows what we do here. 'Sides that chil' ain't stupid. Anyhow, she saw you and Busta, if she ain't know what we do, she do now." Savannah said glibly with her hands on her hip and her head cocked to one side.

"What it look like we start workin' kids. Ya know these folks want us outta here anyway."

"Yeah Lue, I know all this. Ya think I ain't put all this to thought? Well I have, and the first thang I'ma do is put Eva on a train *home* to her mama. I was up late after old Sam went to sleep. I put a letter together for her mother, do ya think ya can carry it to the post later. I gotta get thangs cleaned up 'round here. Then, I gotta go out to the Lambert house and tell that poor gal to come wit' me." Getting up from her knees, Savannah took a deep breath and headed towards the door without another word, holding the letter in her hand.

Taking the hint, Lue soon followed snatching the letter and watching it as if it were going to explode in her hand.

"Lue, thanks hear." Savannah said, with a sad smile.

"Anytime," Lue replied unenthusiastically and rolled her eyes while closing the door behind her.

Heavyhearted, with her head down and a single tear running down her cheek, Savannah said a silent prayer, *Lord I needcha right now...I don't ask for much from ya, but this time what I need is real important to me. Help me find a way to make it all right—and Lord...Forgive me.'*

Event 013.00

Toby was the first to awaken, he lay next to Sarah for a while staring at her wondering what she had been through in her life. Wondering what her face truly looked like under all those bruises. Now though, he thought she was the prettiest thing he had ever seen. He also reflected on the kiss they shared just hours before.

Sarah woke to find him smiling at her, and finding the most awful pounding in her head and a vile taste of stale liquor in her mouth.

"Morning," Toby said rising to his feet

"Jesus, Toby! You still here, you stayed all night?" She asked trying to pull herself together, and smoothing out her hair. Hoping he was too far away to smell her breath.

"Yeah, after the kiss you passed out. I put you to bed. Sorry I kept you in your close. I couldn't find anything else. I just lay next to you and watched you sleep mostly. You all right…you had a great deal to drink last night."

"Fine, just need to get up and get…," she broke

her thought only to start another, with heartbroken tears swelling in her eyes. "Toby...," she said, "I'm alone...I got no one." She hugged her pillow and cried into it.

Tobias searched his mind for the right words to console her, but for a second was met with silence. "Look, you got me now. Sarah, let me be here for ya. I thought about it all last night...and I wanna take care of ya. I mean if that's what you want." He said moving in closer to her.

He sat on the bed next to her and tried to get a peek under her pillow.

"You, take care of me. I don't need anyone to take care of me," she said with her face still buried. "'Sides I don't even know you. I know nothin' 'boutchu. You know nothing 'bout me." Her words muffled by the pillow.

"That's all right, I can get to know you and you me. I won't hurt you. I've already proved that, don'tcha think?" He asked with a half-smile hoping she would agree.

Lifting her head, she replied. "Proven what? You said it ya'self we kissed. I can only wonder what else you—we did." Sarah grew scared at the thought of having intimate relations with a boy she didn't know and not remember any of it. With her heart racing, she jumped from the bed as millions of images raced through her mind of how well her Papa had taken care of her.

"I know how you wanna take care of me! Get out! Get out of here right now and nevea comeback! You hear me boy nevea comeback!" She yelled, standing at the doorway of her room holding tight to the door-knob and trying not to let the shaking in her knees get the best of her.

"Sarah," he called to her, wondering what he had said wrong.

"Just go! Get out I said! Stop talking and get the fuck out!" Sarah walked over to the window with her back to him, praying he would just leave her alone—at least for now.

Toby walked out of the room closing the door behind him. He waited for a moment hoping she would call to him. She never did.

I left my room after what seemed like hours of standing in the window wishing my mama were still here. I walked into the kitchen to get something to take care of my aching head, then out to the porch to get some fresh air. That's when I noticed a car coming up the road. Standing to my feet to get a better look, I saw who it was and walked slowly to the end of the yard—where the walkway met the road.

"Oh damn, now what? Why cain't folks just leave me the hell alone," I asked myself aloud.

Savannah appeared nothing like she did in the past few times I'd seen her. Her hair still in curlers and she didn't have rosy red cheeks and somehow her smile didn't seem real. Her face was showing her age without all the makeup.

"Whatchu doin' here? My pa gone."

"I know ya Pa gone, honey. He come see me yesterday noon. I'm here for you. Can I come in?" Savannah was at the gate waiting for me to open it.

"I s'pose," I opened the gate and led the way up to the house. I couldn't help but to wonder what she was doing here so early and why my pa would go to see her. She had never come here before, at least not that I knew of.

Suddenly it hit me—pa's voice echoed in my head—*'Whorehouse.'*

Savannah walked slowly behind trying desperately to find words to tell Sarah the things she needed to know.

When Sarah reached the door she turned to let Savannah in first, but she was standing at the end of the steps, with a dull painful look on her face. Sarah made no notice of it to her.

"You comin' in?"

"Yeah, right behind ya, honey." Savannah forced a smile.

Sarah pointed to the couch for Savannah to have a seat while she took the chair next to the window.

"You say my pa come see ya?" I asked without looking away from the window.

"He come see me 'bout chu."

"What fo'?" I asked trying not to sound cold and bitter, knowing all along why he had.

"Look-a-here, suga, I—" Sarah was in no mood to hear long drawn out stories about why her papa had left her—abandoned to fend for herself.

"Savannah," she interrupted. "My name ain't suga and ya don't need to beat 'round the bush wit' me. I been through enough shit in the last several years to last me a damn life time. Please just come out and tell me why it is you're here." Looking her dead in the eyes, Sarah waited for a response. A response deep inside she was hoping was different from the one she already knew.

Savannah was taken aback for a moment. The fragile little thing she had only met a few days ago when she chased the Hawkins boys away, was stern and right to the point. Savannah had no idea how to explain any of this to her.

"Okay, Sarah ya right. I'm here 'cause you supposed to come wit' me. That was yo' pa's orders. That's why he come see me." She replied taking a cigarette from her purse.

"His orders? What makes ya think he got the right to be givin' orders when he ain't even here? That man don't give a shit 'bout me, or what happens to me! He ain't cared for me since my mama died—may haps he nevea did! He thinks it's my fault she dead anyway!" Sarah's voice was getting shaky and softer. "Mama had asked me to go with her into town that night, but I told her I wasn't feelin' well. When the truth was…I just didn't want to go. Pa was out in the fields trying to get the last of the harvest pulled befo' sunup, she wasn't supposed to go out alone at night, but she had to have eggs for cookies; she had an order for the next mornin'. So she went out by herself…," Sarah paused, turned back to the window and continued. "Right after we buried her he nevea again said anything nice to me or did anything nice for that matter. Like I said befo', that rat bastard don't give a shit 'bout me. He gave up the right to order me 'round when he up and left—not that I mind—I'm glad he gone and I pray wherever he is, he nevea come back my way."

Savannah leaned forward in her seat. She wanted to go over and comfort her, but she knew that wouldn't have been a good idea, her heart weighted heavy for Sarah.

"Suga, I know ya mad and all right now, but whatchu gonna do here? Your pa say he done already sold this place, ya can't stay here. Whatch'a gonna do 'bout shelter, food and clothes? I'm here to help ya, Sarah, not hurtcha. From what I can tell ya had too much of that already." Savannah knew it would be a hard task to get through to her.

"I don't need you telling me what I need and don't need. My mama dead remember. I'll find somewhere to stay. I got family in the next county they can take me in. 'sides you don't need me there." She took a deep breath and fought back a tear and said, "Where in the hell was all this help when that bastard was fuckin' and beatn' me?" Sarah turned to look at her as she spoke.

Wide-eyed Savannah replied. "Oh my Lord chil' you tellin' me Grady was...," Savannah stopped midsentence. "I knew it," she said softly and walking over to Sarah, "Look-a-here, I know ya angry now and maybe ya needs a bit more time, but I'm here now. And as God for my witness, I won't let nothing happen to ya," Savannah hated lying to her. "Now come on, getcha stuff and let's go. Whatcha say?" Standing in front of Sarah, she tried to find a glimpse of promise in her eyes.

"I need time. I have to thank about it first. I ain't stupid, Savannah, I know whatchu do in that place, and I ain't gonna let no man fuck me no more less'n I want them to, ya hear—on my terms—from here on out, ya hear on my damn terms!" Sarah got up and showed Savannah the way out.

"All right chil', I'll be back later on tonight to see whatcha decided to do," she said, as she stood in the doorway. "Sarah, it won't be all bad, at least give it a chance and ya don't have to do nothin' 'til ya ready, on your terms...I can promise ya that." She said, taking Sarah by the hand and wondering how she could have made such a promise—especially one she knew she couldn't keep.

"Do whatcha want, seems to me that what folk do 'round here anyway." Sarah pulled her hand back and closed the door.

For a moment, Savannah stood there hoping she would open the door with a change of heart. Remembering when she too had said those very same words, *'on my terms.'*

As Savannah set in the car, she thought of Grady and what he had made her do. "Damn you Grady, damn you for making me do this!" She yelled between gritted teeth, as she started the engine.

Event 014.00

Tobias was on his way home, but he couldn't stop thinking of his feelings for Sarah. Could he love her? Whatever the reason, he knew he wanted to see more of her and find out why she'd suddenly been so upset with him. He made up his mind to go back later, after she had time to calm down.

"Hey man, where the hell you been all night? We was s'pose to go meet the Miller twins. How could ya stand them up?" Charlie asked, placing his fist in his mouth.

"I had to stay with a friend. She needed me."

Toby's best friend—which also happened to be his cousin—Charlie Coltrane, stopped him at the soda shop.

Charlie was a drugstore cowboy—of course, the girls in town would have said otherwise. Charlie stood at five feet and seven inches tall, skinny as a rail. Hair thick, curly, black, and shiny as ravens feathers. Skin as black as night—at certain times of the day he almost appeared midnight blue. Charlie was ugly; problem was he didn't know it. The one great thing about Charlie, he had pearly white teeth, and a smile that would light up a dark room.

"SHE...! She needed you? Hey man, she got a sista?" He asked, nudging Toby on the shoulder and giving him one of his pearly white smiles. "Why you ain't call me? It must have been gooood 'cause ya ain't called nobody! Yo' mama gonna have yo' ass ya know. She been lookin' for you too. Who this girl ya was wit'? Come on man, tell me some'em don't hold back." Charlie was talking so fast, which to Toby meant only one thing. He was high.

"Man, would you shut the hell up! It ain't whatchu think!"

"Ain't what I think? You spend all night wit' a chick and you tellin' me you ain't fuck her?" Charlie said with a big grin.

"No, I didn't fuck her! She ain't like that." The vulgarities about being with a girl coming from Charlie's mouth had never bothered Toby before—but Sarah was different—and he was not in the mood for any of Charlie's vulgar commentary.

"Hey man, in this town they *all* like that. Who is she, someone I know?"

"Maybe," Toby replied, looking into the window of the soda shop to see who was there.

"Maybe? That don't tell me a goddamn thang man! Do I know her?" Charlie asked again, looking over his shoulder as if someone was after him.

"Look-a-here, if I tell ya. You cain't say nothing to nobody." Toby was staring Charlie down as he spoke.

"You know me, Tob, I ain't gonna say nothin'. What's wrong wit'a?" Charlie asked, with a smile and moving in closer to Toby, as if he were about to hear a governmental top secret.

"Man, you ain't no good and ain't nothing wrong wit'a. Her name is, Sarah." He told his friend with pride.

"Sarah! The Lambert girl, Maann...you outta yo' mind? Her old man would kill you if he found out you was fuckin' his gal." Charlie looked around to be sure no one had heard what Tobias had said.

"Charlie man, one more time...I ain't doin' her. I was at her place last night 'cause she needed some-one to talk to, that's all. And why would her pa want to kill me for seein' her?" Charlie pulled him into the soda shop and headed to the last table in the back of the store, where they sat to see who was coming and going.

"Look-a-here, Tob man...I don't wanna tell ya who ya should see and not see, but this girl is bad news brotha. It's all over town that her old man is the one who broke her in—and you know what I mean." Charlie had one eyebrow up.

"Broke her in? What the hell you talkin' about boy. She ain't no damn horse, say whatchu mean?" He knew very well what Charlie was talking about, but he needed more information for himself if he was go-ing to get her to open up to him.

"Look Tob, you my favorite cousin-n-all and I don't wanna see ya get hurt. Listen man, let me fill you in on some thangs. Word has it, evea since her mama died, her daddy been puttin' it to her—ya know fuckin'a. She don't go to school with the rest of us and she nevea comes into town to hang out with any of us. Many times we'd see her on the old dried up creek with her face all bruised up—like she been beat. I think her old man fuckin' and beatn' her. Whenevea she see any of us, she just up and runs off like a scared rabbit. One day, the gang and me was going out to the old creek, we had to go past their house to get to the good moonshine. That's when we first heard it," with almost every other word, Charlie would check to see if anyone was listening. "Her screams were so loud, I ain't nevea heard screams like that befo'...we thought the ol' man had killed her for sho'. Not to mention, there was this red glow inside the house...I mean the whole house was *red like fire*, but we was all too afraid to go and check it out. A few days later, I saw her walking up the road and into the woods and there it was again. That strange red light—and she what'n carrin' no lantern either. She seemed to be talking to someone, but no one was there. I'm tell'n ya, Tob, this girl...she bad news bra, leave her alone."

"I saw the bruises on her face when we first met in the woods and again last night when I was with her, but she told me it was an accident from the loft."

"Awww...come on man, you ain't no fool is ya? Accident my ass...her pa did it to her fasho. He beat that girl...I know he did. Man don't get involved with that gal nothin' good can come from it—and those eyes. What person in all of God's green earth you know got eyes black as coal? Them is ravens eyes, now where you think she got ravens eyes from?" Charlie leaned back in his seat with his arms folded, eyebrows twisted, and a curl on his lips.

Both boys ordered a soda, as the store keep told

them to order or get out. After being served, Charlie flicked his bottle cap into the air watching it as it hit the floor and rolled under the next table.

Tobias watched him closely and decided not to say anything more about last night with Sarah. Clearly, Charlie was not the one to confide in. He couldn't help but to wonder though if anything Charlie said was true.

Where did she get all the bruises and why had her pa left her alone like that?

"Look man, I got to get outta here, I got stuff to do befo' I leave for school next week." Toby said, while looking in his coat pocket for the money he'd won in a hand of poker the morning before, to pay for the sodas.

"You gonna leave that gal alone ain'tchu, man?" Charlie asked, not really hearing what Toby had said.

"I toldchu, I gotta to go, not every year a black man gets the chance to go to a fine college?" Toby replied, trying to change the subject and lifting his shoulders high, and pointing his nose upward towards the ceiling.

"I sho' hope ya hearing me man. That gal will only *get you* hurt," he said. "Anyway, come on I'll help ya get ready…, Mr. College man. Hope they can teach chu how to better pick the folk ya hang 'round wit'." Charlie said, with a chuckle.

"I hang wit'chu don't I? Besides, I can do it on my own. I'll catch you later."

"Yeah, catch ya later…and leave that gal alone, she bad news." Charlie yelled, as Toby walked out of the soda shop.

Toby walked up the street a bit trying to figure out what he should do. He knew he was off to school in a few days, but he also knew something happened to him last night with Sarah.

Event 015.00

Sarah made up her mind to go and live with Savannah. She really had no other choice as she saw it. Slowly packing what little valuables she had to take with her, still unsure whether or not this was the right thing to do. Remembering all the times her mama told her to stay away from that place.

She pulled open the top drawer and reached under a pile of clothes, where she had hidden the box of treasures she had taken from the garbage, holding inside it the valuables once belonging to her mama. In it was a bunch of photos she never took time to look over. Most of them contained photos of her ma and pa. Coming across a photo with her mama and another woman, she moved over to the window to get a better look. The photo was old and faded, she recognized her mother, but she couldn't tell who the other woman was. Not giving it any real thought, she put the photo away and began packing the rest of her things.

"Am I really gon' do this," she said aloud. "I'm gonna move in with, Savannah."

She walked out to the front porch hoping she could

think better there. Taking a deep breath and looking up the road, she saw Toby approaching. *What's he doing back here so soon?* she asked herself, as she ran back into the house and into the mirror to fix herself up the best she could. She heard him knocking at the door.

"Who's there?" She asked, coming to the door as if she hadn't seen him.

"Sarah, it's me Tobias, can I come in? I have to talk to you." He asked, watching her coming to the door.

"I wasn't expectin' ya back so soon. I'm sorry for what happened earlier. Reckon I got to get use to people wantin' to help, but in my own time. It's just...you ask so many questions." She was leading him toward the couch. "You hungry, want some'em' cold to drank? I don't got much, but some cold lemon aid and some chicken stew. I make good chicken stew." She asked, trying to be the host she remembered her ma being, also hoping it would make up for her rudeness earlier.

"I have to ask you something." He blurted out, paying no mind to her offerings.

"Damn, Toby...you and yo' fool questions," she replied with a sigh. "Well, have a seat and get on wit' it, I have to pack and head into town." She was a bit annoyed he hadn't taken her up on her offer for food and drink.

"Sarah, there's somethin' aboutcha I want to get to know. Now I know you told me before to leave ya alone, but truth is...well I ain't been able to getcha off my mind since I saw ya in the soda shop. I want to be the one to take care of ya, now ya father gone.

I don't have much…hell fact is, I ain't got nothin' at all. I'm leaving for school in a few days—"

"What ya mean ya—" she was hushed by the gentle rise of his hand.

"Wait…hear me out. I want us to be together," he continued. "I can get a place off campus and get a job while I go to school. Whatcha say, Sarah, will you come with me back to New York?"

He watched her as she sat staring intensely at him. She slowly rose up from her chair walking over to him, kneeling between his legs never taking her eyes off his. She leaned in to kiss him soft on the forehead then, on the cheek, and finally his lips. He returned the favor wondering why she hadn't answered him.

Taking his hand, she led him to her bedroom where the walls were now bear and the window undressed. Things had been carelessly scattered about the floor.

As she lay on the bed, she reached for his hand and pulled him to her. Toby was still wondering why she hadn't answered his question. He stopped her advances.

"Answer me. What about it, will you go with me to New York?" He pulled her hands down to his sides, as he kneeled above her trembling body. He knew she was nervous, he could feel the bed vibrating beneath him.

"Toby, I been tellin' ya since when we met, you ask too many questions." She pulled her hands free grabbing him by the arms pulling him down on her.

Toby's mind had eclipsed by the thought of making love to her. The scars and bruises no longer made her look hard, but somehow in a morbid way, made her appear innocent—angelic. He could no longer hold out the feelings he held inside, he wanted her just as bad as she wanted him.

He kissed her softly and caressed her breasts. Then, he removed her clothing to reveal her soft tender pecan skin. Her curves were like that of a goddess he watched her as she lay opening her legs to receive him.

She was afraid, but his tender touch eased her mind and soul. She was making love to a man who was placid and wasn't going to hurt her. It was a blissful feeling—she wanted the moment to last forever.

Toby was trying to hold out from climaxing too fast, but the feel of her body, the smell of her skin took its toll, and he had to let out what was locked up for so long. In turn, Sarah was feeling a sound sense of pleasure for the first time. In her mind now, she was no longer a virgin—no matter how much her papa had raped her.

When the lovemaking was over, they lay without a word.

Nightfall had come quick, as the two did nothing all day, but make love and explore each other.

It was dark out when Sarah woke turning to look at Toby beside her. She knew she had to make a decision to be with him or send him on his way. She got out of bed and went to the kitchen to refill the water pitcher.

When she returned memories of her father rushed

into her head. She watched Tobias as he slept, and the voice that had been haunting her spoke.

"No man can every love you the way you want." She knew then. With teary eyes, she picked up her belongings and left the house without a word to Toby.

Event 016.00

Sarah had arrived at Savannah's, she stood outside watching people come and go before she found the nerve to go in.

Once inside, she stood by the door to allow her eyes to adjust to the light. Sarah saw a woman walking towards her. She was dark skinned and had on way too much makeup.

"Can I help you?" She asked in a low husky voice.

"Yes. I'm here to see Savannah, she waitin' fo' me." I replied, holding back my laugh.

"Well, she busy...but you can wait fo' her in the kitchen, I'll tella' ya here." The woman led me to the kitchen, along the way I could hear laughter and talking coming from behind the curtain I had peeked behind just a few days before. I thought of the woman and man I ran into there.

The place still smelled of old cigarettes and booze, only this time there was a lingering cloud of smoke in the air. People were poking their heads out of dark corners as we passed.

Once in the kitchen, the girl offered me a drink.

When she turned for my answer—her eyes widened—with her hands over her mouth, she gasped at the sight of my bruises. I quickly turned my head and thought of how I felt from the moonshine and I refused—and I wondered what she must think of me. She left me there without another word.

There was a window above the sink and I thought I would look out to see what was out there. When I pulled back the curtain, at first I thought it was too dark to see out, but then I realized the window had been blocked in. I was getting the feeling this place was about to become my prison.

Nevertheless, I would have a place to lay my head and not worry about Pa coming in. Now all I had to worry about was some other nasty, dirty, liquored up man like Pa.

What am I doing?

"Sarah," I turned to see Savannah standing in the door of the kitchen, she was beautiful. She wore a long red dress with black lace and ruffles, her curls were pulled to the side with a large feather holding them in place. Her lips were full and red, her eyes bright. Her cheeks were as rosy as I remembered them the first day we met. She held a cigarette in one hand and an empty glass in the other. She stood for a moment, watching me and I her.

"Well I'm here," I said to break the silence.

"Yes I can see. Well chil', I guess we have some plannin' to do. You want sumthin' to eat, ya hongry?" She was walking to the sink, as she pulled hard on her cigarette. I watched as the paper got smaller and smaller, it seemed as though she had just smoked a whole cigarette in one puff.

"Can I ask ya some'em?"

"Sho', honey anything."

"Why ya want me here, I nevea asked to come. Why ya takin' me in?"

"Well now, first thangs first. Do ya wanna be here?

"Ain't sho' really, I got nowhere else to go," I thought of Tobias. "And well, I'm not real sho' of what I want right now."

"Listen honey, I told ol' Grady I would take care of ya, as a favor to him."

"Why? Pa nevea spoke'a ya, at least not that I know of." *Why does she keep bringing him up. Grady this, Grady that, fuck Grady.*

She must have noticed I wasn't listening anymore and my facial expression had change at the sound of his name. Because she watched me and kind of cocked her head to the side.

"It's a long story, Sarah, and we ought not get into that tonight, another time okay?" Her face went sullen. Someone would have thought I had said something wrong.

"For now I reckon, but ya will tell me what I want to know." Sarah was coming into her own, she knew she had to be hard in order to survive in this world and she wasn't leaving it all up to chance.

"Befo' you go making demands chil', remember this here is my place, and what I say is what goes. And now with that being said, I'll show ya to yo' room?" Savannah replied with sternness.

"Sho', whatevea ya say." Sarah said while shrugging her shoulders.

Savannah led her up the stairs just alongside the kitchen. The hall was lined with doors that Sarah assumed where bedrooms. The walls were a dark brown with speckles of red in them. The carpet lining the floor was red and worn, seemed as though it had never been changed.

Some of the doors were open a crack and she could see figures moving in the shadows. In some of the rooms, she could see women sitting at mirrors fixing their faces or just staring at themselves.

When they came to the end of the hall, Savannah stopped and opened the door on the right. Sarah stopped behind her, she thought she heard a woman crying, she leaned her body in the direction of the noise to get a better listen. Startled by Savannah's voice, she jumped back into a straight stand.

"Well...this it, t'aint much, but it's yours as long as ya want it."

I stepped in, eyes wide. The room was large, much larger than what I was use to. The bed was in the far right corner of the room and there was a large picture window. I wondered if it too was bricked in, then I saw a flicker of light and knew it wasn't.

"This is nice, but how can ya afford to keep me here. I ain't got no money."

"We worry 'bout that in the morin,' after we all had a good night sleep. It'll be lots to learn Sarah and lots to teach. Tonight is not the time to start, in the morin' we'll talk...good night, Sarah." With that, she closed the door.

I was left standing in the middle of the room. I placed my bag on the floor and went over to look out the window. There wasn't much to see on a count it was dark out. Next, I chose to sit on the bed—it was soft—the covers that lined it were thick and silky.

I had never had anything like this. I lay back to get a better feel, I was in heaven—even if it was only for a moment.

I went over to the mirror to look at myself when I heard a loud disturbance in the hall. I put my ear to the door and I could hear voices. It was Savannah and another woman. The other woman was livid about something.

"Look-a-here, Van...I can take plenty from these nasty ass men, but when they talkin' 'bout doin' me in the ass...they gotta go! Now ya tell'em it's a straight fuck or he gotta go!" The woman yelled.

"Quiet cha'self now...I'll take care of it. We got us a new gal in that room—and I don't want to scare her off—so keep ya voice down. Come in here and let's see if we cain't get him to come to yo' terms." The door closed.

I tried to open my door, but when it squeaked, I quickly closed it back.

I had the feeling I should get up and run, but I was too scared.

I changed into my nightclothes and climbed between the covers. The sheets felt cool on my skin. My thoughts were of Toby and I wondered if he had left the house yet. I thought of how we spent the morning together and how wonderful it felt to have someone lay me down the way he did.

You were wrong Pa..., now I'm a real woman and nothing will ever change that. I feel asleep thinking only of my dear sweet, Tobias.

Event 017.00

Tobias had awakened to silence. He went into the kitchen to look for Sarah. He then, checked the barn and out at the edge of the woods. "Damn, she's gone," He said in a whisper. "Damn."

He went back home feeling empty and alone.

As he was getting ready to go back to New York, he could only think of her, his dear sweet Sarah. Tobias wondered if he would ever see her again.

"Hey man, you here?" It was Charlie.

"Yeah...up here, come on up." Toby walked over to open the door wider to let him in.

"You was wit' that Lambert girl, wasn'tchu? Man, I told you—she bad news.... Anyway fo'get all that, tell me, did yoouu...get any?" He asked, picking through Toby's things to see what he was leaving behind.

"Damn man! I don't get no...how ya doin' or what's hangin'?"

"Yeah whatevea, didcha get any?" Charlie asked moving closer to Toby with his head tilted sideways, a big toothy grin, and desperation in his eyes.

"As a matter of fact…I did. Only I won't make it sound as nasty as you just did. And 'sides that, we spent all mornin' together. But, when I woke up she was gone—just like that—nevea said good-bye…no note…nothin', she just up and left." Toby's eyes saddened with that statement.

"You mean she just left you there, wit' cho ass out?" Charlie replied, surprised that a woman would be the first to get up and leave.

"Yeah man, ain't that what I said, only my ass wasn't out. Why is everything a joke to you…? Ahh, fool neveamind. Like I was sayin', she just up and took off. I got no idea where she went. I looked for her at the woods and down by the creek, but she wasn't there."

"See man toldcha—nothin' but bad news—what kinda woman gets up and leaves a man like that? Ain't that what *we* 'spose to do," Charlie was chewing on a piece of gum he took from Toby's nightstand. "It be fo' the best anyhow, cain't no good come from that gal. You explored yo' wild oats befo' you go back to the big city, and it's done…leave it that way."

"Man, ya think you know all about women don'tcha? The truth is you don't know shit about nothin'. Only thang you know is fuckin', if fuckin wasn't part of the human norm you'd be lost…Man speaking of fuckin', get the fuck off my suit! You sitting on it, gettin' it all fuckin' wrinkled." Toby said shoving Charlie to the side.

"Hey man, don't get bent outta shape with me. I ain't the one left ya wit' cho dick hard, that bitch did." Charlie said jumping to his feet.

Without a word, Tobias rushed in and punched Charlie in the face, falling to the floor with him.

The blood ran fast from Charlie's nose. The two men were rolling around on the floor yelling profanities at each other. It wasn't until Toby's father came in did the fighting get broken up.

"What the hell is goin' on in here? You boys cut this shit out right now! What's going on?" Toby's father was a big stout man, he was able to pull the boys apart—one in each hand—holding them by their collars, as he eyed them both back and forth.

"Nothin' goin' on. 'cept yo' boy done gone and lost his mind over that Lambert bitch!" Yelled Charlie.

Toby went for him again. His father let go of Charlie and held Toby back, pinned against the wall. "Charlie, I think ya said enough get outta here…gone boy get." Father yelled, pointing to the door for Charlie to leave and never taking his eyes off his own son.

"Yeah, later fo' you man!" Charlie spit the blood from his lip onto the floor and rushed out past the two men—bumping into the door on the way out.

"Can I let you go now or ya wanna to take a swing at me too?" Father was a big burley man—as big as an ox—and as strong as five men put together. Toby had no plans on fighting with him.

"Naw, Coltrane, had no cause callin' her a bitch, sain' she bad news and shit." Toby's eyes were red as beets. Father knew his son's anger was genuine, because Tobias only called Charlie by his last name when he was angry with him.

"Look-a-here boy, ya best'a remember who's house ya in. I don't allow no talk like that, you know this.

Now ya talk to me like a man. What's done happened 'tweenst you and him?" After father let Toby go, he watched him for a second, shook his head, and searched for chew in the pocket of his overalls.

"He got no right callin' Sarah out her name like that, he don't know her like I do. He only knows what people in town talking about." Toby had calmed down a bit.

"Who is this Sarah? You gotta start from the beginning 'cause I'm at a loss." His father was sitting in the chair in front of the window—stuffing his face with chew and searching the room for a can to spit into.

Toby took his time telling his father the story of how he had come to know Sarah and how Charlie was from the start telling him to leave her alone.

Toby told him everything, how they had spent the morning making love and how she had up and left without a word to him. He even told him the part about asking her to move with him to New York.

"This gal ya speakin' of...she the Lambert gal?"

"Yes sir," Toby said confused by the way he'd asked.

"Son," he said with his head down. "Charlie right 'bout one thang, you ought to leave that gal alone. The story goes that chil' got evil in her, her whole family do. Her mama, a black woman wit' blue eyes—I don't reckon she was even black—most people seem to think she was a white woman passin' fo' black, 'cause she was in love wit' Grady and it was the only way they could be together. So, they come up wit' this story of her Great-Grandmother being the ancestry of a slave owner. Much easier for folk to believe she got her eyes from her ancestry lain' up wit' a white man. So that's the story I was told. The truth come out in Sarah though, wit' eyes like ravens, everybody knows ravens is messengers of death. They also know ya can tell lots 'bout a person just by lookin' into the eyes. And Sarah had neither her fathea nor her motheas eyes."

"But, Pop...why the color of her eyes make her evil? The Sarah I met wasn't evil—a bit closed off—but look what she been through. That would make any-body hateful to a point."

"Toby, you don't seem to get it son do ya, in time that gal will come to find out who she really is. She ain't no true Lambert—evil begets evil—'twas no mistake that Hawkins killed the woman that raised her. He was tyrin' to get rid of evil."

"Pop, I just don't get it, all this talk about evil. The Sarah I met ain't evil one bit." Toby was hard yet still in his place. The man he was talking to was his father, although he had been adopted.

Toby's father continued his story. "Sarah was tak-en in by the Lamberts when she was just a baby. Her true mama died during her birth, it was awful...ya could her that woman's screams all over town. Sit down son let me tell ya the story as I know it to be."

Tobias pushed the suitcase to the floor and sat at the edge of the bed.

"See son, word has it Sarah's true mama was into devil worshiping, and she would cast spells on peo-ple, ya know voodoo," he said with a shiver. "Well anyhow..., outta nowhere this woman come into town, she was beautiful, most beautiful thang 'round. All the men wanted her and from what I understand, she had most of them. She fell in love with a man called Dewitt. When Dewitt asked her to marry him, she said yes. The folks thought it was the wrong thang fo' ol' Dewitt to do. Folks claim they had seen her in the woods many a night wit' a group of 'bout six others, three women and three men. They be out there wit' a fire lit chanting and putting strange thangs into pots of boiling water. One night ol'lady Harggerdy say she saw them kill a goat and drank the blood. Dewitt's sista was dead set 'ganst him marrying such a woman. So Sista went out one day to let Sarah's mama know how she felt 'bout her marrin' into the family…."

"Look-a-here woman, I know whatchu do out there in them woods late at night, wit' them strange people ya be 'round. I don't want my brotha caught up in yo' mess. You besta leave him 'lone and be on 'boutcho way." Sista was scared at the thought of what might happen to her.

"Get from here, Sista. I loves Dewitt and ain't you nor nobody else gonna tell me who I can and can't have. Now if ya know what best fo' ya I stay out my way." replied Sarah's birth mother.

Toby's father went on. "Sista later told us the woman was cold and her eyes turned black as coal and the light turned crimson, when she told her that she disapproved of her marring Dewitt—at least that's how the story goes. Anyhow, Sista come up missin and ain't nobody seen nor heard from her since. Dewitt married the strange woman after a month or so of him askin. Soon after, Dewitt began actin' strange—like somethin' wrong wit'em. He be out in the fields late at night naked as a jaybird and staring out into space. And, if'n anyone tried to get close to'em, he would go to hollerin' and run after you. Word spread that Dewitt had killed a man in the next town, on account'a he was under a spell to do so by his wife. Some folk say you could walk past their house and see a red light coming from every room. The few folk they let in say it was covered in all that voodoo magic stuff. Ya know dead chickens, bats; even say they had human heads that wasn't nothing but bone. Say it was cold inside—even in the dead of summer. Ol' lady Haggerdy say she saw Dewitt one morin' and he was as pale as a sheet...,"

"Dewitt, what the matter wit'cha? You sho' look awful, ain't you feelin' well?" Old lady Harggdery asked.

"She bleedin' me dry, bleedin' me you hear." Dewitt replied eyes white and glazed over.

"Whatcha mean, she bleedin' ya dry? You need help?" She asked, trying to keep her distance as he walked toward her with every word.

"She bleedin' me dry." He repeated.

After Toby's father spit into the can, he turned his body to look out the window as he continued his story. "Ol' lady Haggerdy say she was too scared to find out what Dewitt meant 'bout being bled dry—'specially after what happened to Sista. Folks assumed the woman killed him after she found out he'd been talkin'.

On the last evenin' the only person what seen Sarah's birth mama was a hunter, he say he was out in the woods when he saw what look like a women being mauled by an animal. When he moved in to help, he saw it was Sarah's mama and a man. He say, he stood there and watched, he say his feet wouldn't pick up and run, although he tried, he couldn't move.

He say it felt like they knew he was there and was forcing him to watch as the man rode her. The hunter say she watched him with tears in her eyes, and was movin' her mouth to scream, but nothing was coming out.

The hunter said he could hear the faint and distant sounds of people screaming and that the air around him smelled of dead bodies.

Next he say, folks came out of the trees when the beast was done and held her down with her legs apart and sewed her up. He say he heard one of them tell her. She had disobeyed and married a human, now the unborn would one day take her place. The beast what was ridin' her was nowhere to be seen. No one saw Sarah's mama, until the day she was heard screaming in the woods, where ol' lady Hagg-erdy found the baby. Mrs. Lambert come to care for the child. Sayin' that no man had the right to kill the baby. If'n it was Satan's spawn that wit' help God, the baby would be all right. She was too, until that day Mrs. Lambert was killed in the very same woods her mama died giving birth to her. Some say she was killed 'cause Satan done come to claim his own.

Folks round here seem to think that's why her Pa went mad, cause it seems, Satan done come to claim his own."

Toby's father just sat for a moment staring out into the distance. His heart was heavy for Sarah, but he was more afraid for his son. He was also scared because he knew things were about to change for the town as they did all those years ago when the strange woman came to town.

"Well I think it's a bunch of shit. I'm sorry, but that's how I feel and I plan to find her befo' I leave." Tobias was to his feet closing up the last of the suit-cases.

"Son, you's a grown man now. I know ya got to make ya own choices in life, but please son…if'n ya nevea listen to me evea again, listen now. Rememba this story and leave while you still can, nevea see that gal again. I'm sure God will take care of ya… but when ya dance with the devil you get burned." His father knew there wouldn't be anything he could say, because a man in love knows nothing else nor does he care.

Toby finished packing and wondered how much truth was in the story father told. Sarah had told him that every story has a bit of truth in it. What part of this story was her truth?

Event 018.00

Sarah was in bed trying to get some sleep, she knew the next morning would be long and trying, she had many things to sort out. Nevertheless, sleep wouldn't come this night.

She got up from bed and went to get the pictures she had brought with her. Maybe seeing her mama would put her mind at ease.

As she studied the pictures, she saw something she hadn't seen before—it was in all the photos. There was a dim glow of red light around her. At first, she thought it was a problem with the photo being a bit old. As she moved closer to the lantern, she could see the photo was old, but there was a red light around her. Where was it coming from?

She moved over to the mirror and studied herself searching for the light each photo held. There was a candle near, she decided to light it and turn off the lantern. She put her face close to the mirror and studied the air around her. Leaning back in her chair she continued to study herself.

The room became chilled and Sarah could see her breath in the air. She looked toward the window and saw it was closed. She turned back to look at the mirror and that's when she saw it.

She jumped up from the chair, cursing at the thump it made as it hit the floor. She glanced back at the mirror, but the image she had seen only seconds before was gone—so was the chilled air.

"Sarah, you all right in there? Open the door. It's me, Savannah," she was twisting the doorknob and knocking franticly. "Open this door."

"I'm comin'," she yelled, relieved that someone had come to see about her.

"What was that noise? You all right in here?" Savannah asked staring around the room.

"Fine...just fell asleep in the fuckin' chair and the damn thang fell over." Sarah was looking into the mirror while she came up with the lie.

"You don't like the bed, is it too hard fo' ya?"

"No Ma'am, the bed is fine...I was...well I just fell asleep in the chair. I didn't mean to disturb ya."

"No worries chil', I was passin' by when I heard the noise. You wanna go down and have a drink with me?"

Sarah thought a drink would be just the thing she needed to put her to sleep. As they walked down the hall to the stairs, Sarah saw a man coming up another set of stairs that led to the front of the house. He was tall and very light skinned—almost white. As the man approached, she saw he was white. He went into the first room on the left and closed the door.

Sarah figured this would be a good time to start asking questions. When they entered the kitchen,

Savannah was going on about something. Sarah wasn't sure what because her mind was collecting questions she needed answers to and she wasn't about to go to sleep without them.

Savannah sat in a chair next to Sarah and poured them both a tall glass of lemonade—adding a bit of whisky to both glasses. Sarah drank fast, placed her glass before Savannah, and waited for her to refill it.

"Somethin' the matter gal?" Savannah asked, as she fixed her another drink.

"Not yet," she replied.

"What is it suga? You know ya can ask me anything. I'm sho' you got plenty on ya mind. I know thangs is happin' real fast for ya right now."

"Whatchu really do here? I see men comin' and going all the time. And Papa told me befo' he left that this place was a whorehouse. Is that why I'm here to become a whore?" She asked, looking into her now full glass and knowing the truth to her own question.

"Sarah listen..., ya don't have to do anything ya don't wanna do. I'm just lookin' out for ya 'cause ya papa asked me to. He was a good ma—" Savannah was cut short with the pound of Sarah's fist hitting the table.

"He what'n shit..., and as for bein' a good man, look at my face! It really look like he was a good man to you? Stop the bullshit and tell me the truth! Why am I here?" I was angry, and as I watched her face for truth I thought, *how could she tiptoe around the matter with such bullshit.*

"All right, ya want the truth. Just like that ya want me tell you why you here. Grady thought it be good fo' ya to come here and live and work for me. Be one of my girls. So, yeah suga, you were brought here to be a whore. I owed him for helping me so many years ago and your bein' here was how he wanted to be paid back. 'sides that…, he ain't wantchu and was gonna leave you in the street…there that enough truth fo' ya. I know ya pissed as hell, but you will respect me." Savannah had had enough of her fits and angry questions.

Sarah sat for a moment, glaring into the eyes of her new mistress. The words that came out of Savannah's mouth didn't make Sarah mad, but relieved, she felt she needed to hear the truth one last time in order to come to full grips with it all.

The two women sat in silence for a while and drank. Savannah wondered what she was thinking, what was she feeling.

Sarah took the whisky bottle and poured another tall glass. She drank until the glass was empty. "All right then…, if this is to be the life for me…then I should get use to it right? After all, Pa did tell me he broke me in good and I should be ready for anything that come my way. So when do I start?"

Event 019.00

Tobias thought he would go back to the house in hopes Sarah would be there.

Arriving to the house, he found it still locked up and the note he'd left on the door was still there. He retraced all his steps, still she was nowhere to be found. He headed back to town in hopes he would see her in the soda shop or possibly run into her on the street.

He asked around wondering if anyone had seen her last night. No one had an answer for him.

Where could she be? He gave up and started for home, his heart longing for her.

Tobias replayed the morning they had spent together repeatedly in his mind. How could he have allowed himself to sleep when in his heart, he knew she would get up and leave.

Was father right in the stories he told me?

To him it all seemed like something out of a horror story, with devil worshiping and demons having sex with women.

He needed to find out from Sarah was it true? He had so many questions and not one answer that satisfied him.

However, time was getting away and he had to be on the next train to New York.

As Tobias was heading for the train station, he saw Charlie at the corner of the soda shop trying to gain the attention of a group of girls walking by. He waited a moment before deciding to go over to him and apologize for belting him one in the face. He thought about it and figured he couldn't leave town with two people angry with him.

"Yo, Charlie," he called out.

When Charlie made eye contact, he turned his back and went into the soda shop. Toby ran behind him, thinking it might be the last chance he had to settle his differences with his best friend.

When he entered the store, he searched for Charlie and found him sitting at their favorite table—looking in his direction. Toby walked over to him—slowly—hoping he wouldn't get up and leave. The two men eyed each other as Toby approached the table.

"What the hell ya want man?" Charlie asked.

"Wait a minute man...no need to be so cross. I come to say I was wrong for last night."

"Man, you was more than wrong," Charlie leaned around him to get a glimpse of girl entering the shop. "Daammn! Wouldchu look at that. Sho' is a beautiful site." Toby turned to see what was more important than him trying to make amends.

"Man, you listenin' to me? I said I was wrong." Toby

tried to regain his attention.

"Yeah man, I heard chu, now sit down...you standin' over me like I'm some sort of big shot. Sit yo' ass down so I can see." Toby knew then he had forgiven him.

"I was on my way to the train station, it leaves this afternoon."

"So, ya really finna do this? You finna go up to that fancy school. Man sho' wish I was you or at least going wit'cha. I hear there is some baadd asss pussy up there!" Charlie said, as if it was a love song, holding himself tight and swaying back and forth in his seat.

"Maann, yo' dick gonna be the death of you if you ain't careful." Toby laughed, glad his friend was no longer angry with him.

"So didcha find that gal?" Charlie asked.

"Naw, I went back to the house, but she wasn't there. I don't know where else to look."

Charlie thought hard about telling him he'd seen her going into Savannah's place. He watched Toby searching the store as he went on about her. His heart heavy for Toby, he figured since he was leaving for school, it wouldn't do any harm to tell him where she was.

"Look-a-here man, I know where she is. I spotted her last night—"

"You saw her last night, here in town, where?" Tobias's head spun around so fast, he got a small crick in his neck.

"Look, Tob man, I'm only telling ya this 'cause...I whatchu to gon' and leave this place like ya plan on doing, don't get stuck here like most of us...and damn sho' don't stay 'cause of that bit—...that Lambert gal." He said, not forgetting they fought because he called her a bitch.

"Save the speech and just tell me where she is. I gotta see her. Now where is she?" Toby found himself trembling at the thought he might see her again.

"She over at Savannah's place, I saw her go in last night and she never come out." Charlie's heart hardened.

"What...? I have to see her."

"Hey man—" Before Charlie could get out any more words Toby was up and heading for the door. He sat and watched his friend run to the old house that held a den of no good and wondered what Toby saw in her.

"Sho' hope that fool know what he doin'." He said aloud and turned his attention to the girls at the counter.

Event 020.00

The place was quiet outside and Toby couldn't see anything through the thick of the curtains. While he was contemplating what he was going to say to Sarah, a woman opened the door and stood before him. Suddenly, he was at a loss for words.

She stood short and stout with a cigarette hanging from her mouth and her hair was a mess, her make-up smudged. She wore a long gown that hung just so around her ankles. There was an odor of stale cigarettes and booze coming from inside. He thought for a second, *Why this place?*

"Can I help you, son?" The woman asked. "We ain't open yet."

"Ummm…I'm here to see Sarah. Is she here?" Toby asked, with a tremble in his voice.

"You ain't heard what I said," the woman stated with a twisted face and placing her hands on her hips. "We…ain't…open…yet. Hell, hoes gotta sleep too." The woman repeated.

"Hoes," Toby said taken aback by her comment. "Sorry Ma'am, I'm not here for pleasure, this visit is about business. I have to see her please tell her,

Tobias is here, please Ma'am. I gotta see her, this is my last chance." He pleaded.

"Look, ya wait here, ya seem harmless enough and I'll check see if she here. We did have a new gal come in last night. However, don't get use to it ya hear. Comin' by at all hours of the morning." The woman was mumbling as she closed the door without waiting for his answer.

Toby stood wondering why Sarah would choose to live here instead of coming to be with him. *This place can't give her what I can.* He said to himself. Then the door opened.

"I understand ya here to see Sarah. Well come on in, I'm Savannah." Savannah's beauty and the smell of her perfume rivaled Toby's senses.

"Look Ma'am, I'm just here to talk to her, that's all."

"I didn't ask ya why ya were here suga, I just said come in. So you comin'?" She asked, with her hand out to lead him in. She showed him to the parlor. Told him to wait there and she would get Sarah.

He watched her as she walked slowly up the stairs, and now knew why so many men would come to see her. Her walk was like an angel, although he had never seen one. He figured if he had, it would move like her. He could see her figure through her nightgown, as it clung to her every move; her skin was like butter—smooth and creamy. Her smile was bright and although her eyes seemed to hold a longing, they were still beautiful.

Toby had to collect himself—fast—because he looked down and saw his manhood getting the best of him. He tried hard to think of something else, by then Sarah had come into the room and he had to turn and face the wall so she wouldn't see what he had gotten himself into.

She stood for a moment watching him. When it was safe he turned and walked over to her, taking her hand in his and pulled her close, he could smell the booze on her breath, but he didn't care. He kissed her softly. He could see she still had bruises on her face. He also noticed she was healing unusually fast and more of her true skin was showing through.

"Whatcha doin' here?" She asked.

"I come to see you. Why did you leave and not tell me?" Still holding her hand, he led her to the couch in front of the curtained window.

"I don't owe you nothin', not even an answer to your questions." She was cold and knew it would hurt, but that's the way it had to be.

"Sarah, why you so upset? I know thangs ain't been easy for ya, but I wanna change that."

"Look man, you cain't change nothin'. Now what-chu come here fo' and how did ya know I was here?"

"Charlie saw ya come in last night and told me just a few minutes ago. Sarah, I don't wanna rush ya into anything and I didn't come here to fight wit'chu, but I'm leavin' this afternoon and I need your answer. Remember I told ya I was going off to school and wanted you to come with me?"

"Yeah, I remember and ya seem not to get the message. I aint goin'. 'Sides I cain't. I ain't got any money and I won't have ya payin' my way. I don't wanna owe ya nothin' in the end."

"Whatchu gonna do here? Let these women turn

you out; you know what will happen to you here? These men will eat you alive."

"Now look-a-here, Tobias, you got no right comin' here and telling me how I should live my life. I know what go on in here and Savannah done talk to me. Now I have to get some sleep befo' this evening and it's time you get goin'. And for the last time...I'm not goin' to no New York wit'cha—ya hear—I'm not goin'!" Sarah was shouting and Savannah hearing this, came to see what was going on.

"What's goin' on in here gal, why you yellin' like that?"

"Please sho' him to the door." Sarah ran from the room crying. Savannah was left standing bewildered and Toby called to her, but she didn't return.

"Will you please tell me what the hell this is all about? Whatchu say to her. She got loads to deal wit' already...and who the hell are you anyway?" Savannah asked, holding him back so he wouldn't run after her.

"Ma'am, please let me go to her. I got to see her one last time befo' I go. I love her, Ma'am. YOU HEAR ME, SARAH, I LOVE YOU!" He shouted.

Sarah was in her room with her head to the door, she had heard his calls, but wasn't about to go to him. She heard him yell out that he loved her. She knew she felt the same way about him—she has loved him since day one. There was no way she was going to allow herself to trap him in her world.

She could hear footsteps coming. Then, there was a knock on the door.

"Sarah, its Van, open this door," she called out.

"Open it now!" She was in no mood for childish fits.

"It's open, you can come in as long as he ain't wit'chu!" She shouted back through the door.

"Girl, it's time you grow up. You playn' a dangerous game, you need to see that boy and tell him how ya really feel. You love him too don'tcha? I know ya do, 'cause I ain't nevea known a woman to have such a fit 'bout a man wantin' to take care of her." Savannah wanted nothing more than to hear her say she did.

"No, I hate him!" The pillow she had buried her face in was soaking up her tears.

"Gal, who you think you talkin' to? I been where you are too many times in my life *not* to see how ya really feel. At least talk to'em like a woman. You owe him that much, he still waitin' downstairs for ya. Now I'm gonna call him up and you gonna talk to him, ya hear." Savannah took a deep breath and went to get Toby.

Tobias knocked gently at the door. It took Sarah a few seconds to get herself together before letting him in.

"Come on in and have a seat." She said softly, as she took one herself.

"I didn't come here to upset you. I just wanted an answer about you coming with me."

"Did you mean what you said down there?"

"Yes...I want you with me."

"No...not that. Do you really love me?" Her eyes filled with tears, as she thought of a man really loving her.

"Yeah, I love you and I want you to come wit' me. I

don't have much, but I'm sure we can make do." He studied her, looking for a sign she was giving in.

"Look, I ain't going to New York wit'cha. Cain't you understand my place is here. I would be no good for you, and 'sides I don't got money to make the trip." Sarah was fishing for reasons, anything not to hurt his feelings.

Toby stood from his chair and walked over to her. He took her by the hand and pulled her up to him. He held her close and gave her a slow deep kiss. She returned his kiss with a passionate one of her own. Once again, she could feel her heart beating with his.

Sarah stepped back and lay on the bed. She motioned for him to come to her. She felt she had to have him one last time before she showed him the door.

Toby removed his shirt and pants and climbed into bed with her. Slowly he removed her gown, then her panties. He softly kissed her breasts working his way down to her navel. She inhaled and trembled with every warm breath hitting her body. For the last time she would be in heaven and hope the moment would stay with her forever.

Toby wondered if this was going to be his last time holding his beloved. He made love to her in a way he never thought possible between to people. He wanted her to feel the way he thought the women in the movies felt when a man was making love to them.

The noonday was fast passing and Tobias knew he'd already missed the first train, but he figured he would catch the next one or leave in the morning.

"Toby?"

"Yeah," he replied.

"What time you say your train leavin'?"

"Don't worry 'bout that, it's ok." He was hoping the next thing out of her mouth was that she would go with him.

"You gotta get goin' now. Get up and put your thangs on." She got out of bed and handed him his clothes. With a confused look, he began to put his clothes on. When he was done, he stood for a moment and watched her as she stood by the window. He watched her wondering what she was thinking about.

"Sarah," he called to her.

"What," she replied without looking at him.

"I think ya know what, what's it gonna be?" He walked over to her, taking her by the arms swinging her around so he could see her face.

"Tobias, I told you...I cain't be wit'chu, not right now."

"Didn't you hear me say I love you? Sarah, I love—" She stopped him before he could say anymore.

"I know ya do...and yes...I heard whatchu said. There is something ya don't understand though, I tried not to hurtchu—but, I...I don't really love you." Tears welled in her eyes, she knew she loved him and wanted to be with him, but she couldn't shake the words the voice had said to her. *'No man will love you the way you want.'*

"Now why you wanna say some bullshit lie like that? Ain't a damn thang here for you! You said it ya'self. Yo' pa gone and yo' ma...well she dead! You act like you like this life or somethin'. This here, this here whatchu want? A life wit' all kinds of men in and outta ya all day and night. Beatin' on you like your papa use to—"

Sarah had heard all she was willing to hear. Reaching back with all she had, she slapped him on the face. Repeatedly, Sarah beat on Toby until he was able to gain control grabbing her and pinning her to the bed. Then he lay atop of her holding her until she stopped fighting—trying his best not to hurt her, she had already had too much of that.

His words repeated back in his mind. Then he realized, he had hurt her too. Maybe far more than a fist to the face or a busted lip could have ever done. He let her go, standing up and unable to face her.

"What right you got to judge me? Who the hell told-chu, you got the right to explain my life to me! Get the hell out! Mista, you don't know me like ya think ya do. Now get the hell outta my life fo' you get hurt!" Her voice was wounded and deep. She was hurt and he knew it.

Thoughts began to fill his mind of what life had put her through. Her mama killed and her papa not loving her, but blaming her. Now him—in a frenzy—angry over her not wanting to be with him and talking before he thought it through. Tobias knew there would be nothing left for him to say now. Slowly he walked to the door, searching his mind for words to make up for what he had said.

"Sarah—" he started, looking back to her.

"Toby, geeett ooutt! There ain't a damn thang left fo' you to say now. You done said all I'm gonna listen to! *Now go*," She yelled throwing a glass that sat on the edge of the dresser near her. It missed his head by inches. "Oh yeah…, leave the money with Savannah on your way out." She added.

"Sarah, whatchu doin' this for?" Toby turned to her, with tears in his eyes.

"Leave the money, ya may as well be my first, you heard me trick…I ain't got nothing left in me. Now get the hell out!" She walked over to the door and opened it for him while she stood behind it. Wanting nothing more than to take him in her arms and apologize.

Toby left with his head down and his heart heavy— not forgetting to leave more than enough money with Savannah.

"Don't tella it was from me."

Event 021.00

"Toby man, you still here? Didchu find whatcha was lookin' fo'?" It was Charlie coming out of the soda shop when he saw Toby walking by. Charlie noticed that he hadn't looked in his direction or flinched when he called out his name. "Hey man, didn'tcha hear me? Slow down what's the hurry... you already missed the first train—of course I know ya know that," Charlie was puzzled by his friend's reaction. "Hey man, what's up. Why ya look like somebody just died?"

Still, Toby said nothing, not even slowing down to let Charlie catch his breath. He just kept walking and staring in one direction.

"Man, she must have really put it on you in there. What's it like in there anyway? I tried to get in, but they say I'm still a boy and come back when I grow some hair. Boy look-a-here let me tell ya, that's one task I am truly workin' on...ya know what I mean?" Charlie was trying to break the ice—he could see something was heavy on Toby's mind.

The two walked in silence the rest of the way to the train station. Once they arrived, Toby went up to get his ticket, still not having one word for Charlie. Toby found a seat near the window inside the stations waiting area. The window had been broken out and carelessly taped to hold in the remaining pieces of glass. He still hadn't made notice of Charlie, which by this time had no idea what to say next. So, he sat next to Toby without saying a word and hoping he had realized that Sarah wasn't worth it.

Toby was thinking back on the days leading up to this one. *Why did I fall asleep? If I had been awake, I could have stopped her from leaving the next morning. Maybe if I had nevea heard her cryin' out in the middle of the night, I would have nevea saw her again.* "Damn, Sarah. Why would you choose that life?" Toby was now thinking aloud.

"Whatcha say?" Charlie asked.

"I was thinking man—I said some nasty shit to her just now. Now she'll never let me back in her life." Toby replied.

"Ya need to back up and start over," Charlie wanted to know everything. "I ain't got a clue whatchu talkin' 'bout."

"I'm talkin' about Sarah, I messed up....I said some mean shit to her." Toby was rubbing his face, trying to hold back the tears.

"What did you say?"

"Man...open your ears. I may have lost the most beautiful thang I have ever seen in my life. I called her a *hoe*, told her she was *nothin', an orphan.* Charlie man, I opened my mouth without thinkin' of how it would affect her. I'd hoped she'd just get *mad*...tell me I was right and come with me. Instead, she got *pissed*...told me to get the fuck outta her life. Damn man, I fucked up." Tobias was feeling alone and he wanted to go back and tell her how he really felt, but he figured it would do him no good now.

"Look man, ya know I care aboutcha, but it's like I toldchu befo', ya best to leave that girl where she at. I don't know why ya family evea came back. You don't know how thangs really is 'round here. You doin' right by goin' gettin' out—hell, I wish I could go wit'chu. Man look, ya only knew the girl for a short time, when ya get up to the big city...and see aww'la that big fine city ass. Man this small time shit here, be a fade in the dark."

Tobias was staring at Charlie. He wanted to knock him one in the mouth for saying it, but he figured he had almost lost him once and he wasn't about to do it again.

"Look man, I'm gonna pretend you didn't just say whatchu said and call it a day. Let me ask you something though?"

"Sho' man, anything fo' ya." Charlie said with a big smile.

"Will you look out fo' her while I'm gone? Ya know, look in on her—see how she doin'."

"Sho' man, I'll do that. But, won'tcho pops be kinda mad 'bout me comein' 'round to see his ol' lady?" Charlie said with a sarcastic grin.

"Come on man, this is serious will ya watch out for Sarah or not?" Toby wasn't sharing his cynicisms.

"Yeah, well I s'pose so. Look man, you askin' me to do an awful lot. Keepin' my eye on that girl, that part is easy. It's what I just might see that got me worried." Charlie agreed shaking his head.

Now annoyed by Charlie, Tobias stood to ask him what he meant by all the sarcasms.

"Hey man, look yo' train, best you get goin fo' ya miss this one too." Charlie said feeling a bit of relief

"Saved by the train bell, but you'll have to explain to me one day why you hate her so much. Hey man, I have to go!" Seeing the train ready to pull away, Toby ran to catch it with his friend in tow. He waved good-bye to him and said a silent good-bye to Sarah.

Charlie was left standing alone with his thought, as he watch the train roll and scream out of sight.

What is it about the Lambert girl that fool sees and I don't...?

Toby did ask him to keep an eye on her and that is just what he planned to do. His birthday was coming soon—he was going to be twenty-one.

The way Charlie saw it Savannah and her house couldn't refuse a young man and his money. This would be his chance to find out what Toby saw in Sarah. He would be able to find out what kind of spell she had him under. Charlie laughed a deluded laugh and ran off behind a young woman fumbling with her suitcase

Event 022.00

Sarah stood at the window with tears in her eyes, wondering why Toby had said the things he did. She knew he was upset about her not wanting to go to New York with him, but she couldn't help wonder why he was so mean about it.

Why should he be any different from pa—after all he is a man. That's when she came to the realization she was starting a new life.

She dried her face, walked over to the vanity and watched herself in the mirror, then said. "There's no room for love. You besta learn to live wit' it and learn to fight back with just as much hate." With that, she smiled and noticed her mirrored reflection dancing in the red mist.

Unmoved by what she'd seen, her thought was interrupted by a knock at the door. "Yeah, who is it?" She asked.

"Its Van honey, ya all right? I saw the young man fo' he left. He left ya a little somethin'." Savannah tried to sound as caring as she could about the money, knowing how most new girls felt their first time taking money for sex.

"Yeah, well you keep it. I don't want nothin' that boy got or gonna evea get, nothin' ya hear! Nothin!"

"Sarah, open this door. We need to talk about this," Savannah was fed-up with it all and thought it was time to nip it in the bud. "Open this damn door. You got some explainin' to do. I have to know what's goin on befo' I letchu stay. Now this place ain't much, but it is peaceful and—"

"It's open," Sarah interrupted. "All ya gotta do is turn the knob. No need to get all upset about it," Sarah was sitting on the bed staring in the direction of the door when she opened it. "See...toldchu."

"Now look gal, no need to get sassy wit' me. I was the one that took ya in—and I can be the one to put cha out. Now ya got a great deal on yo' mind, I understand that. I'm guess'n it got much to do wit' the way ya actin'. Nevertheless, You just remember who's boss 'round here. I don't mean to sound uncarin' or sound like I ain't got no compassion, but even I got limits to how ya gonna talk to me. Do we have an understandin'?" Savannah was sound, firm, but treading lightly.

"I'm sorry, I ain't meant to hurtchu, Savannah, just thangs seem to be happin' so fast. After my mama was killed and all I been through wit' Pa. Now this place? I feel like I'm losin' control of everythin'," she said, as she looked into the mirror, thinking of the figure she had been seeing. Not to mention, her dancing reflection. "I even think I'm startin' to see thangs." Savannah watched her as she fell back onto the bed.

"Well chil', maybe ya just need a good night's sleep.

For now though, I want to talk to you 'bout the young man that was here. He comin' back anytime soon?"

"No Ma'am, I don't reckon he is. As a matter of fact, I know he ain't." Sarah said, watching a roach creep across the ceiling.

"And what makes ya so sho'?"

"Well I told him to get the hell out of my life."

"May I ask what you do that fo'?" She was looking for a reason to send Sarah packing. Hoping she would see he might be able to give her a better life than she could.

"Look, he said some thangs that he ain't had no right to say. Sticking his nose in places it don't belong. He was like that from the start. But, today it was worse. He..." She stopped midsentence and broke into tears.

Savannah stood up from her chair and walked slowly over to her. Fishing for words to say when she got near. Taking Sarah in her arms, she pulled her close and held her tight.

"Hush chil', I know thangs is hard right now, but in time you'll grow and adjust. You'll see, ol' Van won't letcha down. I'll show ya how to survive."

Sarah pushed her back. "I know how to survive—I wanna know how to live." She said sadly, dropping her head back on Savannah's shoulder.

The two women sat for some time without a saying word, as Savannah rocked her and waited for her to cry it all out.

After Sarah was quiet and Savannah realized she had fallen asleep. She eased Sarah over to her pillow and crept out of the room.

Event 023.00

Afternoon, Ms. Van nice day ain't it?" Eva asked with a smile.

"Yeah, so far so good I s'pose, I'm glad ya here I need to talk to ya 'bout somethin'. Have a seat, I'm havin' lunch, you want some?" She was putting out the bowls and getting the soup from the stove as she spoke.

"Sho', I'd love some?" Eva replied, as she watched her move slowly across the kitchen.

"I changed my mind on you not havein' that baby. Now, I already sent a letter forward to ya mothea, and I told her 'bout the baby you expectin'—"

"Oh no, Ms. Van! Whatcha go and do that fo'?" Eva asked frantically.

"Calm down chil', you ain't let me finish. I told yo' mama you was gonna have a baby, and that I didn't think it would do you any good to get rid of it. Told her you was a good girl wit' a strong mind. She might be mad at first, but I know she wantchu to be wit'da...you and the baby."

"No, Ms. Van, I cain't do that. You don't know my mama...ya thank she would want me back fo'real?"

Eva had wide eyes as she spoke and hoped what Savannah was saying was true and that she wasn't just trying to get her to go back home. The mother Eva knew wouldn't want her back, unless she got something in return.

"Have I ever lied to ya 'bout anythin'? Anythin' at all?" Savannah knew she had, she was hoping Eva didn't know it.

"No Ma'am," Eva replied.

"Then, I ain't gonna start now. You can be on the next train in the mornin'," Savannah was sipping a spoon full of soup, although her appetite had gone.

"Oh, Ms. Van, how can I ever repay ya fo' whatcha done for me? It sho' gone be nice to get outta here."

"Chil', ya payin' me by goin home, where ya belong. This no place to be raisein' a chil'. This be fo' the best. You'll see thangs will work out when you're home and settled. Remember it might be ruff for a while, but it'll pass. I promise ya that," she said with a wink. "Now eatcha soup. Ya have to keep up yo' strength fo' that lil' one in ya belly." Savannah got up from the table and put her bowl in the sink, she felt like she was carrying hundred pound weights to the grave.

Eva stood up behind her, giving her a heartfelt hug. "Ms. Van, I'm too happy to eat, I'ma go pack my bags right now so's I don't fo'get nothin', 'sides I got a trick to do in 'bout a hour, least I can make a few more pennies fo' I go. Wow, Ms. Van…home," Eva was high on life and full of energy from the news. "Home…home…home!" She sang as she left Savannah alone in the kitchen with her own thoughts.

She thought now would be the best time to get Sarah up and have a long talk with her about what was expected of her. She knew there was no sense in putting it off any longer.

"Now how am I gonna say this?" She thought aloud.

"Say what?" Lue asked coming into the kitchen when she heard Savannah talking to herself.

"Oh, Lue ya scared me, ya know for a fat woman you sho' walk like a cat in the night." She replied laughing.

"Girl, now ya know I ain't one bit fat! Just big boned, ya know damn good and well my daddy was a Mandingo and that's where I get it!" Lue replied, as she pushed passed her trying to contain her laughter—knowing deep inside, she was fat. "So whatcha goin' on 'bout in here anyway, ya back to talking to yo'self again?"

"No, I gotta go up and tell that chil' that tonight is gonna be her first night workin'. Ya know how hard it is when its yo' first time."

"Cain't be too hard for her, whatin' that boy up there just this mornin'? Ain't no man and woman got that much to talk about. He was up there all mornin'. So she ready to do whatevea ya ask her to, you'll see. If'n it was me, I'da had her ass workin' the first night—bruised up face and all." Lue gave Van a wink and a smile, and then walked out the kitchen—nibbling on a slice of chocolate cake.

Again, Savannah was left alone to dwell in her own thoughts. *"Damn I hate this...damn."*

She closed her eyes, hung her head, and began walking slowly up the stairs and down the hall to

Sarah's room.

Event 024.00

Sarah had awakened and was thinking about Tobias. She still couldn't get out of her head the nasty things he had said to her.

Was he tryin' to hurt me? Why would he say such thangs? I thought we had somethin' good—

"No man can love you the way you want." She heard the voice say, turning fast to see who was there. She saw no one. Then, looking at her image in the mirror—her bruises still visible—she appeared tattered and broken.

Was it all a bad dream? Perhaps Tobias was just someone I'd dreamt up to get me through the day.

She knew he wasn't, but she knew she had to believe the lie to make it without him.

"Soon, Sarah wait…soon." A faint voice proclaimed. Startled, she turned once more to see who was there. She lifted herself slowly from her seat and walked over to the window pulling back the drapes. She peered over the window seal and scanned the ground and the skies for the person speaking. Still, no one was there.

"Who's that out there? This shit ain't funny, I ain't in no mood to be playin' games wit' nobody." Sarah yelled into the dusk.

The sun was going down and a picturesque array of oranges, pinks, and yellows filled the fast darkening skyline. She waited to see if anyone would come out to confess their nasty little joke, when her thoughts quickly ran to her mama.

Thinking on the days her mother and she used to sit out by the old oak tree at the creek and watch the sun go down.

"Mama, where the sun go when it ain't shinin' on us?" Young Sarah asked.

"Well I s'pose it go and shine on other people like us. Maybe it goes and gets some sleep—like you ought to be doin.' I reckon yo' pa be home by now. I gotta get him his supp'a. Come chil' let's get goin'. We got a long walk and I don't want to much dark to catch us," Her mama was putting the empty containers of food and drink back into the small wicker basket. "You get the pillows and covers, fold'em up nice now."

"Yes Ma'am," Sarah replied, smiling up at her mama.

The colors of the setting sun made her mama look like an angel in her eyes.

Her thoughts ceased when Savannah knocked at the door.

"Come in."

"Evenin' chil', whatcha doin' here all alone?"

"Just got up and was watching the sun set. My ma and me use to do that when she was still alive."

"Ya miss her somethin' bad don'tcha chil'?"

"Yes Ma'am, I reckon I do." Sarah said looking away.

"Well ya keep the memories of her alive within ya like ya doin'. When thangs get too hard to endure, her memories will getcha through." Savannah had only said this in hopes it would help when she told Sarah she had to pull her first trick tonight.

"Sarah," Savannah took her by the hand and led her to the bed. "Sit here I got somethin' I need to talk to you about."

"If it's about Tobias no need...I'm over him." Even though it was a lie and she felt Savannah knew that.

"No. it ain't 'bout him, it's 'bout whatchu have to do here. Now...I know...ya ain't gonna like this, but ya gotta start workin' for yo' keep."

"I knew my day was comin and I'm ready. You'll see. Like I already asked...when do I start?" Sarah's head was down and she could feel her body began to shake.

"It ain't that easy chil'. These men can be mean and nasty. Some of them just plain mean and some just plain nasty. They gonna want you to do stuff you ain't likely heard befo'. You have the right to say no to anything, but they have to right to get what they pay for. Ya understand that."

"Yeah, I 'spose I do. But, I am afraid." Sarah was shaking so hard she knew Savannah could see it.

"Look chil', I'm gonna be right down the hall at all times, so if you run into trouble you just yell out and I'll be here. I talked wit' a longtime friend of mine, he's one of the good ones. He's kind, and gentle, won't make ya do anything ya don't want to. He's gonna get ya started. Make ya feel at home."

Savannah was rummaging in a bag she brought with her, trying to find something to put on Sarah's still visible bruises.

"Savannah, I'm afraid what if I cain't do it. What if I mess up? I cain't do this...I just cain't. I don't feel right 'bout it." She was pacing the floor back and forth, rubbing her hands together, as Savannah watched her from the mirror.

"Come over here and sit. I'll be right back." She left and went to her room to retrieve a few things. Sarah was left to think about what the night would bring.

Softly the voice whispered again. "I'm here with you," Sarah sat very still, holding her breath and careful not to make any sound, she waited. "I'm here." She heard it again.

"All right now, let us see what we can do 'bout that pretty face of yours." Savannah said, as she reentered the room.

"Ummm..., didchu say somethin' to me befo' ya come in?" Sarah asked hoping she had.

"No chil'. But, you know, there was an ol' woman I befriended when I was about yo' age and she used to tell me, *'if ya hear somebody talkin' to ya and no one is around, it be yo' guardian angel talkin'. Just sayin' hello'.* So see chil', you have an angel. Somebody to look out fo' ya."

"Well so far it's doing a shitty job." Sarah replied in whisper.

"Ya say something suga?"

"No..."

Savannah was putting the contents of the bag in line on the top of the vanity. "We gonna get you all fixed up and lookin' like somebody. Ya evea wore makeup befo'?" She asked, trying to find just the right shade of red.

"No Ma'am, Papa wouldn't let Mama wear it. He said it was fo' whor..." Remembering where she was and whom she was talking to—not to mention what she too was about to become—her brain wouldn't allow her to finish her statement.

"Was fo' who, suga'," Savannah asked looking at her with a half grin. "Whores...is that whatchu was gonna say?"

"Well...yeah," Sarah was ashamed, because she knew that once the makeup was on, she would be what other people in town despised—she would be one of Savannah's whores.

"Well just you pay no mind to any of that. A lady can were makeup and still be a lady, no matter what kind of lady she be. Don'tchu evea forget it. Now lift ya head. It's time you stop draggin' it on the ground." Savannah went to work smearing, wiping, pulling, plucking, and admiring her work in between.

When she was done, she handed Sarah a hand mirror. "Well...that ought to do it. Whatcha think?"

Surprised by what she'd seen, she swiftly turned to look in the larger mirror on the vanity.

"Oh my God, Savannah, is that me?"

"Yes chil', who else it gone be," Savannah said, finding her ignorance heartwarming.

"Look at my eyes, and my lips...they as red as cherries. You made my bruises go away."

"No chil', they still there, they just covered up for now—and be sho' they stay that way—don't need you scarin' off my customers wit' all those bruises. And 'sides, tain't nothin' worse than a man thinkin' they can beat on ya, 'cause they think another man did."

"Whatchu gonna do wit' my hair. I ain't nevea had curls. I want curls like yours. Can you do it for me, Van? Can ya?" Sarah had never felt this pretty in her life, even though her mama did all she could.

"Okay..., but ya have to pay close attention, I cain't be in here all the time gettin' you ready, Sarah. Ya have to learn to do it yo'self. Sit down and let's get finished."

Sarah was in heaven, she had lost sight of the real reason for the complete makeover. Savannah watched her work as she pulled out a diamond in the ruff.

Sarah was truly beautiful Savannah thought. She was reminded of how she looked for the first time when she too had put on makeup, fancy clothes, and big spiraled curls. She remembered how all the men in her old hometown eyed her as she walked the streets. Now Sarah was her and she was more beautiful than she could have ever imagined.

After Savannah was done, she took Sarah into the kitchen to show her how to eat and drink without smudging her makeup. She also taught her to, hold a glass, sit like a lady, have a halfway modest conversation, and last how to show a man politely to the door when the job was done.

"After all time is money. Now you need a dress. Let's go up so's I can find somethin' old of mine that I haven't worn in years."

Savannah rumbled through an old trunk and found a red dress made of silk and lace.

"This thang use to cling to *all* my curves, driving the men wild—hum—but that was a *loonng* time ago."

The back of the dress hung low, forming a V-shape at the small of the back. The front, adorned with a laced patterned diamond shape on the chest, that spread up to the neck and hook tied in the back. Savannah eyed Sarah for moment, who was standing close by with a big grin. Savannah knew the dress wouldn't fit. Nevertheless, she had taken it in and let it out so many times before; she knew it wouldn't take long to make it fit.

"Well now. Let's see what this look like on ya, gone in my bathroom and try it on for size. We may need to take it in a bit." Savannah watched a giggling girl enter the bathroom and watched a smiling woman emerge.

"Hey, you sho' are swanky now, real fine. We may have to beat the men off wit' a stick when they get an eyeful of you gal! Hot damn!"

Savannah was pleased but still not happy.

Event 025.00

The other women were curious to see what this new girl looked like. Although Lue already knew, she still had her head stuck in the middle of the whispers and chatter among the other women.

"Oh shit, she ain't much, a skinny little shit wit' nappy hair, big coal black eyes, not to mention, she got all them damn bruises on her face. She won't last the night here, I can tell ya that." Lue said.

"Oh Lue, ya always goin' on 'bout how somebody is ugly and won't last here. I remember when it was me, and you saw me fo' the first time. You look like you was gonna rip my eyes out." One of the women replied.

"Yeah, maybe I did," Lue said laughing. "'Sides, I ain't told you lately, ya still ugly." All the women laughed. When Lue stopped laughing, she was looking up at the staircase, all the other women stopped and watched too.

It was Savannah standing waiting to introduce the newest girl to the house. "Ladies, I have someone I want ya'll to meet. Some of you have seen her here already in the halls and such. And one of you, she done already seen in action." Savannah was playfully eyeing Lue and smiling.

"Stop that foolishness and get on wit' it woman." Lue said, rolling her eyes.

"Everyone...meet, Sarah Lambert." Sarah stepped out from the dark and stood next to Savannah. She could hear some of the women whispering to each other, when one of them yelled out.

"Look out y'all, y'all ol' hoes in fo' a fight! She's a real look'a!" said a woman coming into the kitchen.

"Oh shut up ya nasty scank! Ain't nobody ask you to open yo' mouth, we all can see her." Lue yelled back.

"All right ladies, we have two hours befo' the doors open, so let's begin to get ready. Al, you have the refreshments out?" Savannah asked.

"Yes Ma'am," said the woman smiling with no teeth.

"Oh for-petes-sake, Al, where are yo' teeth? I done told you over and over keep them thangs in yo' mouth." Savannah said shaking her head.

"I got'em, they right here," she replied, pulling a set of teeth from her bosom and placing them in her mouth.

"Van, you sho' know how to pick'em. We all a bunch of misfits! Folk walkin' 'round wit' no teeth, Pat, got an awful stutter, it's a good thang this job don't require ya to talk much. Oh and what about Denver—the gal wit' one leg? Let's not forget the newest memba...lil' orphan Sheba over there." Lue said with a mouth full of corn bread.

"Oh Lue, shut up, you ain't nevea got nothin' nice to say," someone said as they were leaving. "And her name is Sarah."

"I know what her damn name is."

"All right enough of that," Savannah interrupted laughing and thinking Lue was right—they were a sight to see. "Please be sure we have fresh candles in the parlor. Lue, may I see you please? Sarah, gone down and talk with the ladies, I'll call you up later."

As Sarah passed Lue on the steps, Lue gave her a nasty look, rolled her eyes, and pointed her nose in the air. One of the women took notice and took Sarah by the hand leading her to the parlor.

"Neveamind her, her bark more harm than her bite. Don't know what her problem is though—we all hoes—no matter how we look. I'm Gina." She said, pulling up two chairs and getting two glasses from the bar.

"I'm Sarah, why she like that?"

"Girl, yo' guess as good as mine, she been that way in the three years I been here. I pay her no mine—here have a drank. This being yo' first night-n-all you gonna need it...trust me. Ain't no women come in here and the first night not get loaded befo' some ol' nasty ass man climb on top of her. Here take it down fast." Gina handed Sarah a small glass filled to the top with whisky.

Sarah figured she knew how to handle a nasty man on top of her, after all her papa saw to that. Nevertheless, she figured a shot would calm her nerves. With her head up and her eyes shut, she poured the liquor down her throat.

The burning in her chest made her cough and cringe with chills.

As the two women sat and drank, Sarah wondered what it would be like. Would it feel like being with her papa or would it be more like being with Tobias? Either way the time had come—and she had to be ready.

"Say, I got some stuff in my room. Wanna come up wit' me?" Gina asked.

"Some stuff? Whatchu mean," I asked feeling inexperienced and out of touch.

Gina took me by the hand and led me up to her room.

Gina's room was much larger than mine. It was decorated in velvet and lace, with lots of bright colors. Her bed had silk sheets and covers. The vanity sat near the window. I noticed a rug in the middle of the room. It was the ugliest thing there. It appeared like it had been there for years and she never cleaned it. It was torn and shredded on the edges.

"Look-a-here, Sarah, this some good shit. Last me all night long. You want some?"

"What is it?" I asked now knowing I was inexperienced and out of touch.

"Its coke girl, ain'tchu evea seen coke befo'?" Gina asked, snorting a line up her nose.

"No I ain't nevea seen it befo'. Look like flour. What it do to ya and why ya puttin' in yo' nose?" I watched her as she took another line into the opposite nostril.

"It make ya feel real good, 'sides it helps me get ready fo' certain men that come to see me on a regula'," Gina said, as she sniffed and wiped the extra residue from her face. "Girl, this one man that comes to see me, he real fat and ugly. He just be pourin' wit' sweat all the time. I feel like I'm…sloppin' hogs or somethin'…and he smells so bad. See that perfume bottle over there? Well it ain't perfume, it's soap and water. I tells him it be fun fo' me to wash him befo' we fuck. He don't care…he like it. You know you sho' is pretty in that dress. You do yo' makeup?" Before Sarah could answer, Gina was back to doing another line.

"No, Savannah did it fo' me. She done my hair and give me this dress."

"Sho'nuf, is that what she tell ya?" Gina replied snickering. "I know that dress…and I don't think she give it to ya. She let all the new girls wear it. It's so's the men know ya new. I wore it when I first come here, even though I had my own. I was told, the V-shape in the back meant ya was a virgin, but I'm not sho' how much truth in that though, 'cause Lord knows, I was no virgin. Hell, ain't no virgin gonna hardly come up in here, Ya know."

Gina held back nothing, she said whatever was on her mind and she said it fast. She was getting ready by putting on her makeup and clothes, as I watched—she was in no way shy at all.

There was a large cut on her left breast. She says that's where one of the men's wives tried to cut her heart out. The woman told her, if she could fuck a married man, then what she need with a heart. She says the men love a woman with a scar—some of them think it's sexy. It just looked downright ugly to me. It protruded slightly from her chest, it was dark, and it hadn't healed well at all.

"Hey girl, gone and get ya'self a line. I got mo',"

Gina said on her knees pulling a pair of stockings from under the bed. "Damn, fine time to have dirty stockings. Oh well...nasty hoes for a nasty hoe." She said shrugging her shoulders and giggling.

"Maybe another time, I'm good with the drink I got." Although I was curious about the coke and wanted to see what it was like, I was too afraid and thought I would stick to the whisky.

After about an hour of drinking and talking, Gina thought it was time for the us to go down and mix with the early guests.

"Here fix ya lips, the lipstick is gone, ya have to learn to drink wit'out messin' ya lips. It's the first thang that attracts the men. Well anyway, it takes some time to learn. Why ya lookin' at it like that? Don't tell me...ya cain't put on lipstick? Girl you do got lots to learn. You...you can fuck cain'tcha," Gina asked laughing, "I'm only kidding, anybody can fuck. If ya can move yo' hips—you can fuck. Just remember to keep those hips movin' and when ya ride'n him, turn ya back to him, so's ya ain't gotta look'em in the face."

"Ride'em? Turn my back to him? Gina, whatchu talk'n 'bout?" I asked puzzled.

"Well I'll be...Sarah, you *is* a virgin?"

"I ain't no virgin...just ain't got no idea whatchu talk'n 'bout is all."

"Well no time to sho' ya know. 'Sides if I know Van, she gonna set you up wit' ol' Sam, Lawd he is ugly, but he sho' ya what to do. All the new girls get'em. There, ya look great—you can keep that one. Let's get downstairs now."

"You go on…I'll be right there, I've gotta somethin' from my room." After Gina was out of sight, Sarah slipped back into Gina's room and poured some of the coke onto the table. Unable to snort it like Gina, she opted to put it in her whiskey glass.

Sarah was midway the staircase, when she was stopped by the sound of Savannah's voice. "Sarah, glad I caughtcha. Would ya come in here please? Someone I'd like ya to meet." She walked slowly back upstairs with her heart trying to find its way out of her chest.

Stepping into the room, she could see a man standing in the corner. She couldn't make out his face because he was in the shadows. She scanned the room and it was something different about it. The lights were out, all that illuminated the room were ten candles, and it smelled of sweet perfume.

"Sarah, this here is Sam, the man I told you 'bout. Sam, get out of the corner and meet Sarah." Savannah was holding out her hands to the pair.

"Hello, Ms. Sarah, how you be tonight." Sarah noticed it was the somewhat round fat man, with blood shot eyes, and the beard that hadn't filled in on all sides.

"Fine," she said with a hiccup. "'scuse me."

"Yeah, whisky does that to me to." He replied with a chuckle hoping to calm her.

"Well you two stay here, and I'm gonna go see 'bout my other guests." Sarah's eyes widened as she watched Savannah shut the door behind her. For a moment, the pair stood in there respectful places and stared everywhere, except at each other.

Sam broke the silence. "You want anoth'a drank? Savannah brought this up when I come, so's we didn't have to be wit' the others. Savannah tells me you her newest gal," Sarah moved in and sat on the edge of the bed without a word and watched him as he prepared two glasses of whisky and handed her one. "We can just sit here and talk all night if ya like, Savannah uses me to break in all the new gals like you."

Sarah wasn't sure if the whiskey was catching up to her or if it were the coke. But, she knew she didn't want to spend the rest of the night listening to the old man fish her bullshit lines—especially listening to him use phrases like *'break you in'*.

"What the hell am I? Some kinda fucking cattle. I've heard that line far more times then I care to mention. I feel ashamed enough as it is already. Savannah give me this damn dress to let all the men know this my first time. Well…let me tell ya somethin' mista. I been—*'broke in'*—as you say already! So ya here to talk or ya here to fuck? 'Cause I ain't here to talk, this hard enough already wit'out all the damn talkin'." I was afraid I would lose my nerve if we talked. When really all I wanted to do was get it done and over with.

Sam sat watching me wide eyed and puzzled at my sudden outburst. But, I'm sure he was use to the new girls taking their anger out on him.

I reached over uneasily and too fast to undo his shirt. I hit his glass spilling his whisky in his lap.

The cool from the liquid must have alarmed him, because he sprang up so high, he could have touched the ceiling.

"Oh Sam, I'm sorry...I'll get that right out, just wait here!" Sarah said.

"No worries gal, these ol' anyhow," replied Sam, as he shook the whiskey from his pants.

"No problem, won't take but a second." Not paying any attention to her, he grabbed her by the hand and pulled her to him fast, strong, and hard. Sarah gasped. That's when she saw something unusual. Sam's eyes were no longer a soft shade of hazel, but jet black and he seemed not to be looking at her, even though he was. She began to feel light headed.

"We are here with you." He said. It was Sam's body but the voice was different. "We have always been with you. You're afraid, this we know, Your time is soon approaching." The smell of his breath was intoxicating, and Sarah felt engaged by the man that was no longer Sam.

Sarah recognized the voice, she had heard it just hours before. She could feel the room spinning as he spoke.

Her body was weightless, as if she just hung in midair. The room was cold and growing colder.

"Who are you? What do you want?" Sarah words were soft and weak.

"In time you'll see and know what we are, Who you are. For now stay. Stay in this house. No longer be afraid. We are with you."

Sam's body went limp and fell to the floor. Sarah was left standing over him—light headed and dazed—with a bottle of whisky in her hand.

As she slowly regained her composure, she saw

Sam was on the floor and bleeding from the ears and nose.

"Savannah!" Sarah yelled, dropping the bottle. She had yelled so loud everyone in the house heard. Most of the woman, including Lue and Gina, ran to see what happened.

"What's goin' on in here?" Savannah asked as she and a few of the other women burst into the room. "What happened to Sam?" She asked, noticing the blood. "Gina get me some clean towels and cold water, hurry he's bleedin' real bad. Sarah, Sarah," Savannah called, "what happened in here, chil'?" Sarah still in shock was unable to find an answer.

Lue thought this would be the perfect time to slap her for coming in on her and Busta. Lue smacked Sarah hard across the face—she came too. Lue stood in silence while Sarah rubbed her cheek.

"Now Lue, ya ain't had to take her head off." said a woman standing behind them.

"Oh hell, I ain't hit her that hard. Anyway, she back ain't she?" Lue replied, watching Sarah while she was still rubbing the side of her face.

"What the hell is everybody doin'….Why is Sam bleedin' like that?" Sarah asked in shock by the site of Sam on the floor. Quickly images flashed in her head of Sam and a figure she couldn't fully make out. Then suddenly she knew. *The voice….*

Without saying another word, Sarah bent down to help clean Sam's face.

Savannah was feeling for a pulse—there was none. "He's dead!" Savannah said in shock.

"Oh no," replied Sarah, then passed out, hitting the

floor with a dull thud.

"Dead! What the fuck ya mean dead!" Yelled Lue, "let me check you ain't doin' it right." Lue felt his neck to check for herself. "Yep, the poor ol' fool done worked himself to death." Lue said looking up with a grin.

"Lue, this ain't no time for that fool mouth of yours. What we gon' do? Somebody get this chil' up and take her to her room." Some of the other women picked up Sarah and walked her to her room.

"Put her on the bed and get back to Savannah, I'll stay here wit'da." said Gina.

Meanwhile, Savannah and Lue picked up Sam and placed him on the bed. "Call the doc over and tell'em we got a man dead over here, hurry. The longer we wait, the more trouble we're likely to get into."

Savannah watched her longtime friend lay lifeless. She remembered he was the first man to defend her when things got rough. What was she going to do without him?

"All right ladies, nothin' we can do now, he's gone. We wait for the doc to get here. Y'all gon' back down and see 'bout the others." Savannah was trying to keep her cool in front of the other women. "Lue, ya think ya can keep yo' trap shut long enough *not* to let this get out?" Savannah was in no mood to put up with her tonight.

"I know when to keep my fuckin' mouth shut, and when not to. But, how in the hell I'm 'spoes to make any damn money wit' this dead man in here?" She said and walked out the door with the others in tow.

Savannah was left alone with Sam. She continued

to clean him up the best she could and thought of a story to tell the doctor and sheriff when they came to get the body.

"Oh Sam, what the hell happened in here?" She said aloud, and looking around for a sign of a struggle. *Okay Van, don't go lettin' ya mind get ahead of ya now. You gotta hear her side.* "Oh Sam, I'll never hear yours, but I know ya ain't done nothin' to hurt that child. I'm so sorry, Sam honey, I will miss ya, and I love you."

Lord, I pray this ain't that chil's fault.

Event 026.00

Everyone had done as they were told and were with their guests when Savannah went to see about Sarah. Gina was with her and cooling her head with a cold cloth.

Savannah walked over to the bed and studied Sarah's face, looking for clues that Sam may have hurt her.

"Is she restin'?" Savannah asked.

"Yes Ma'am, just lay here and went fast asleep. I ain't nevea seen nothin' like it. She just lay down and was out."

"Damn..., maybe I pushed her into this too soon. She been through some real shit wit' men. The shit wit' Grady—*that sinful ass bastard*—dealin' wit' the death of her mama, the fight she had this mornin' wit' some boy who wanted to take her to New York with him, and now this." Savannah held her head down for a moment to collect her thoughts. "You gon' down with the others and I'll stay wit'da. When my company comes you take him."

Savannah sat on the edge of the bed and took a deep breath. She was growing tired with all that was happening. With Sarah just starting, things were sure off to a bad start and Savannah knew she had some explaining to do.

The folks in town already wanted a reason to put her out, now they were going to have one. With all this, how was she going to deal with the death of her beloved friend?

Night was ending, the house was quiet, and Savannah could hear some of the women in the hall outside Sarah's room. They were waiting to hear what happened to Sam.

Savannah got up and walked out to meet them. She assured them everything was going to be all right, and that she didn't know what happened. But, they would be the first to know when she did.

Back in the room with Sarah, Savannah woke her up.

"Sarah honey, get up now." Sarah awakened, still sleepy and groggy from the whisky and coke.

After yawning and stretching, she stared at Savannah asking, "Sam…, how is he?"

With no other way to put it, Savannah replied. "He's dead, Sarah."

"Dead!" Sarah replied, with eyes wide open.

"That's what I say ain't it? Now you got to tell me everythin' that happened in there wit' the two of ya."

"I cain't remember it all…, I do remember spillin' the whisky on him…and he grabbed me. That's all I remember, I swear." The two sat in silence, staring at each other. Sarah searched her mind to find answers to what happened. She remembered the voice, but dared not say anything to Savannah about it. Savannah watched her looking for a sign she may be remembering something.

"I have to call the sheriff and let'em know what happened. You up for it?"

"Yes Ma'am, ain't like I got much choice now do I?" Sarah got up and walked down the hall to wash up.

Did I kill Sam? He was alive when he grabbed me. He was standin' just fine. Oh shit I cain't remember. Think Sarah…Think damn it! As I stood in the mirror, I searched for anything that would help me remember. *We was there—just him and me, talkin'—the voice! Whose voice was that? Shit! Why cain't I remember?*

I ran the cold water and splashed my face. I planned on telling the sheriff as much as I could.

I heard voices speaking in a low mummer outside the bathroom. It was the sheriff and Savannah. My heart tried to break free of my chest when I heard Savannah call my name.

"Sarah, come to my room please. The sheriff wants to ask ya some questions—it won't take long. The doc done took Sam away. So, you won't have to see'em." Savannah had taken off her makeup and pulled her hair back into a bun—again her age was showing.

"You Sarah?" asked the sheriff.

"Yes sir."

"This won't take long. Can you tell me what happened here tonight? You may want to think about the fact there was a dead man here all night, and you ladies waited to call me out." The sheriff was staring from under the brim of his hat with a note pad in hand.

"All I remember is…I spilled some whisky on his pants…I went to get a clean towel to clean it off and he grabbed my arm. Then I must have passed out. 'Cause all I remember is waking up and all the ladies were standing around him. Later, Savannah told me he was dead." Sarah watched the floor while she recalled the events of the evening.

"Well, that's all I need to know for now. We'll wait and see what the doc says later. Young lady, don't leave this house 'til you hear from me." He left the house without another word.

The sheriff really didn't care what happened to anyone coming in or out of the house, one less bad apple in town he thought.

Everyone began leaving the room one by one, with all eyes on Sarah, as she continued watching the floor.

Savannah waited to see if Sarah would say anything more. She never did.

Sarah left the room with her head down and her heart still banging against her chest for freedom. She felt like it was the last walk of her life. She had no explanation for anyone about the evening.

Back in her room Sarah sat at her mirror watching herself, wondering what could have happened.

The sun had come up, but she couldn't remember when. The day was long and quiet. The women of the house went about doing their daily routines without a sound. Even Lue wasn't able to muster up one single sarcastic word.

Event 027.00

Tobias had made it to New York—he was like a kid in the candy store. His roommate was another black kid from out of town—they were both majoring in science.

Tobias managed to put Sarah out of his mind long enough to get his classes and schedule in order. Being introduced to many new faces and many new things, but as time went on his mind was always taken back to Sarah.

"Hey Toby, why you always tellin' the girls you cain't go out with them?" His roommate asked.

"No reason man, just not interested." Toby said, looking up from his partially dissected frog and having a quick thought of Sarah.

"You know, you keep that up word is gonna get around you like boys or somethin'."

"Now who in the hell is gonna believe a tale like that? You sound like my cousin back home. 'Sides I like girls just fine. As a matter of fact, I have a girl."

"Oh yeah! How come I ain't never seen her. If you ain't in class, you in the lab with your face stuck in some lab rat's ass." He said with a grin.

"Look man, I'm not here to find a girl anyway. And 'sides neither are you, Mr. Dean's list." Toby said, throwing a frog leg at his friend.

At that moment, he wondered if Charlie was keeping an eye on Sarah like he had asked.

"Check it out, Toby, there's this party tonight see, why don't you come and check it out? What's one night of fun gonna do to ya?" As the boy was leaving his seat, he tossed Toby the invitation that was floating around campus.

Toby thought for a while and decided he was right, one night of fun won't hurt, and besides he was going to have plenty of time to spend with the rats.

"Yeah man, I'll be there!" He yelled back, realizing what he had done, he gave the teacher a shy smile and went back to his frog.

It was Charlie's birthday and he had his mind set on going out as well. He had showered and put on the new clothes his parents had given him that morning.

"Charles, whatcha plans fo' the night?"

"Uncle Busta comin' to get me, he gonna get me a woman!" He yelled back with a big woo hoo at the end.

"A woman," His mother yelled. "Whatchu mean a woman?"

"Now you know what the boy mean, calm yo'self woman. It be time fo' the boy to sew his wild oats." Charlie's father replied in his defense.

As he walked to Charlie's bedroom, he pinched his

wife on the butt and whispered to her about his wild oats when Charlie was gone. With a girlish giggle, she smacked him on the hand and went into the kitchen.

"Look-a-here son, I know yo' uncle won't let you get hurt or nothin', but just be careful who ya fool wit'. If I know yo' uncle Busta, he plans to take you to that house on the edge of town. I hear it be some *fine* women in that house. Here's some extra money, if'n ya find the need fo' it. Don't tell ya mama, she'll have my hide fo' sho'."

"Thanks, Pops, you's all right. As fo' being careful, no worries. It be a new woman in town...," he said with a wink and a slap to his father on the back. "Well how I look?" He asked as he turned to the mirror.

"Fine son—just fine—like I did when I was yo' age." His father replied, sucking in his gut.

"Good, I'm outta here, gonna meet Unc at the soda shop." Charlie was half way down the hall when he finished his statement. Yelling good night to his mother, he was out the door and down the walk before she could come out to say good night to him.

"That's my boy!" His father said. But, he couldn't help but think about the words Charlie had said. *There be a new woman in town.* The last time a new woman came to town, strange things started happening and his friend, Dewitt went mad, and folks went missing.

"George, you okay? You look like you just seen a ghost." His wife asked.

"...Ohh, I'm fine, just fine. Now woman...back to

you, and *my* wild oats!" He said as he chased her back into the kitchen.

Charles walked as fast as his legs would carry him to the soda shop. The main thing on his mind was that he was finally going to have his chance to see why Tobias had fallen so fast in love with Sarah.

He had arrived at the shop to find his uncle hadn't been there yet. He moved back outside to see if he was by chance standing outside the brothel. There was still no sign of him.

Charlie saw a woman he knew and decided to have a talk while he waited for his uncle.

"You really gone get a woman from over there? Ain't none of them women gonna want your skinny ass." She said.

"Look, you just jealous it ain't yo' ass I want. Anyways, it be this gal over there my buddy told me 'bout. You remember the Lambert girl?"

"Yeah, I thank I do." She said with her eyebrows turned up trying to remember.

"Well she the hoe I'm after." He said in a low tone.

"She works over there?" The woman asked, with a surprised look in her eyes.

"Yeah, ain'tchu heard yet? Her pop's put her to work over there after he was the one what fucked her first. He done gon' off to another state and left her here to work over at that house. Toby done had her too and he done ask me to look out for her while he gone—*and that's just what I intend to do.*" Charlie said licking his lips.

"You so nasty, how you gonna do that to yo' best friend girl while he away." She asked pushing him.

"Easy, she let'n all those other men do her ain't she, so why not me?" Charlie turned his back to the wind to light a cigarette and spotted his uncle coming up the road.

After saying his good-byes to the young woman, he ran over to meet him. His uncle explained the way things worked at the house, and that he wasn't to make him look like a fool for bring him there

"No worries Unc, it's only *one* woman in there I want tonight!" Charlie proclaimed, rubbing his hands together and leading the way up to the house.

Event 028.00

Sarah was in her room trying to get rid of the memories of the night before. She refused to believe she had anything to do with the death of another human being. Although her life after her mama's killing wasn't a good one, she could never bring herself to execute another human—even if the other human was her own Pa.

She was lying on her bed downing whisky as if it was ice-cold water, one glass after another.

The words Savannah had spoken to her about Sam played repeatedly in her mind. The look on the other women's faces as they passed her in the halls or saw her in the kitchen made her feel uncomfortable and unwanted. She thought perhaps her life was destined to be cloaked with evil, she wasn't sure. However, one thing was for sure, she was slowly losing sight of what being wholesome meant.

There was a knock at the door, she allowed the unwanted visitor to knock several more times, before frustratingly yelling for them to go away.

"Sarah, it's me Gina," she said softly. "Let me in, I got somethin' that will cheer ya up."

"Go away, Gina, I'm in no mood." Sarah said, to jaded to sound convincing.

"Come on and open the door. Let me in...it ain't all that bad. Let me in." Gina wasn't going to go away and Sarah knew it. She rose up and unlocked her door.

"Gina, make it quick I wanted to be alone."

Gina stood in the doorway for a moment and watched Sarah as she stumbled back to the bed and lay down. While Sarah lay on the bed, she saw the way the full figured girl watched her and wondered for a moment what her reasons were for working in the house.

How could anyone choose to work in a place like this?

"Whatchu want, Gina?" I asked.

"I wanna help ya get through this. Ya need a friend right now, and I want to be that friend," Gina was sitting on the edge of the bed, running her fingers through my hair. Not wanting to be touched I pushed her hand away. "Sarah, I was in yo' place once, when I first came to this house. Only, I didn't kill nobody though—"

"Gina? You think..."

"Oh, Sarah, no...I didn't mean...I'm sorry, bad time for a joke, huh? Calm down, I didn't mean nothin' by it. What I should have said was. I had no friends either and all the other women hated me. I guess what I'm saying is, they see you as a threat to them—and the tricks they already have—you young and pretty, just like a new doll. Everybody wants to see it first and be the first to play with it. See what I'm sayin', they just old dolls. They wantchu to be the one to have killed Sam. But, see—Sam was old—and one thang ya don't know. He had a bad heart. So maybe you ain't the one killed him, maybe it was his bad heart." Gina got up and went over to get the hand mirror from the vanity.

"Whatchu mean he had a bad heart?" Sarah asked with renewed optimism.

"Savannah told me about a year ago, Sam was in the hospital with a bad heart. She said nothing more of it after that. So see, ya ain't got nothin' to worry about. Maybe he was nervous 'bout being wit'cha and his ticker just gave out. It was bound to happen one day. It just happened to be on yo' day...I mean really, look at'cha. Those eyes of ravens bound to scare any man to death."

"You sho' it may have been his heart?"

"I ain't sho' 'bout nothin', except that when ya been here long enough, ya become all numb to what happens to men that come in here."

"How ya get use to it, Gina?"

"Look. I'ma help ya get use to thangs 'round here, fo' ya up and kill off all us." Gina said, hoping to bring a smile back to Sarah's face.

She opened her pouch and pulled out a little white tin cup. Sarah could see the white powder inside. She watched as Gina poured it out and split it into four rows.

"What's that?" Sarah asked.

"It's the same shit from last night ya remember...a bit of *heaven* and *courage*, it can be yo' best friend— just like I wanna be. Watch me and do what I do."

Gina bent over with the tin tube to her nose, sniffing as hard as she could until one of the lines was gone. "That's all ya have to do. Here take the straw and put it in yo' nose to start. I'm here to help."

"I cain't," Sarah replied.

"Ya could last night when ya thought I was gone out of my room. Thought I wouldn't know 'bout that." Gina replied with one eyebrow raised.

"I just put some in my drink is all."

"Well, this way better, it won't give ya a stomach ache and it last longer. Won't sneak up on ya. Come on now, it'll help take away all yo' fears and worries. It helped me get through tons of shit. Still do." Gina helped Sarah for the first time snort coke.

The powder made her sneeze and then she felt the burn. She watched Gina as she took another hit and then it was her turn again.

On the second snort, she could feel the room begin to spin, she got up to open the window and take in some fresh air. It helped some, but not enough to stop the spinning. Sarah lie on her bed and let the drug continue to take effect. She could see Gina in the dime light standing over her, watching her. Sarah reached out her hand to Gina. She took it and lay next to her. The two of them lay in silence for what seemed like an eternity.

Sarah thoughts flashed back and forth from her ma, to her pa, then to Tobias. She wished he was there with her, holding her, kissing her, and making love to her. Her body became light as a feather and she longed for someone to hold her.

"Hold me," she requested of Gina.

"What?"

"Hold me," Gina turned to hold her and before long, the two were in a passionate kiss. Sarah thought only of Toby as Gina's hands probed her body.

She had never been with another woman and never thought she would. Gina found spots on her body never felt before by anyone. She made Sarah feel better than anytime she could remember.

As Sarah's high was ending, she asked if she could do another. Gina again helped her to get it right. Nightfall had come and it was time for the women of the house to get to work.

Gina was gone and Sarah was alone getting ready for the night. She didn't think much of what happened between her and Gina, she was thinking of the old man.

I hope tonight will be different? I sure hope it brings good things. At least as good as it gets here anyway.

Gina had shown Sarah how to cut the rows of coke and told her not to overdo it the first time, but Sarah really didn't care—she just wanted to zombie through the night. And have no recall the next morning.

No recall...no guilt...no shame...

After taking in a few more snorts and having several more drinks. Sarah sat at her vanity allowing the high to consume her. She took a moment to examine herself in the mirror. Her eyes heavy and glazed over. Flashbacks of her papa's hands striking a blow to her head, his foot in the pit of her stomach, the smell of stale booze on his breath—as he kissed her. Images of him thrusting his body in and out of hers and the pain of her mama's death began haunting her awakened mind. The memories quickly turned to rage and her blood began to pump through her veins like raging seawaters.

Then, the voice she had been hearing for several weeks was back. "Sarah, wait for us, we're coming to bring you home, we're coming for you. Wait."

In the mirror, she could see a face, more of a blur then a face, but she could see it was still a face. The room once again turned a crimson red and the blood that raged through her body now felt as though it had been set ablaze. She had become hot and pouring with sweat. Sarah felt the urge to get up and run, but she had to know who the voice belonged to and where it was coming from.

"Who are you?" She asked.

"You'll find out soon. Do not be afraid. Soon we shall return." With that, the face was gone.

Sarah blinked and rubbed her eyes to clear them. Only her reflection remained in the mirror. She figured it was the effects of the drugs or perhaps, the time had finally come, that she was truly losing her mind. She got up and went to the bathroom to splash water on her face.

Standing there, watching the water run, she slowly lifted her head to look into the mirror. The bruises that covered her face, were now gone.

When did that happen? What the hell is going on with me? With no time to worry about it now, she quickly washed her face and returned to her room to get ready for the night.

After using the practices Savannah had shown her when putting on makeup, she found the dress one of the girls had given her and slipped it on.

Inspecting herself in the mirror—she felt beautiful—just as beautiful as the other women looked when she first saw them. Her face was clear of bruises, her lips weren't swollen, and her eyes were as bright as a shiny black stone.

Look out world here I come!

As she entered the parlor, she could see most of the women had already started to work and some were just hanging out near the bar at the far corner of the room. She saw Savannah waving to her. With a smile, she walked over to find her there with the sheriff.

"Working late, Sheriff?"

"I'm off duty, but I come 'cause I got good news for you little lady."

"Yeah, what is it?" I asked, hoping there was no powder on my nose.

"Ol' Sam had a fit," the Sheriff said watching the confused expression on Sarah's face. "A heart attack, according to the doc." He added. "So little lady, looks like ya in the clear. It ain't yo' fault he's died." The sheriff said, throwing back his drink.

Sarah thought the news was good. But, from all the cocaine and booze she had consumed, she felt numb to the news and replied dispassionately. "Yeah, well thanks. I s'pose that's good news for me. But, not for that ol' fool. Savannah ya seen Gina?"

"Chil' ya hear what he say, Sam had a bad heart, ya had nuttin' to do wit' it." Savannah was shocked by her none interest in the matter.

"Yes Ma'am, I heard'em." Sarah replied with her

head down.

"Well, anyhow Sheriff, ya got yo' pick of any woman here tonight, for bringing us the good news. We all can rest good now knowing none of us had anything to do with it. Now if you will excuse me, I got work to do and Sarah needs to be joinin' me." Savannah took Sarah by the arm and turned her to the kitchen.

As the two of them walked through the house, the others watched like hawks. Sarah grabbed a drink from one of the trays she passed on her way to the kitchen.

"What's wrong wit'cha chil'?" Savannah asked as they entered the kitchen.

"Whatchu mean, ain't nothin' wrong wit' me."

"I think ya need to lay off the booze the rest of the night, your eyes are as red as fire."

"Savannah, I know ya mean well and all, but I have had to deal with much mo' then I can handle in the last few days. I am sorry yo' friend is dead. Is that Whatchu wanna hear? I'm here to do a job, not to worry 'bout folks that kill ovea." Sarah went to take a seat at the table with Savannah in tow.

"Sarah, I don't know what's wrong wit'chu, but as long as ya can handle it, then that's fine by me. We ain't got much time to talk and tonight is gonna be a busy one. Ya sho' ya up for it?" Savannah asked watching Sarah with her head sideways. Wondering why she was so nonchalant about everything.

"Yeah, I can handle it, Gina give me some tips."

"Gina?" Savannah knew if Gina had anything to do with it, things weren't going to be good for long. "Sarah you watch out for that girl, she can misinterpret what is help and what is hindrance. She mean well, but thangs have a way of going wrong when she 'round."

"Well I had my share of thangs going wrong when other people are around. Don't worry, I can handle more than foke think."

"Good to hear. Now fo' business. You had your first request. It be a young man's first time here and he's perfect fo' ya. He seems to be 'round yo age. Let's manage *not* to kill this one." She said with a giggle. Her last words hurt more than she thought. Tears weld up in her eyes, but she fought them back.

Sarah took notice. With her heart heavy and not finding the kill joke funny, she replied. "Savannah...I...I am sorry for yo' loss."

"I know ya are, Sarah, 'sides ya done said it already. We all deal with tragedy in different ways." Savannah gave her a friendly tap on the wrist. "By the way, have I told ya that ya lookin' lovely tonight? You did your makeup just fine, just fine indeed. Covered ya bruises like a pro. They look like they're not there at all."

Sarah gave Savannah a smile, got up and went over to get herself a slice of cake from the tray.

Savannah was left thinking of her last moments with Sam, and wondering who would be there to protect her now.

"Savannah ya hear me?" Sarah interrupted.

"No chil' what is it?"

"They callin' ya."

The women were outside calling for Savannah. One of the men had come in drunk and was fighting with another man over one of the women.

Upon reaching the parlor, she saw a crowd around a man trying to hold him off the other. As Savannah stepped in the middle of all the commotion, she saw it was the town drunk and knew that nothing she did was going to make this customer happy.

"Sheriff, can ya take this one out. He ain't nothin' but trouble."

"Glad to Savannah, we been lookin' for a reason to lock him up." Sheriff took the drunken man out and led him to the jail.

"All right, all is well, ya'll gone back to whatchu was doin'. Ladies get yo' men a drink—on the house."

Savannah noticed the man that had requested services from Sarah was standing at the bar looking in her direction.

"Sarah honey, come with me. Some people I want you to meet." Savannah directed her to the bar where the men were waiting patiently. "This here is Busta and his nephew. This the one I told ya wanted no other woman here, but you. This be his first time here." Savannah was pushing Charlie up so Sarah could get a better look. "Sarah, meet Mr. Charlie."

"Hi," he said.

"Hi, how are you?"

"Just fine Ma'am." He replied with a big grin.

"The drugstore cowboy. I've seen you around." Sarah said with her eyebrow arched.

"Sho' you have."

"I've mostly seen you at the soda shop." I remembered him chasing around any girl that would look at him.

"Yeah, I seen ya there too. Anyway, today be my birthday and my uncle done brought me here."

"Well nice of yo' uncle," I replied in a monochromatic tone. I knew all about Charlie and could have really did without him being my first request. Not to mention, he was Toby's friend. "So ya want a drank and a lil' conversation befo' we go up?"

"Sho', ya got whisky." Charlie was afraid of being alone with her only because of the stories he'd heard about her, but he was more interested in finding out why Tobias had fallen so hard and so fast for her.

He could see she wasn't the same beaten up girl he remembered. Her face was like carmel. Her lips had bright red lipstick on them. Her dress hung well on her long slim body. For the first time he saw what Toby had seen in her.

"I seen ya with Toby, ain't I?"

"Yeah, he my cousin, but best friend first though. Ya know he out in New York at some fancy school for colored fokes?"

"Yeah, I know, ya come here to talk 'bout him? 'Cause I really don't want to hear anymore. Anyway, why don't we go so's we can have more privacy." Sarah was in no mood to make new friends.

"Naw gal, I'm here to celebrate my twenty-first birthday. I'll go with you anywhere!" He said downing his glass of whiskey.

Sarah led him up the stairs to her room. She couldn't help wonder what Toby was up to now that he'd been brought to the foreground of her mind. Did he think of her?

She watched Charlie from the mirror as he undressed and made the bed to fit his needs. She excused herself and went into the bathroom. She took out the small pouch from her corset and placed it on the counter. She watched herself in the mirror for a few seconds before opening the pouch. Pouring out a small amount of the white powder into her hand and taking a long sniff. She held her breath for a bit and exhaled. She turned on the faucet and splashed cool water on her face, wondering why Charlie had chosen her for his date. Anyway, it really didn't matter, she just wanted to get it over with. Upon returning to the room, she found Charlie peeking in her closet.

"What the hell you lookin fo'?" she asked slamming the door.

"Nothin' just thought I would take a peek," Charlie replied embarrassed he was caught. "You ready gal, I know I am?" Truth is, he wasn't ready, he wasn't sure if this is what he really wanted to do.

"Yeah, let's get it ovea wit'. Whatchu want done?"

"Damn gal, that the way you treat all yo' tricks?"

"Don't worry 'bout my other tricks. Now again, whatchu want?" The coke was kicking in and I was in no mood for his games.

"Well, why don't ya surprise me and I'll tell ya what I like and what I don't."

"Fine wit' me, on the bed then."

I stood in front of the bed frame while Charlie lay there licking his lips waiting with anticipation for what I would do next.

What the hell am I doing?

Trying to figure it out, I stood watching him, studying him. Slowly I began to take off my dress one button at a time. I allowed it to fall slowly to the floor in a neat pile around my feet. Next, I removed my corset and tossed it at him.

Watching her, Charlie smiled and sniffed the air, as her sweet perfume danced around his nostrils. He watched her in the candle light and thought about the beauty that stood before him. She was gorgeous and like no other girl he had been with before. Her flawless figure enchanted him.

As she slowly removed his clothing, the stories he had been told escaped his mind. All he wanted was her. He wanted to engulf himself around her, taste her. Charlie wanted to explore every inch of her being. And for a moment, he wondered where these feelings were coming from, the more he studied her the real reason for him being there dissipated.

Sarah watched him, she noticed he would seem to get lost in her and she questioned what he was thinking.

"What's on yo' mind?" She asked in a low sultry voice. There was no answer. "What's on yo' mind?" Still there was no answer. He had heard her every word, but he couldn't open his mouth in response.

She could feel his manhood as hard as a rock. She slowly removed the rest of his clothing. Her eyes locked on his, she moved into position, slowly kissing his lips and working her way down to his chest. Nibbling his nipples and making warm breathing circles around his navel. She lifted his hardness and placed it into her mouth. With the warm touch of her tongue, Charlie took in a deep breath. He closed his eyes and arched his back. Sarah reached up to feel for the 'I am pleased' shiver of his body.

She pondered on what people saw in it all—lost in her own thought—she suddenly felt his hand on her head. Charlie had pushed her head so far down his manhood she gagged. She wasn't sure if it was her fault. Then, she remembered the hand on her head.

"What the fuck ya think ya doin', man?" She yelled.

"Whatchu talkin' 'bout bitch get back to work!" Charlie hadn't realized what he'd done.

"Look man, I don't know whatchu do wit'cho other girls, but you...don't run nothin' here!" Sarah tried to take back control.

"Look-a-here hoe, I paid good money fo' yo' ass and you gonna do what the fuck I tell ya to do, and ya gonna like it." All he wanted was for her to finish what she'd started.

Sarah watched him for a minute not sure of what to say. Then, "why don't we both calm down, ya got caught up is all, let's have a drank, call it even, and start over? Whatchu say?"

Sarah was learning to think fast on her feet and she had her papa to thank for that.

Mayhap that shitty rat bastard taught me something useful after all.

Charlie agreed to the drink and said nothing more of what she was supposed to be doing for him.

Sarah was pouring the two a drink when Charlie asked for the bathroom.

"Hey gal, a man got to take a leak!" He blurted out holding himself.

"Take a right at the first door down the hall, that's fo' tricks only." Sarah wanted him to know he was nothing special.

"Good gal, I'm 'bout to bust, this break just what I need. Make my drink strong gal, 'cause I'm gone make you forget all those other dudes ya had befo' me." He yelled as he ran down the hall to the bathroom.

Make me forget? You gonna have to do more than have a strong drink dumbass.

A knock on the door broke her thought. It was Savannah. "Hey honey, I saw your friend go into the bathroom, thangs okay in here?"

"Yeah, he tried to shove his dick down my throat, We takin' a break to have a drink."

"Good, those kinds of thangs will happen in this business, but remember we here to help if thangs get too heavy."

"Yeah, I'll keep it in mind." Sarah said downing her whisky. At that moment, Charlie returned.

"What's this...I get the two of ya?" He asked smiling a big white smile.

"Ya wish...I just come to find out what was goin' on. I saw ya leave," replied Savannah.

"Damn." Charlie said snapping his fingers.

"Well, now I know thangs all right, you kids have fun now." Giving Sarah a wink, she closed the door.

Sarah watched Charlie as her body cringed with the thought of having to finish what she started. Eyeing her pouch at the end of the nightstand, she came up with an idea. "Say, why don'tcha put on some music."

"Yeah girl, now ya talkin'," he replied.

While he found a record to play, Sarah put a bit of

the powder into his glass. When he returned he lay on the bed and asked Sarah to join him. "Come here gal."

"I'm right here."

"No, come closer. I want to hold ya for a bit."

"Look fool, I got money to make, and if ya want to take time to hold me, it's gonna cost ya more."

"My uncle got it gal, he say I can have ya all night if I want. Don't worry 'bout the money ya gone get paid."

"I'm not worried 'bout the money."

"Then what is it gal, I know it ain't Toby." He said with a smile.

"Toby, now whatchu bring him up fo'? I ain't thought 'bout him since he left here. He told me it was you that told him I was here."

"Enough 'bout him gal, this night 'bout me," Charlie lay back with his arms over his head, quickly changing the subject.

Sarah was relieved he didn't want to talk much about Toby, it would have only made things harder than they already were.

"You're right, so fool how am I gonna getchu outta here?"

"Bitch, the only way ya can get me out…is to get me off! Now enough stalling let's get to it." The tone in his voice was all too familiar. Her heart once again began a marathon, in which it was the only racer and her body began to shiver. Sarah had no idea of what to do next, she had lost all train of thought.

"Come on gal, I been here wit'chu too long already— it's all kinds a women out there fo' me. You ain't the only hoe in this house." Charlie was cold and growing annoyed.

Sarah wondered if it had anything to do with the dope she put in his drink. Suddenly, he snatched her down to the bed.

Pulling from him she jumped up. "Hey man, what's wrong wit'chu? Don't be so rough wit' me."

"Look-a-here hoe, I know how ya like it, everybody knows y'all hoes like it rough. I'm tired of playing games wit'chu. I come here to get laid—and laid is what I'm gon' get." Charlie jumped from the bed grabbing Sarah by her arm, throwing her again to the bed and this time ripping her panties off. Taken aback by his own actions, his eyes widened.

Sarah lay petrified and stunned as Charlie climbed atop of her. The memories of her pa flashed back. Her fears quickly turned to anger. Then the room turned a crimson red.

"Stand...we'll make him pay for that, do what you have to do. Do not be afraid." The voice proclaimed. Looking down at Charlie who was now kissing her breast, she knew it wasn't him.

"I'm not." Sarah replied aloud.

Looking up Charlie asked, "You ain't what gal?"

Smiling a mischievous smile and knowing she was no longer alone, Sarah responded with, "Nothin'... say whatchu doin' down there anyway? This yo' birthday," she stated, remembering what Gina had told her about riding them with her back to them. "On ya back...I'ma try something new." She ordered.

"Yeah girl, now ya talkin', come on let's get wit' it." Charlie said as his head spun from the laced whisky.

"Damn too much whisky, my head is spinin'."

"Stop ya fussin' ya just fine."

When they were finished, Sarah had gotten up to go get cleaned. Charlie laid there for a moment looking up at the ceiling—thinking. He had been wondering for a long time what it was Toby had saw in Sarah—now in his own way—he knew.

As Sarah reentered the room, Charlie sat up. "Now I know why Toby fell fo' yo ass so fast! You got some good shit 'tween yo' legs!" Charlie said smugly.

"Look fool, ya got whatchu come fo', now get the fuck out!" Sarah replied pointing to the door.

"I know damn good and well you ain't getting' uppity?" Charlie rose to his feet and rushed towards her.

"You touch me and you'll be sorry ya ever entered this house." She took a step back with every one he took forward.

"You think you a bad bitch, huh? You think you can handle me?"

Sarah remembered her Pa saying the very same words. "Charlie, let go of me and get out. I ain't gon' say it again, ya done had too much to drank and ya askin' fo' trouble. You keep it up…you just might find it." She said as she thought about Sam.

When he released her she bent over to get his shoes, when she stood back up she saw a glimpse of horror in his eyes and he was frozen—dead—in his tracks. As she watched him she saw him break into a cold sweat and began to tremble.

"What the hell wrong wit'chu now?" She asked. He just kept staring into space without a word. She turned to see what he was looking at.

Behind her was a red light, more like a mist lingering in the air. Like when the dust moves about when kicked up from a gust of strong wind. It took all she had not to run, but she was curious and wanted to know what it was. Did this have anything to do with the voices she'd been hearing and the figure she'd seen in the mirror? She waited to see what would happen next.

Looking back at Charlie, standing frozen. Then, back to the mist.

"What are ya?" She asked, wondering why she was talking to red mist. "Why ya doin' this?" Still she received no answer. She walked over to Charlie and tried to wake him but it was no use. "You let him loose, ya hear, whatevea ya is or who evea ya is. You cut him loose...now...right now I say."

At that moment, Charlie fell to the floor out of breath, as if something had been cutting off his air supply. Sarah watched him and waited for him to catch his breath.

"What the hell ya do to me? What the hell ya show me them thangs for?" Charlie was crawling away as he reached in all direction for his clothing.

"Whatchu talkin' 'bout? I ain't did nothin'." She said as she watched him cowering on the floor.

"Them thangs ya was showin' me, you can really do them thangs? The stories are true girl, and that be the work of the devil, you be one of his slaves. Stay away from me gal!" He shouted.

Sarah was enjoying this, for once in her life, a man was afraid of her. She didn't know exactly what it was Charlie had seen, but she thought it had something to do with the mist and she intended to take full advantage of it.

"Look-a-here fool, I toldchu if ya mess wit' me ya was gon' get hurt. Now you gon' do anythang and everything I wantcha to, ya readin' me? You tell anybody whatchu done seen and I'll end yo' black ass. I'll do so many nasty thangs to you, you be wishin' death to come, ya here me nigga? Wishin' fo' death to come." Sarah sat on the edge of her bed and smiled.

"Oh Jesus, the stories...! They was true. You are the work of the devil." He said with tears in his eyes.

"Fool, I don't know whatchu talkin' 'bout, I ain't the work of no devil. Look at ya..., still a little boy—helpless—and don't know what to do. Cain't even handle ya whisky." She said feeling powerful.

Charlie stood slow to his feet.

"Ya tell anybody Charlie, you'll be wishin' for death to come." She stated one last time.

Sarah had no idea what Charlie was referring to or what he had seen, but she indulged and marveled in the thrill it gave. She was going to enjoy every minute of it. No one was going to treat her worse than trash anymore...no one.

Event 029.00

"Has anyone heard from Sarah and the young fella she was wit' tonight?" Savannah asked a group of women sitting in the kitchen drinking and smoking, instead of entertaining the guests.

"I saw the young blood in the parlor with his uncle, not just two minutes ago. He had a strange look on his face, like he done seen something and it spooked the bageeves outta him." One of the girls stated, without giving it a second thought. Then, walked out when she thought Savannah was going to ask them why they were in the kitchen, instead of out in the parlor where they should've been.

"Maybe that high yellow heffa's eyes scared the poor young thang to death, he done probably dropped dead somewhere here in the house." The women laughed and went back to smoking and drinking.

"I won't have that kind of talking in this house... that's enough of the killer jokes. Shouldn't y'all be out in the parlor anyway? There is money to be made—unless y'all don't need it." Savannah scolded, while thinking of Sam.

The women rose from their seats and walked

away—some complaining under their breaths.

Savannah thought she would go up and check on Sarah. As she approached the room, she could hear the faint mummers of whispers. She waited, trying to get a better listen, but the voices stopped. There was a crimson light emanating from beneath the door. When she reached out to knock—the door opened— and she saw there was no one there to greet her. The air was cold, stale, and had an emptiness about it.

"Sarah, honey," she called out.

"Yes," Sarah replied.

"You all right in there chil'?"

"Yes, why wouldn't I be? You coming in or you gonna stand out there and yap at me from the hall?" Sarah's tone was different, Savannah couldn't put her finger on it, but she knew Sarah wasn't right, she was changing like the wind since she come to stay.

Savannah moved slowly into the room, it was dark and cold, even though the window was closed. She could see Sarah's shadow in the corner of the room. She didn't move or say a word when Savannah entered.

"Why ya in the dark suga," Savannah was careful, she wasn't sure why she suddenly felt the need to be on her P's and Q's. "Ya trick didn't hurtcha did he?" She asked as she looked for the lantern.

Sarah came out of the corner. "No...he ain't done nothin' to me. Nothin' I ain't want'em to anyway. 'Sides why you up here? I was on my way down to meet the rest of the guests."

Sarah was much more sultrier in appearance

then Savannah had remembered. Her cheeks more blushed, her lips where fuller, and her eyes seem to glow with the flickering of the lantern. Not to mention, if she hadn't known any better, it seemed as if Sarah's breast size were a few cups larger.

The way she spoke was calm and at ease, not at all nervous like she had been the past few days or just hours ago for that matter. Savannah watched her as she refreshed her lipstick, redid her hair, checked the back end of her dress, and ran her hands up her legs and unwrinkled her stockings from around her ankles.

"I'm ready to make some money, 'cause yo' stockings are way too big fo' me...and I can't keep the men interested if I have wrinkled ankles." She said giggling and watching Savannah in the mirror.

"Yeah, I guess ya have a point there. You sho' you up fo' mo'? That first trick had you tied up for a while, you can rest if you have to. We got all night—them lounge lizards ain't goin' nowhere 'til the sun come up."

"I'm ready let's go." With one last look in the mirror, she tossed Savannah her tube of lipstick and was out the door before she caught it.

Sarah walked slowly, so that all in her path could get a good look at her. She wanted them to know she was in the room and demanded attention.

At the top of the stairs, she stood and watched everyone below her. All the men seemed to find her there. They all came walking in to get a better look— pretending to be going into another room—some were bold enough to just stand and stare. She stood with one hand on her hip and the other resting on the staircase railing, in the dress with the V-shape in the back.

It hugged every curve in the right place, her lips where painted worrier red, her cheeks had a light blush that held on to her innocence. It would be her eyes—those coal black, raven like eyes—which had most of the men in a trance. They had taken on a large almond shape, twinkling in the dim lights.

"Hey gal, why ya standing up there like that, you need some company?" It was Busta at the bottom of the stairs licking his lips like some sort of hungry beast.

"Ain't that whatcha come here fo'? To keep us ladies...company?" She asked, her voice soft, deep and slow, her smile breath taking.

"Ooh woo, Savannah show no how to pick'em, you sho' is fine as hell in that get up," He said as he ascended the staircase. "Damn, put a gal in a fancy dress and some paint on her face and look out!" He said in her face as he reached the top step where she stood. "You know my name?" He asked

"No, and I don't really care." I said knowing full well who he was.

"I'm Busta, you 'member you walked in on me a while back."

"Well now. I do seem to recall somethin' like that, but I had no idea that was you. I wasn't lookin' atcha face at the time." I said, peering over Busta's shoulder watching Lue as she came charging up the stairs.

"Busta, what the fuck ya think ya doin wit' this

gal?" Lue yelled before she reached the two of them.

"I...I...was....a...I...was askin' her 'boutchu. Wasn't I, Miss Sarah?" He said as he eyed me to play along.

Shit this fool really is a busta!

I watched the both of them before I answered, then my eyes locked with Lue's.

"No." I said, with a smile.

"No...What the hell that mean?" Lue asked.

"No, Busta wasn't askin' me about you. He wanted to fuck me. My answer to him is...No. I was gonna tell him that when you came charging up the stairs like a mad heffa."

"Whatchu mean askin' her to fuck you...I told ch'a, you don't fuck no bitch in here 'til I fuck you first..."

Sarah moved on, while Lue laid into Busta.

When she reached the bottom of the stairs, she turned back and caught Busta looking at her over Lue's shoulder. She gave him a tongue wave and went into the parlor.

All eyes turned to watch her as she made her way over to Gina and the other girls standing by the window. Gina greeted her with a smile and a drink, as the other women parted like the Red Sea to allow her to take her place next to Gina.

"It's a bit busy tonight." Gina said.

"That's all right, I have plenty of time."

"Yeah, that's all we got is time. 'Sides it's still early, it'll slow down later. So, tell me what happened with your first trick, did he go all right fo' ya?" Gina asked pulling her to the two empty chairs in the corner. Gina was about the same age as Sarah maybe a year or two older.

"Yeah, he'll be back—no doubt 'bout that." Sarah saw Charlie watching and gave him a wave. His eyes widened and he turned back to his drink, she could see his knee still shaking.

"You all right, there is something different about ya. That coke still workin' on ya. Ya much more mellow then you was earlier. Or did that young buck work it out?" Gina gave her a punch in the arm. Sarah cut her eyes at Gina and laughed punching her back, a bit harder than she had punched her. Gina grabbed her arm, not sure how to interpret what just happened.

Sarah went back to watching the rest of the people in the parlor and thought if she was going to get her hands dirty, she may as well get down to it.

The door opened and in came a breath of fresh air. The man wasn't tall for what you might think a man's tall should be. His clothes were neat and pressed. His skin was creamy, eyes bright. Sarah watched him as he walked over to a group of women standing at the lower end of the staircase. He leaned into one of them whispering something in her ear and she pointed to the kitchen. The creamy skinned man looked around and caught Sarah's gaze, he gave a smile and a wink, then walked into the kitchen.

"Who was that?" She asked Gina, who was trying to steal a snort hoping no one saw her.

Wiping her nose, she looked in the direction of Sarah's gaze and caught the last of a man's body going into the kitchen. "Humm...I have no idea, but I'd love to get to know." She stood to her feet, only to have Sarah grab her and pull her back down.

"Heeyy!"

"You know, you need to lay off that shit." Sarah said without looking at her.

"What the hell is wit'chu?" Gina asked in disgust.

"Calm down girl. I'm just sayin' go to the bathroom and freshin' up a bit. In this light ya makeup lookin' cracked." Sarah said with a smile and wink.

"Oh you an expert now? Anyway, ya might be right, it's been a while since I checked it."

She wasn't happy with the tone Gina had taken with her. She decided to let it go for now.

Sarah took her alone time to sit and watch the others at work. A few men came to see what she was about, but she turned them down. By the time she decided to get up and get a drink, she saw Gina coming back. This time she just stood next to her instead of sitting down.

"Girl, sometimes I do thangs without thinkin', sit down and get calm."

"No worries girl, I know how it is." Gina replied, when really she knew nothing.

"I want to find out who the suit is. You say you nevea seen him here befo'?"

"No. at least I don't remember. Ohh girl, one of my regula's is here." Gina said giving the old man at the parlor entrance a wave.

"You like these old bastards all over you?"

"Hell naw, but it pays my bills. That's why I don't have to live here in this shit hole."

"You got your own place?" Sarah asked with new interest. Nevertheless, Gina was gone before she could get an answer.

Her own place? It's time for me to get a bit closer with, Miss Gina.

Just then, she saw Lue coming towards her with her finger out and waving it in the air.

Oh shit

"Who the fuck do you thank you are? Everybody in this damn house know that Busta belongs to me, and me only! Me and him gonna be married someday. I evea catch you tryin' anythin' wit' him again. I'm gon put my foot so far up yo ass, you got me gal?"

Sarah was afraid at first, but the more Lue talked the madder she became. She wasn't sure what was happening to her, but she liked this new feeling—not being afraid of anyone. She could feel rage boiling in her blood once again. Sarah rose slowly to her feet standing a head and shoulders above Lue.

"Look-a-here…you…ol'…wrinkled coochie, bad bodied…ball headed heffa. Yo' man come to me and wanted to fuck me. I told him no 'cause Van told me the scoop on him and you. But, because ya wanna handle it like this, I suggest you keep yo' dog on a short leash. 'Cause I might take him up on his off—" Before Sarah could get out another word Lue grab her by the hair and pulled her to the ground.

The two tossed each other around on the floor, knocking over tables, while yelling out profanities.

Someone called out to Savannah, who came running out of the kitchen, surprised to see her best friend and her new girl rolling around on the floor.

It had been a long time since anyone had a fight in the house.

"What the hell is goin' on out here? Someone help

me break this shit up!" The creamy skinned man grabbed Sarah by the waist, dragging her into the kitchen, kicking and screaming.

Lue was left on the floor with Savannah eyeing her in disgust.

"Lue, you know better. I'll deal wit'chu later. Somebody get her big ass up off the flo'." she ordered, before walking away.

Now embarrassed with a house full of guests she ordered everyone to return to what they were doing.

"What the hell is goin' on around here?" She yelled to no one, as she returned to the kitchen.

Event 030.00

The creamy skinned man and Sarah were in the kitchen, standing face to face. His eyes and the smell of his cologne captivated her. They had said nothing to each other when Savannah came in.

"Girl, ya got to tell me what's going on wit'chu and tell me somethin' right now. You've been acting strange and shit all night. I cain't have that shit here," Savannah was eyeing her, waiting for an answer. She noticed Sarah hadn't bothered looking her way. "Sarah, you hear me talkin' to ya?"

"Yeah Van, I hear ya, but I'm thinkin' 'bout what you asked." She said still watching the creamy skinned man.

"Well peel yo' eyeballs away from Franks face and talk to me!" She yelled, pulling her by the arm and turning her around to face her.

Her raven eyes widened, and then voided. Savannah taken aback by what she'd seen, took a step away from Sarah. The change in Sarah's face made the hairs on Savannah's arms stand on end. As a chill rose up her back causing her to shiver.

"Frank, you say." Sarah turned back to the man

now standing at the window puffing on a cigar.

"Sarah, this here is Frank, he been comin' here a long time now, he's been away, but just stopped in to say he's back for a while. Now back to you missy. What the hell is goin' on wit'chu tonight?"

"Oh that thang with Lue and me, don't pay that no mind, I'll take care of her later…What I mean to say is, I'll apologize to her later." Sarah replied.

"No…we need worry 'bout it now."

"She told me to stay away from Busta, but it was Busta who come up to me. I told that ol' heffa I didn't want him, but she hit me in the mouth anyway." Sarah was trying to sound like she hadn't done anything wrong.

"Gal, I told ya how she feel 'bout Busta." Savannah said, not sure if she believed what Sarah was saying.

"Well, Busta had me cornered on the stairs and befo' I could get away, Lue saw us and come chargin' at me and him. 'Sides it was her that hit me in the mouth or did ya forget I just told you that." Sarah protested menacingly.

"Look-a-here gal, don't take that tone wit' me. I don't know what's gotten into you, but tonight you have been very disrespectful to me and to some of the other guests here. Now that's gonna have to change." Savannah was lighting a cigarette and she could feel the cold coming from Sarah's back stare.

"Okay, Van, I don't wantcha mad at me. I mean it was you that came to take me in after my pa left. You gave me a place to sleep and work. Did I ever say thank you? Thank you, Van." Sarah said, stabbing a knife into the kitchen table. Frank thought it was time for him to step in.

"Sarah...that's it right. Ya name I mean. Why don't you pour me a drink, and let's have a chat."

Sarah turned slowly in the direction of Frank and watched him as he moved over to the table, carefully taking the knife from her. He took Van by the hand, pulled up a chair next to her, took his seat, and placed the knife on the floor under the table.

"Savannah and I been friends along time and she good people, young miss. There ain't no need to be acting like that, fighting and carrying on. I know if ya got a problem with some of these ol' gals, just come to Van and talk to her. Some of these ol' gals get jealous when a young pretty thang come along. They feel like they bein' moved out. Ya just got to know how to handle'em. Let them know they still the shit, ya know." Frank was trying to bring peace back.

"Let them walk all over me ya mean, let them tell me who I can and cain't fuck ya mean. No sir, done had me enough of folks walkin' over me, pretending as if I'm nothin' and actin' like I'm not there. Done had me enough of it, ya hear and tonight that came to a joyous end."

"Frank, she done had a rough go of it. She comin' into her own and just tryna find her place. I understand it ain't her fault." Savannah was trying to explain.

"No need in ya explainin' fo' me, if I want everybody to know about poor little battered and orphaned me, I'll be the one to tell it." Sarah said as she slammed the bottle down on the table.

"Gal, I'm 'bout done with you tonight!"

Sarah eyed Savannah, wanting to reach out and jab her in the throat. However, she remembered Frank had taken the knife from her. The two women watched each other.

Frank interrupted by asking Savannah to step outside and get some fresh air with him. The two walked outside and left Sarah in the kitchen alone.

Sarah suddenly realized the tone she had taken with Savannah and wondered what was happening to her. She went over to the sink, spread her arms over the counter, and held her head down exhaling. For the first time, she didn't feel like crying. She felt more like killing anyone that got in her way. Mostly angry with her papa for all the things he had done, and then leaving her there for more men to do the same.

She remembered the vow she made to herself, that no one would do to her what she didn't want them to anymore. She also promised herself that she would get even with her pa—if it was the last thing she did.

It's his fault, all of it. My rage, this house. I hope where ever you are Papa hell is following.

"*Soon, Sarah...wait...*" the voice whispered. "*Wait...*"

Feeling restlessness surging rampant through her body, she took a few deep breaths and after pouring herself a drink. She once more, unwrinkled her stockings from around her ankles, and went into the parlor.

Leaning against the wall, she eyed a group of men playing a game of cards. She watched and waiting for one of them too meet her gaze. When one did, she winked a long and slow wink. He winked back and she walked over to introduce herself to him. The man wasn't handsome, but then again, none of the men in the house were—with the exception of Frank, and she figured she would work on getting him later.

"Hey suga, ya come here to play cards or what?" She asked sitting in his lap and playing with his ears.

"Whatchu thank I come here fo'?" The man asked with a big grin. His teeth where yellow and his breath was foul, he smelled as if he hadn't bathed in days and his face was rough from not shaving. His eyes were beet red and he was as cockeyed as a chameleon—you know the ones with eyes that move in all directions.

Trying to get past the oddness of his gaze, she said. "I dunno, looks to me like ya come here to play cards. I got somethin' better for ya to play with."

She got up and walked to the stairs, never once looking back to see if he was following her—there was no need, she could smell him.

Sarah walked slowly up the stairs, giving her John an eye full—teasing him with her hips. At the top of the stairs, she looked over the railing at the rest of the men and women wondering, was it worth it.

Once in her room, Sarah asked the old man to take off his clothes and come with her to the bathroom. There she washed him with the lye soap they used for washing clothes. The man had so much liquor in him, he hadn't notice it burned a small hole in his leg. Sarah put a bandage on it and they both returned to her room. She snorted a line of coke, and went over to the old man lying on the bed, waiting patiently to receive her.

She climb atop of him, he helped her guide himself inside her. She burned a little from the lye soap residue, but the coke was kicking in and it didn't matter much anymore.

While, the old man moaned and groaned. Sarah was in another world, remembering back when she first made love to Toby. It was truly the first time she had uninterrupted thoughts of him since he left for school. She really did miss him at that moment. She closed her eyes and permitted her mind to fill with him. She could feel the old man's hands on her body. She grabbed them and held them as if they were Toby's.

"Toby," she called out.

"Gal, my name ain't Toby." The old man said.

"Who gives a fuck you old bastard...yo' name Toby tonight, now shut the fuck up." Sarah said without stopping or looking at him. "Toby," she called out again.

"Look here gal, you ain't gonna be callin' me no other man's name. I'm payin' good money for yo' ass and you here to do what I tell ya. And I'm tellin' ya don't be callin' me no other man's name." The old man shouted after slapping her across the face.

"All right—ya ol' fart—we play the love game yo' way. Whatchu want me to call ya?" Sarah asked stopping long enough to await his answer and allowing her fury to take over as she massaged her cheek.

"Oh baby girl, don't stop just call me—Papa."

"Papa...is it." Sarah's eyes voided, the old man saw

the change in them even though the light was dimming. The room grew cold. Sarah was rough and wild, calling out the name, Papa, over and over again.

The old man yelled out for her to stop. It was more than he could handle. Sarah dug her nails into his chest and held on, throwing her body back and forth yelling out. "Papa, is this what you want? Is this how ya like it, Pa?" She was moving back and forth with such force, that the old man thought he was going to lose his manhood.

Frightened and engaged at the same time, he watched her. He watched her young tender breast fall up and down. Her skin glowing in the moonlight, her untamed beauty took him in. He wanted her to stop, but he couldn't bring himself to mouth the words.

"Is this whatcha wanted, Papa? Is this how ya like it, Papa?" Sarah was still watching him. The old man opened his mouth to speak, but found he no longer had a voice. His body heavy and now unable to move. Suddenly, the room illuminated a crimson red he saw another figure standing at the end of the bed watching them.

Tears welled in his eyes, as he felt life draining from his body. He could see Sarah atop of him her eyes glazed over and void of any expression. He could feel her moving about. It all became a morbid and intriguing haze. Sarah wrapped her hands tightly around the old man's neck as the images of her pa trying to take her life flashed back in her mind.

"Wait…not yet, soon child…wait." With that Sarah let the old man go, rolled off and waited.

"What the hell was that, you 'bout ripped me to pieces?" The old man tried to stand, but his legs were weak.

"The beast."

"What gal?"

"The best ya ol' fool." She replied with a smile and walked over to her vanity, took a seat and watched the old man struggle to his feet through the mirror.

As he went for the door, Sarah called him back. She gave him a big kiss and then bit his tongue. He managed to break free and then slapped her so hard she fell to the floor.

With her head still down, blood dripping from her mouth, and caressing her face, she turned up her eyes to him. The old man felt the cold return.

"What the hell ya do some crazy shit like that fo' gal?" The old man asked, examining his tongue in the mirror.

Sarah sat with her eyes on him without a response.

The old man turned to Sarah, ready to grab her up and demand answers when he spotted a woman's figure standing behind her. Afraid he backed out of the room slowly with eyes wide open. Without a word to anyone he went in search of Savannah. Finding her still outside with Frank, nervously he said, "Savannah, that new gal she ain't right, that fool bitch damn near bit off my tongue. She did thangs to me no human should be able to do. There's evil behind her, I saw it. I saw it in her eyes too."

"Oh, I'm sorry if you weren't happy wit' her, I can give ya another gal. No charge." Savannah said, wondering why she would bite a man on the tongue, and then noticing Sarah peeking out the front window.

"No need...'sides I don't wanna be in that house wit' the likes of her. If'n I was you I'd be thinking the same way." The old man said nervously. Then, tucking his scarf into his coat he headed up the road.

As he walked, he couldn't get Sarah out of his mine. As he neared the forest opening, he could see a light not too far in the distance. Wanting to know what it was, he walked over to get a closer look. He could see a fire going and called out to see if anyone was near.

"Anybody out here?" He called. Walking closer to the fire and seeing no one around, he tried to put it out. "Damn kids, don't they know this how fires get started. Last thang I need is fo' another fire to kill my crops." Just as he was putting out the last of the fire, he saw a shadow standing in front of him. Looking up slowly he saw it was a woman.

"What ya doin' out here, gal?" He asked in fear.

She didn't answer.

The old man let out a scream and disappeared in the night.

"What I'm gone do Frank? That gal been through some real shit in her life and I think she might be close to snapin'. She just so different from the gal I saved from the Hawkins boys some weeks ago. The look on her face when I asked her 'bout what happened between her and Lue. And, her attitude is changing like the wind. Lord Frank, I don't know what I'm gon' do?" Savannah felt a chill run through her, as she noticed the curtain closing.

"You're a smart woman, you'll think of somethin, come on let's go inside, your shivering."

<<<>>>

The night was ending—most of the men had gone. The only ones left were the ones that had no real home to go to.

Savannah stood with her back to the door as the last guest left for the night. Her mind was heavy with worry—mostly about Sarah, and why she had changed so. She took a deep breath and headed to the kitchen. To her surprise, Frank was still there. He was gazing out the open door when Savannah walked in.

"Frank, I thought you left." She said.

"I was going to, but it's been a long time, Savannah and I've missed you." He was walking towards her with his arms out stretched. He grabbed her by the waist and pulled her close. Stroked his hand across her cheek and planted a deep kiss on her lips.

From the landing of the stairway, Sarah watched.

Event 031.00

People were leaving their seats and exiting the class before Toby realized what time it was. He couldn't keep his mind off Sarah and wondered why he hadn't heard from Charlie about her. He had called Charlie several times since he'd left, but his father always told him he was out or asleep.

Toby needed some answers and he needed them now. He walked over to the building that housed phones for campus students to use. A small room which contained about thirty phones for a campus of two hundred plus people. He waited for a booth in the far corner—it was far enough away so one felt as though they had a little privacy.

He allowed Charlie's phone to ring several times before a voice came over the other end.

"Hello!" Charlie yelled, upset because he had to get out of bed.

"Hey man, I been trin' to getchu." Toby replied, grateful he had finally caught up with him.

"Who dis?" Charlie asked rubbing his eyes.

"It's me fool, Tobias. If ya returned phone calls ya wouldn't have forgotten me already." He replied with a smile hoping he could feel the love.

"Oh hey man…yeah I been meanin' to get back to ya…, but I been busy. You know how it is."

"Yeah, I suppose, but anyway man. How's my girl, have ya seen her?"

"Yeah man, I'm good, thanks for askin'," Charlie replied annoyed he hadn't asked about him first. "And what girl ya askin' 'bout?"

"Sarah fool, who else?"

"Oh, yeah that bit…look man she ain't right. She ain't right fo' you man. I told ya befo' ya left, leave that girl alone. Forg—" Charlie was cut off.

"Man, what the fuck is wrong wit'chu I asked you to keep an eye on her. I bet you ain't even been back to that house have you?" Toby knew Charlie didn't like Sarah, but he had promised him he would look after her.

"Look man, like I said I been busy. Whatcha want wit' a girl like her anyway. She up in that house and ya know what she doin'. All that fine college ass 'round you and you stuck on this small town hoe. Tell ya what, *you* come back here and *I'll* gladly take yo' place." Charlie was in the hall sniffing the air, he could smell the breakfast his mother had prepared, before she and his father went off to church.

"Look man, first off, I know how ya feel 'bout her, but you need to watch how ya talk 'bout her to me and 'sides you promised me. Have you seen her at all?"

"Yeah man, I seen her," he said reflecting back on the night of his birthday. "And like I said, you don't need to worry 'bout her. Ain't nobody in their right mind gonna fuck wit' that hoe. Tobias man, you gotta believe me, she ain't right, she bad news." Charlie wanted to tell him what happened, but he knew Toby would be upset about him sleeping with her. He also knew he would never believe the story about the figure he'd seen or the images he'd been shown. So he decided to keep it to himself, for now.

"Yeah, yeah, that's what you keep tellin' me, but chu ain't given me one good reason why ya think she ain't right. Is she well?"

"Man, I don't know and I don't care. Look-a-here man, we been pals for a long ass time and I ain't nevea said nothin' that would get you hurt. So man please, just let this hoe go."

"Whatevea man, I thought we was boys, but ya seem jealous or somethin'. What happened, ya tried to get wit' her, didn't ya? She turned ya down, 'cause that's what ya actin' like. I don't know what's up, but you disappointin' me. I just asked for one favor from you and you cain't even do that fo' me. Bad mouthin' her every time you talk about her. Why? 'Cause of some fool story about demons and devils. Coltrane fuck you!"

"Look man, it ain't even like that, I just—"

Toby hung up. He was walking slowly back to his dorm trying to come up with a reason to get back to Sarah. He wanted to be with her so badly it was ruining his concentration on his schoolwork—and the holidays were too far off to wait. Toby ran down to the Dean's office to talk with someone that might be able to help.

Charlie was left holding the phone listening to the

dial tone. His heart was heavy. "Fuck!" He yelled slamming down his end of the receiver. With his head in his hand he walked into the bathroom. He stood in the mirror for a moment reflecting on old times spent with Tobias and wondered how he was going to get through to him.

He pulled off his pants and began running a bath. He sat on the toilet with thoughts of Toby and all the good times they shared together. The thought brought tears and smiles at the same time.

"Ha Ha, look at that fool, Charlie, ain't it time for his daily mud bath!" A kid yelled, throwing mud balls at him.

"Hey, look what y'all did to my new shirt. Why don't you assholes leave me alone?" Charlie yelled back, trying to rub the mud off. A second kid hit him in the back of the head. This time Charlie went to the ground in pain. Through the mud, one of the bullies noticed blood coming from the point of impact.

"Yo man, whatcha trin' to do, kill'em?" Tobias, one of the bullies shouted. "This ain't funny anymore we really hurt him, he bleedin'!" Tobias ran over to see if the injured Charlie needed help.

"Hey man, we was just foolin'…we ain't mean to make you bleed. Let me help ya up," Toby reached out his hand and Charlie pushed him away. "Come on man, I'm tryin' to help."

"I don't need yo' help, you just don't want me to tell on you and those fools you hang out wit'." Charlie got

Sarah Rose

up and tried to clean himself off the best he could.

"We ain't meant no harm, we was just—"

"You was just what, man? Look at me, my mama gonna kill me coming home with another ruined shirt, we ain't made of money ya know."

"Look, come to my house, my mama will clean the shirt for ya befo' ya go home." Before Charlie could make up his mind, mud balls were flying from every direction, bashing into every part of their bodies.

"Run man!" Charlie yelled forgetting his books on the ground.

"Don't run, that's what they want, you got to fight back." The boys ran behind a large oak tree and began throwing mud balls back at the other group of boys. Toby had good aim thought Charlie—because none of his mud balls hit anybody. After several minutes, the other boys ran off yelling obscenities and making finger gestures. Toby and Charlie gathered their things and laughed all the way to Toby's house.

"Hey man, you sure yo mama can get this mud out?" Charlie asked holding him back.

"Yeah man, my mama is a wiz wit' the wash," The boys entered the house from the back door that led into the kitchen. "Hey Ma! I'm home," Toby yelled. "You want some lemonade, man?" Toby asked, as Charlie stood by the door. Toby could hear his mother coming down the hall.

"What the hell is wrong wit'chu boy? Look at the mess you done brought up in here. Look at my floor, I just spent all day on my hands and knees scrubbin' it. Get yo' raggedy little behind out...get back outside and hose yo'self off!" She never noticed Charlie standing at the door, until Toby called to him to come get his glass.

"Mama this here is, ummm...man, I don't even know yo' name." Toby handed him his glass.

"Sorry Ma'am, I'm Charlie."

"Who...? Doggonit, I don't give a damn who ya are. Right now just getcha asses outta my kitchen. Gon' now...get." Toby grabbed his new friend by the arm and went out to the east side of the house, and they rinsed off their faces, hands, and feet—cringing and chuckling as the cold water hit their bodies.

"Damn man, yo mama was pretty mad."

"Aww man, her bark worse than her bite, she all right as far as Mamas go, she the best there is. Damn I forgot, I'm Tobias, just call me Toby." From that day on, the boys became the best of friends.

Shortly after, Toby and his family moved to New York. It was only when Toby returned did Charlie find out they were related through marriage. He had been told they were distant cousins. To Charlie they were true blood no matter how far, down, up, across, or around the family tree they were.

Charlie's thoughts were interrupted when he felt warm water under his feet. "AWW SHIT!" He yelled, jumping off the toilet, he went to turn off the water. He'd been so engaged in thought he'd forgotten he was running a bath. After towel drying the liquid mess, he pulled off his shirt, flexed one good time in the mirror, and slid himself down into the tub of hot water.

Steam and the smell of rose scented soaps his mother kept on the face basin filled the room. He was back to thinking about Toby and trying to figure out a way to get him to understand what it was he was trying to tell him.

Charlie pulled a rag from the rack, dunked it into the water, slid down into the tub so only his head was visible—he placed the soaking wet rag over his face. The water felt good on his body and he was now relaxed and able to think clearly about how he was going to tell Tobias about the other night.

"Charlie," he heard, "Charlie."

He removed the towel from his face yelling back. "I'm in the tub Ma, whatchu want?" He received no answer.

"Charrrlieee," sitting up he heard it again. "Charrrlieee."

"Damn!" Wrapping a towel around his waist, he went to see what his mother wanted.

"Yo Ma, where you at? I was in the tub," he yelled, searching the house for his mother, only to find she wasn't there. "Damn! I must be losing my mind." When he turned to go back to his bath, there was a woman standing in the middle of the hall staring at him.

"What the fuck you doin here? And how you get in?" Charlie was shaking from head to toe.

"Charles, didn't ya hear me calling you?" She asked.

"That wa...how you get in here?" He yelled once more.

"Now Charles, is that any way to speak to company? I came by to see how you were doing." She said, moving closer to him. The closer she came, Charlie could see she wasn't walking at all. He ran to his room and closed the door behind him.

"I don't know who or whatchu are girl, but leave me the fuck alone." Charlie yelled out as he turned from the door and saw her standing behind him.

"Now Charles, that's no way to treat a friend. We are friends now, aren't we? I mean I shared my deepest secrets with you the other night. Don't tell me.... You didn't like your birthday present?" She grabbed him by the neck and gave him a long deep kiss. He fought to get away, but she was too strong for him. She pushed him to the bed and pulled off his towel.

"Someone's glad to see me."

"Look-a-here, I don't know who or what ya are, and if this is about me not thanking you for the gift. I'm so sorry and a belated thanks to ya."

"Don't be foolish, Charlie." She replied and climbed atop of him. Unable to scream Charlie took in a deep breath and fainted.

Event 032.00

Savannah woke to find that Frank had left. He left a rose for her on the dresser. He always thought leaving money made things seem dirty and aloof. He would return later in the day to bring her the money, which she usually didn't take. After a while, he started leaving it in the mailbox or giving it to one of the other girls to give to her later.

Savannah picked up the flower, held it close to her nose taking a long sniff, smiled, and then went to the bathroom to get showered.

Time spent with Frank made things seem a bit better—even if just for a moment.

Her thought quickly turned to the nights events and how her best friend and Sarah had fought. She wondered what she was going to do about Sarah—something about her wasn't sitting right. As she played with the running water, she heard a knock on the door.

"Come in," she called. The knock came again. "Come in," Savannah, now annoyed, turned off the water and went to open the door to find Sarah standing there with tears in her eyes. Both women stood in the doorway watching each other.

"Come, let's go to your room and you can tell me what's goin' on." Savannah took Sarah by the hand leading her to her room. Set her down slowly on the beds edge and then took her place next to her—but not before reaching to the bedside table for a tissue.

The way Sarah's makeup had smeared about her face. The way her gown hung carelessly from her body. Savannah could see the innocent girl she saved from the Hawkins boys had returned. Savannah pushed Sarah's hair back from her face. "Talk to me chil', what's wrong?" Savannah asked, concerned.

"I...I...," Sarah hung her head down and sobbed. She tried to speak, but words evaded her. Savannah reached out and held her close until she was able to talk. Finally, Sarah sat up and wiped her face with the tissue that Savannah had given her only moments ago.

"Can ya tell me what's goin' on in that little head of yours?" Savannah asked.

"I'm not sure what's happenin'. I...I feel like I'm in two worlds, like I'm two different people. Thangs is happenin' so fast, my life is goin' by so quick. I awoke today feelin' so sad and confused. I cain't remember much of last night—maybe I drank too much. I keep seein'a boy..., I thank I might have hurt him. I even think I may have..." she said with worry in her voice and decided not to finish her sentence—remembering what happened to Sam, she decided not to mention the vision of the woods and the old man.

"Whatcha talkin' 'bout chil' hurt who? The fellas you was wit'," Savannah was worried that she had done something wrong, because Charlie did look distraught after he left her room. And the old man had complained about her as well. "Tell me, Sarah, what do you think you did?"

"I don't know that I did anythin' fo' sho'. I just feel like I did. Last night was so strange...*Gina*! Where's Gina? I got to talk to Gina." Sarah jumped up and ran to her room. Savannah ran after her.

"Gina left before dawn, she got her own bed to sleep in. Whatcha need to see her fo'?" Savannah's heart raced.

"Where she stay? I got to see her she give me somethin' and I just need to talk to her." Sarah was running from room to room, as Savannah ran behind her.

"Gal, stop and listen to me," she grabbed her by the end of her gown. "She don't live here. She leaves at the end of the night, but she'll be here this afternoon, ya can talk to her then. Now tell me what she give you?" Savannah asked even though she had a good idea. She had instructed Gina in the past not to go around passing her cocaine out, as if it were candy.

Damn her.

"Sarah, what she give you?" Savannah asked again, taking Sarah back to her room.

"I cain't tell ya, she told me not to."

"Look gal..., I been in this business far too long fo' ya to play that game wit' me. Now tell me what she give ya. Or should I tell *you* what she give ya?"

"If you know already, then why ya askin'? Now who's plain' games?" Sarah responded, stopping to see her reaction.

"Sarah, I don't like my girls doin' that shit. It do bad thangs to ya, how much did she give ya and was it just coke?" Savannah asked, looking around to see if there was any left anywhere.

"How am I to know? I ain't nevea had it befo'. She told me it would take the edge off. Told me it would make the night go by faster, but she never told me it would do some of the shit it did to me last night." Savannah knew it had to be more than coke.

"Look chil', don't take nothin' else from Gina, she ain't nothin' but bad energy."

"Then why ya keep her here?"

"The men love her and she the only one that will sleep wit' other women. Have to give it to her, that hoe bring in real good money. Sometimes I think a few mo' like her and I could get rid of some'a y'all. 'Sides I don't need to be telling you 'bout my money," Savannah giggled and hoped it would relieve some of the tension. "Sarah honey, promise me ya won't mess wit' that stuff anymore, it won't lead to nothin' but trouble." She waited, but Sarah said nothing, she just stood there watching her. "Speaking of trouble, do ya remember you and Lue had a fight in the middle of the parlor?" She asked, changing the subject.

"Yeah, I remember and I remember what I said to her too—I meant every word of it. She done had it in fo' me evea since I got here." Sarah said nervously.

"Now Lue is my best and oldest friend, I can't have ya comin' in here stirring thangs up. There are plenty of men in and out of here, just leave Busta to her—'sides I hear he ain't much in the sack anyway. So see, ya ain't missin' nothin'."

"Cain't miss what I ain't had."

"Ya say something honey?" Savannah asked, straightening her bathrobe.

"No Ma'am, I'm gonna take a bath and get dressed...I feel as bad as I look." Sarah took her things and went to the bathroom down the hall.

Before Savannah left her room, she peeked in her closet and saw that she had nothing to wear. The things she did have weren't going to do around the house. She liked her girls to look presentable at all times—just in case a man came calling. Even if all they had on were there evening gowns.

"Sarah, when ya done come to my room. I got some'em fo' ya." Savannah called through the bathroom door.

"I hope it's a boot through the front doe!" A voice yelled from the opposite end of the corridor. "That little heffa betta watch her back, 'cause I'm *waitin'* on her." Savannah watched Lue as she walked past her and down the stairs still talking to no one.

Sarah heard Lue from behind the bathroom door, she squinted her eyes and curled her lips. *It ain't always good thangs come to those that wait.*

Event 033.00

Charlie awoke in a daze, his head was spinning and his stomach was nervous. For a moment, he couldn't remember what happened or if anything had happened at all.

He tried to get out of bed, but his legs buckled beneath him. He fell to the floor in pain. There was a horrible pounding in his head and a sharp pain in his stomach.

The woman, Charlie eyed the room for the mysterious woman and waited for a moment before trying to get up again.

He'd made his way to the bathroom to get cleaned up. When he examined himself in the mirror, he saw his face had changed.

He was much older in appearance, his hair had fallen out in patches and his skin was ashen and cracked. "What the hell did that bitch do to me?" He said aloud.

Charlie scrubbed his face with scolding hot water, when that didn't help, he went to get his mother's face cream. He figured the way his mother went on about the stuff—it would work faster for him if he used the whole jar.

After doing the best he could with his face, he dressed and found one of his old ball caps. It was small and sat tight on his now bald head. He could feel his head quickly numbing from the absence of adequate profusion—that didn't matter though—when he was done positioning it around, he'd noticed he'd pulled the wrinkles taut and he no longer appeared as decayed looking. Now he just appeared as though he was stuck in some sort of G-force with an excessive amount of oil on his face.

Hearing his parents coming in the front door, Charlie ran back to his room throwing the items he'd used to clean up into the closet.

"Charles, we home." He heard his mother call out.

"Boy, you up yet?" His father yelled as he walked down the hall to his son's room. Charlie took one last look into the mirror. His face—a greasy and slick mess—he tugged at his ball cap once more, trying to regain a bit of feeling to his head.

He heard his father getting closer and then there was the knock on the door. Charlie stood for a moment, thinking.

How in the hell am I going to explain this to them.

"Boy, getcho behind outta that damn bed!" His father yelled through the door.

He heard his father grab the doorknob, but before he could open it Charlie swung it open for him.

"Damn boy! What...the fuck ya been doin'...in here? Smells like somethin'...up and died!" His father proclaimed, standing in the doorway covering his nose and trying to catch a fresh breath between words. "Hell the whole house smells like dirty ass. What the hell you been doin' while we was gon'?"

His father went to the end of the hall to open the single pane window. "Open up the windows and let some good air in," walking back to Charlie, he noticed his face. "Boy, what the hell done happened to yo' face? Why you got on that hat? It seem too small for yo' head and 'sides, you know yo' mama don't like ya wearing those thangs in the house, take it off," his father continued as he walked away. "One night out wit' yo' fool uncle and ya look like death warmed ovea." Not giving the matter any real thought, because Charlie was always up to something and this time he wasn't in the mood for any of it.

"Pop."

"What is it, boy?" His father asked, turning back to face him. Charlie didn't answer because he wasn't sure what he was going to say.

"Neveamind," Charlie remarked sullenly and closed the door, then went to open his bedroom window.

Outside beyond the garden his mother was working on, was an old weeping willow tree. He thought he saw someone standing there watching the house. When he blinked his eyes to clear them and get a better look, the figure was gone.

Charlie thought he'd get out for fresh air. He decided to go to the soda shop—it always made him feel better. Before, he could get out the gate, his mother called him back.

"Charlie, telephone they say it's important. Charlie."

With great qualms, he turned back to see whom it could be.

"Yeah, who dis?" He said into the receiver. He noticed his mother standing at the end of the hall trying to listen in. He turned his back because he knew it made her strain harder to hear.

"Hey man, it's me...don't...don't hang up," It was Tobias "I gotta tell ya somethin'."

"Ya hung up on me and now ya callin' back. I think it was more like..., fuck you...or didcha forget?"

"Boy! Watch your mouth in this house," his mother said passing by and hitting him upside the head.

"Yes Ma'am," he replied, ducking in pain from the ball cap being too tight. "Look man, I don't know whatchu want. But if ya callin' back to say fuck me again, save it. I'm done watchin' out over that evil bitch, ya hear me man, I'm done. Don't ask me about her again, and you should be thinking the same way." Charlie was looking at his reflection in the mirror.

"Boy, didn't I tell ya to stop all that damn cussing in my house, Oh Lawd...now ya got me cussin' and I just come from the house of the Lord." His mother yelled, poking her head out of the bathroom. He watched her until she pulled it back in.

"Look man, I was wrong okay. I was just upset at how ya keep talkin' 'bout my girl. But look-a-here, I found a way to get back home. All I need is fo' ya to do me one more favor. Can ya do it?" Toby was excited at the thought of seeing Sarah again and nothing was going to spoil it.

"What is it?" Charlie asked, with reservation, but willing to do what he had to in order to help Toby find out what he's been trying to warn him of since finding out he was in love with Sarah.

"Aww, man you're the best. All right this is what I need from ya." Toby laid out every detail, as if he was planning the largest heist in history. Charlie stood listening and shaking his head while Toby explained.

Event 034.00

Sarah finished her bath and was dressing when she thought about the words Lue had spoken to Savannah. She took a deep breath and let out a long sigh.

You're the new doll... the words Gina had said echoed in her head. She left the bathroom with her heart heavy. As she woefully walked down the hall, Lue was coming back up the stairs.

"There you are ya little bitch. If ya ever come near Busta or me again, it'll be the last thang yo' ass ever do." Lue shoved passed her and continued walking down the corridor.

"Lue," Sarah called out. "Lue," She stopped not turning around. "I'm sorry." Sarah said, as an image of Lue burning in flames danced in her head. Lue walked away without another word. "I tried you scanky bitch," Sarah whispered to herself. "Savannah you in here?" She called out as she let herself into Savannah's room.

"Just stepping out the tub, sit down, I got somethin' I want to give to ya."

"You don't gotta give me nothin', ya done enough

for me already, lett'n me come here and all." She replied with slight disagreement in her voice. "Girl cain't ask for much more than a place to stay, food, and all the men she want." Sarah yelled back with a shiver, thinking of the end of her statement.

"Okay miss thang, no need to be glib," Savannah laughed aloud, knowing she wouldn't be there either if she knew how to do anything else. "Look-a-here, I pulled these thangs out for you," she said as she was exiting the bathroom. "They just been sittin' in my trunk making food for the moths, thought ya might like to have'em. Some of them's a bit out of style, but they'll do ya 'til ya getcho own thangs. Ya like."

"Yeah, they okay I 'spose, kind'a fancy though." Sarah was holding up the gowns to her body.

"They 'spose to be, after all when a man comes to call, ya want to look ya best."

"What's wrong wit' what I got on now, these my best overalls? I always wore them when I went into town with Mama," Sarah asked looking down.

"Nothin'…if you goin' to farm," Savannah said with her nose turned up. "It's all new suga, give it time. After a while ya gon' find ya can't do without the finer thangs." But, what Savannah was more concerned about, was the way Sarah's attitude had been changing since she came into the house. "Sarah, while ya here I want to ask ya 'bout somethin'."

"Sure, what is it?" she asked while looking at herself in the mirror, admiring the new dresses against her body.

"Are ya angry 'bout being left here?"

"Yeah—I'm mad as hell—but what am I gon' do, I

plan to make the best of it while I'm here. Save up some money, and get out this hell. Why ya askin' me this again, we talked about this already." She replied, letting her shoulders fall and losing the smile that lit up her face only seconds before.

"Yeah I know...it's just...ya changing like the wind, so's I can't tell if ya happy or not—not that this life anythin' to be happy about."

"Look, Savannah, I'm gon' do what I got to while I'm here. But there is no need for ya to get in my personal business, if I need to talk, I'll find ya. Thanks for the gowns, I'ma go into town for a bit." Sarah was out the door before Savannah could ask any more questions.

She went to put the gowns in her room. Stopping in front of the white pouch sitting on the vanity, she thought of what Savannah had said about not taking anything from Gina.

Nevertheless, to muster up courage in order to ask Gina about what was in the stuff she had given her, she had a few drinks and decided to do one last line anyway.

Her first stop was at the soda shop. Too ashamed to ask anyone about anybody that worked at the house, she waited for courage and bravery to kick in. As it did she dove right in asking anyone and everyone that made eye contact with her about Gina.

There was no luck, no one seemed to know who she was, How could anyone miss her? She was a full figured, beautiful woman. She decided to give up and go home—before she did though—she wanted to go by the old house for one last look.

As she walked up the old dirt road, her thoughts fell to Toby, she wondered what and how he was doing. She walked past the woods at the point where she first met him—seeing a little boy—she wished it was Toby standing there holding the rifle instead.

As she approached the house, her heart began beating faster with each step. Reaching the front gate, she wasn't sure if she wanted to be there. Everything was the way it had been when she left—no one had been by to disturb anything.

Sarah claimed into the house through a window and then walked slowly down the hall to where her bedroom used to be. It was hard being there again, but she was able to cope. Thoughts of her and her mama flashed back and forth through her mind. Her papa came in at times, but she would quickly try to think of something else. She gazed out the window towards the barn and she saw a person going in. Pulling up the window, she called out to them. She quickly ran down to the barn to see who it could have been.

As she approached the barn, she called out to them again, but still there was no answer. Pushing back the door as slowly as possibly, she couldn't see anything. It was dark and her eyes needed time to adjust. She walked in slowly.

"Is there anyone here? I know there is…I saw ya come in from my bedroom window," She called out. An owl that sat perched on a beam was the only thing that returned her calls. "Don't be scared, I don't even live here anymore, so if ya claimed it…it's yours." She heard a rustle up in the loft.

She claimed the stairs slowly and poked her head into the loft opening—she could see the figure of a woman.

"Who's that up there? Come on out now." The figure came out the shadows and into the light.

"Gina, Gina, that you?!"

"Sarah?"

"I been lookin' fo' ya all over town."

"Sarah, you had me so scared. Stay down I'm coming down too."

"Ya know, no one seems to know who you are or what you look like. Whatcha doin' way out here on my farm?" Sarah was happy to see her, but surprised at the same time.

"Yo' farm?" Gina was dressed in a red skirt and a white shirt, it was a bit dirty, but Sarah figured it was from climbing up into the loft.

"Whatcha lookin' fo' me for? After last night, I thought ya was done wit' me?" Gina said watching her.

"Seems last night I done a great deal of thangs I cain't remember, and stepped on a whole heap of toes doin' it. Look, I'm sorry, I don't know what's been up with me lately. Savannah seems to think thangs is moving too fast. Do ya accept my apology?"

"Yeah girl, it's all good I guess," Gina responded jumping off the last step. "We all been where you are now."

"I really don't think ya have, anyway I wanted to ask ya something?"

"What is it?"

"The powder ya gave me, was it just coke?"

"Why ya askin' that?"

"Well Savann—" Sarah started to say but was interrupted.

"Savannah always got her fool mouth open 'bout somethin' she ain't got no control over. Watch out for her, she'll be yo' best friend as long as she can tell ya whatcha can and whatcha cain't do. Then, she'll turn on ya like the sky on a nice day. As long as you fuckin' fo' her, with no questions asked, ya good." Gina's tone disturbed her.

"Damn, why is everyone so fuckin' up tight? Watch out fo' this one, watch out fo' that one…" Sarah took the bottle from Gina's hand and took a big drink.

"AAAGHHH SHIT...! WHAT THE FUCK IS THAT!?" Sarah yelled dropping to the barn floor, chocking and holding her chest.

"Good ain't it? It's a little somethin' I been workin' on. Get up—you'll be fine—you cain't go suckin' it down like that," Gina smiled and took the bottle from her. "Anyway whatchu mean yo' farm?"

"Not anymore…," Sarah said between coughs. "My pa gave it up and now the bank owns it back. I saw ya through that window over there." Sarah was eyeing the bottle Gina held in her hand. She let out one last cough and tried to get up, but her head was spinning. "My head don't feel right."

"Girl ya gon' be just fine." Gina told her with a giggle. "Let's go for a walk and get ya blood going again, this shit really kicked ya in the ass, huh?" Gina helped Sarah up and waited for her to regain her composure. The girls went out back and headed for the woods. "I know a spot we can go and be alone, no one will find us." Gina grabbed her by the arm and pulled her along. Sarah had no idea where she was going, and she still didn't get an answer from Gina on why she was out there.

"Look over there ain't it beautiful." Gina was pointing to an old wooden lean-to in the middle of a field at the edge of the woods.

"Who's place is that, I don't remember seein' it befo'?"

"Mine. Come on." Gina was already about ten paces ahead of her.

"Wait fo' me." Sarah wasn't sure of the feeling' she felt—something wasn't right—but she paid no mind and followed her anyway.

As she approached the lean-to, it seemed to get larger. Gina walked in, while Sarah waited by the door until Gina fired up a lantern in the middle of the room. The lean-to was much larger than it appeared from the outside. It had one table in the middle of the room, with four mix-matched chairs. The windows were painted black, with no window dressings. Sarah saw another room to her left, it appeared to have a bed in it, but the light wasn't bright enough for confirmation. She wasn't sure if she should stand or go and sit down. So, when Gina sat, she did too.

"Ya hungry, I ain't got much, some dried cow hide in my room—you're welcome to it if ya want."

"No, I'm okay. You live here?" Sarah asked

"Lawd, naw girl. I just come here when I don't want to be bothered."

"I ain't never seen this place befo'...and I'm sure I've been this far into the woods, I never saw the path you took either." Sarah said with her head turned sideways.

"Well don't know how you missed it, been here for years." Gina said taking a swallow of the chest burner in a bottle.

"So whatcha doin' out here?" Gina asked.

"I was in town lookin' fo' ya, then I decided to come out here and see what the old place looked like."

"Why ya lookin' fo' me?"

Sarah took a deep breath. "I want to come and stay wit'cha. Ya gotcho own place ain'tcha."

"Stop right there. Come and stay wit' me. Damn ya ain't even known me long enough for me to even consider ya stayin'—and after the way you treated me last night, ya think I'ma up and say sho'."

"I'm not sho' of what happened last night. Matter fact, I'm not sho 'bout much anymore, but I already said sorry. It wasn't me."

"It wasn't chu? Hell, could have fooled me. Look like ya, talk like ya. What next, you gonna tell me ya got the monkey on ya back or somethin'?" Gina laughed and took another swallow and passed the bottle to Sarah.

Sho' felt like it. she thought, before swigging chest burner and pleading her case to become a live in companion.

"Look, we can be a good team together, you and me, whatcha say? Just let me come for a few days and if I get in the way...ya can put me out. Gina, ya cain't just leave me in that house with all them hateful old bitches." Sarah pleaded with a sullen look and then took another sip of the chest burner. This time taking care not to swallow too much at one time. "Smooooth," she said.

"I don't know." Gina replied with uncertainty.

"Just thank about it. Hey…ya got any more of that stuff." Sarah thought if she could get Gina to trust her, then she would be in.

The two sat chatting about nothing, doing blow, and drinking chest burner the rest of the day.

Event 035.00

Toby was back at his dorm packing for the trip back home. He paused, yearning for the moment Sarah would be back in his arms. His reflections interrupted with the notions of what his mother was going to say when she discovered he was dropping out of school—dropping out for a girl no less.

His plan was to stay with Charlie until he could find a way to tell his mother. He knew this would be no easy undertaking, but if it was the last thing he did, he was going to get his girl back.

Toby opened his trunk and discovered a hair tie, he'd taken from Sarah the night he found her drunk in the barn—he smiled and tucked it back into the corner of the suitcase.

After packing, he headed for the train station.

Meanwhile, Charlie headed into town for a stop at the soda shop. Along the way he scratched at his itching face and removed his ball cap several times to calm the throbbing of his bald head. He came across an old spoon on the road, picking it up to take a look. He saw he appeared no better looking than when he'd left home. "That bitch!" He said aloud.

He wanted nothing more than to get his hands on her and rip her to pieces. He was glad Tobias was coming back, because now he would be able to see for himself what he had been saying all along. However, he had to come up with a plan that would show him what he was trying to say.

Now nearing to the edge of town, Charlie could see what he now considered, "**The Den of Evil**." The sight of it made him cringe. He wondered if Sarah was still there and if she was could he burn it down fast enough to kill her. He had plans on finding out what was going on, but wasn't going anywhere near that house—at least, not until Toby came back.

As Charlie continued on to the soda shop, he began to notice all eyes were on him. Now he loved when people eyeballed him, but not the way people were eyeballing him today.

When he'd reached old man Cutties, he peeked into the window and at a mirror that sat on the opposite wall. His face was worse than when he'd checked it a few moments ago. His skin was paler and appeared more decayed and ashen. The longer he stared the worse he began to feel.

Charlie headed on to the soda shop, he thought it would be best to go up the back of the buildings instead of out front where everyone seemed to notice him.

Not soon after he was out of the public's watching eye did he begin feeling the presence of another.

Stopping and taking a moment to survey the area around him—he saw no one. Chills rose up his back and his vision blurred. He could feel the wind picking up, so he pulled his cap down a bit more, folded his arms and continued.

"Charlie," he heard. "Charlie."

"Who's there come out so I can see ya. This been a fucked up ass morning and I ain't in the mood for nobodies funin', now bring yo' ass out." He was turning in all direction to catch a glimpse of whom it could have been calling for him.

"Charles." The voice came again. He no longer wanted to know or cared about who it was, he ran until he was at the back door of the soda shop. He waited a minute before reaching out and opening the door.

Something ain't right.

But, he figured he was just being paranoid. Pushing the door open, the air inside was stale, cold and still. Reluctantly poking his head in—seeing nothing in the pitch-blackness—he stepped in to give his eyes time to adjust.

The room was dark and dank, he could barely see past his own hand. However, there was a small flicker of light coming from the middle of the room; he walked slowly towards it, squinting to get a better look.

"Charlie." The voice came again.

Oh I'm 'bout to regret this shit. "Who are you and whatchu want wit' me?" He asked, his voice trembling.

"Oh Charles, don't act like that." The voice said.

"I don't know who ya are, so show yo'self 'cause this

shit ain't funny no mo'." Charlie was standing still because his feet would no longer move.

Suddenly he felt a hand on his shoulder. "Oh how quickly they forget." The voice whispered in his ear.

Turning slowly, he was able to make out the hourglass figure of a woman. "It's you again ain't it?" He asked his voice still trembling. No answer came from the figure. "Answer me! What did you do to me? Look at me."

"I see you...and ya wanna know something. You're just as ugly as your personality. Really, Charlie, you should try using a skin cream. You're literally cracking up." She said.

"Why don't you just leave me the fuck alone! If I wasn't scared shitless I'd kick yo' ass." He replied trying to sound as bold as possible.

"Oh Charlie, stop acting like a bitch. Besides, I'd watch who I was taking too if I were you. For generations, your family has been talking a whole lot about what they nothing about—and it really makes us look bad. You're family painted a nasty picture of us—been that way for a millennia. Now it seems you've become quite the chatterbox as well. You see we've been waited for that girl to come of age."

"What girl," he asked.

"Who else."

"I...I...th—"

"I...I th—, They said you were stupid. Glad I wasn't born a minion."

"Look lady, I don't know who ya are or what the fuck ya are, or whatchu talking about, but I ain't said nothin' to nobody 'bout nobody."

"Delusional little Charlie, caught with his tongue hanging out," The woman reached out and grabbed Charlie by the tongue, pinching it between her long and sharply pointed fingernails. "Well, I've had enough of your delusions, time for a dose of reality." Still holding onto his tongue and with her other hand, she backhanded him across the face. Charlie flew through the air as if he had been catapulted out of a canon, hitting the wall and leaving behind only his small framed imprint, before hitting the floor.

After getting his head together, he got up and sprinted forward toward the woman. Before he could reach her, he was stopped in midstride. She slowly hoisted him into the air—watching him as he dangled helplessly. Tears began filling his eyes. "Still a little boy, helpless and don't know what to do." She dropped him to the floor and turned her back to him. Charlie had a flash of the same words being spoken by Sarah, as he tried to catch his breath.

"I want you to see something, Mr. Charlie, up on your feet." Before he could open his mouth to respond, with a twist of her hand, she winched him up into air with straps on his arms and legs, dangling him like a puppet. Not one part of his body mobile.

"I'll have you know the straps are purely for my amusement. Enjoy the lesson."

Charlie screamed in horror, wiggling, and trying to break free, but it was no use. His voice had been silenced and his wiggling was done in vain. What felt like an eternity of anguish was finally over, exhausted and petrified he cried out, "Oh my God, what the hell was that?"

"Charlie, give credit where credit is due, God, had nothing to do with this. What's wrong, a little too much for your first lesson?" The woman asked, standing in the shadows. "We've come to reclaim what is ours and you're gonna help. You need to know what it is your doing so you don't go fucking it all up. We need you Charles, she needs you, and well let's face it, your gonna need us," the women moved in close to him, "we'll be keeping an eye on you."

The straps that held him suspended loosened. Charlie fell and quickly sprang up to his feet and tried to run in the direction he'd come from, but he ran into a wall, fell to the floor realizing he was in the dining area of the soda shop—with everyone watching him.

Event 036.00

The house had brought in much more than Savannah had expected. Between Gina and Sarah, things might be picking up. Nevertheless, she wondered what things would really be like with the two of them in the house. Savannah wasn't concerned with Gina though, it was more the way Sarah had been acting, she couldn't tell from one moment to the next what might happen.

"Lord, I ain't sho' what's goin' on, I know I ain't much on praying and going to church. But, can ya find it in ya to let me know what to do?" Savannah was putting a tray up when Lue and the others walked into the kitchen.

"Van, we got to talk. The women and me been talkin', and we done come to the conclusion that… well…it's Sarah, ya know the stories 'bout her and that strange family of hers. It ain't right her bein' in this house." Lue said.

"Yeah, we all think she needs to go," said another woman. "I was upstairs most of the night and every time there was a trick in the room…. Well how do I say this?"

"Just gone say it," Savannah said.

"Well, they scream out in horror. Like they bein' done-in or somethin'. I waited, peeking out my doe when I heard one them scream out. When he'd come out he was pale and looked like he'd seen a ghost or somethin'. I ain't nevea seen a black man turn white befo'. But, last night I seen it...twice." The woman proclaimed.

"Yeah, and she tryna take my Busta," Lue said. "Did ya see the way she was lookin' at us all when she come down stairs, like we was all in for it. There is somethin' wicked 'bout that girl." Lue said nudging another woman to agree with her.

"Now ladies, she just tryna to find her spot in the house. I'm sho' she ain't meanin' to step on any toes. We all did it when we first come here. Just give her a chance. Thangs will change, you'll see. 'Sides I done had a good talk with her this morning," Savannah replied hoping to relieve their fears. "Now, let's see how thangs go tonight, and if need be, I'll talk to her again. But, we cain't just up and put her out so soon. Now ladies...please go and rest and try to put it out ya minds, thangs will work out—they always do for us don't they?"

Those that were sitting rose up from their chairs and walked out with the rest. Savannah could hear several conversations going on as they all went their respectful ways.

"Lue, wait a minute. Come and sit. We been friends a long time and gone through some thangs together. I need you to be understandin' most of all. I spoke to Sarah 'bout Busta bein' off limits. She says she understands and it won't happen again."

"Yeah…well…We'll see 'bout that won't we. I'm tellin' ya, Savannah, somethin' foul is in the air—somethin' wicked I tell ya—And it's been here ever since that gal step foot though that front doe. Somethin' evil is behind her, somethin' awful." Lue was never a person to scare easily. But, as Savannah listened to her she knew she was afraid.

"Now Lue, ya don't really believe that do ya? All that craziness 'bout her birth mother and she being the devils spawn. If it is true, then why now? Why it come to pass now? After all these years. Lue, really…it's just small town talk from folk that ain't got nothin' better to do then spread gossip. 'Sides look who doin' all the talkin' anyway…Bible thumpers. Honey, put it outta ya mind it's just stories. The wrong family just brought up the poor chil'. I blame Grady for that. He was a mean man. But, on the other hand, Anna did the best she could." Savannah wasn't all too sure if she believed the story she was telling herself.

"Maybe ya right…. Still there's somethin' 'bout to happen—some'ems comin'—I just know there is." Lue said as she got up from the table and went out to get some fresh air. Leaving Savannah to wonder if Sarah was the devils child.

Event 037.00

Toby was on the train and almost back home. The first thing he wanted to do was see Sarah. He wondered if she would embrace him or push him away.

He thought about how proud his mother was when she found out he had been accepted into college—and how is father took on an extra job to help with tuition. Now he was going home to tell them he was quitting. But, he felt he had no time to worry about that right now.

"Sir, something to drink?" A woman asked, holding a note pad in her hand.

"Yeah, I'll have a whisky." Toby said with a half-smile. He noticed the man in the seat across from him watching.

"Anything for you, Sir?" She asked the stranger.

"I'll have the cheapest whiskey ya got." He replied with a wink. "Boyy. That's a nice piece a tail ain't it, young blood?" he asked as the server walked away.

Toby didn't reply he faked a glance down the aisle and gave the stranger a smile.

"Say, young blood, I was watchin' ya for a while there. Ya look deep in thought. Need someone to talk too?" The man in the seat across from him asked.

"Naw, I'm cool" Toby replied.

"Say man, where ya headed. I'm on my way back to Wisconsin."

"Yeah, me too." Toby really wasn't in the mood for conversation, but he figured he might as well indulge the man, as it would pass the time.

"By the way, the names Grady, what's yours?"

"Tobias, but most just call me, Toby."

The man reached out his hand for a shake and Toby obliged.

"So, ya from there or just visiting? I was a farmer, had to get out though wasn't nothin' left fo' me."

"I'm just goin' back, got some business to tend to. If there ain't nothin' there for ya, why ya goin' back?" Toby never understood why people say their leaving a place because there isn't anything there for them then they return.

"Well, when I got to where I was goin', there was nothin' there either, so I figure...I might as well go back to what I know best. I'ma try and get me another farm goin'," The attendant had arrived back with their drinks. "'Sides I got some family there and I know they sho' be glad to see me," Grady said holding his glass in the air for a toast. Toby did the same. "So, what business ya got...if ya don't mind my askin'?"

"Well, I got to get my girl back. I realized I cain't be without her."

"You goin' back fo' a woman? Young blood she got

yo' nose wide open, huh," Grady said with a chuckle. "Well here's to love, young blood. It ain't fo' me no mo', but good luck to ya…, to young love." Grady made another toast and they rode the rest of the way in silence.

Event 038.00

Sarah and Gina squandered the day away, drinking and filling their noises with powder.

Sarah stood to her feet trying to catch her bearings. She went out to get some fresh air when she saw a woman approaching. Running back into the house she called to Gina, who was in the other room squatting over a pot on the floor.

"Gina, somebody comin'!"

"No one knows we're here!" Gina said, not taking time to finish peeing.

"Well, somebody knows somethin', cause they comin'!" Sarah was peeking out a tiny scratch in the black paint on the window.

"Shit...the coke! Get it up and hide it."

"Hide it?! Where in the hell ya thank we gone hide it? There ain't shit in here."

"Damn! The pot in the other room."

"You pissed in that!"

"Sarah, we gon' be in a world a piss we get caught wit' this shit." Gina grabbed it, ran into the other room and tossed it into the pot. The girls then took their seats at the table and waited for the person to knock.

"Sho' takin' them a long time to get here. Ya sho' ya saw somebody?" Gina asked.

"Yeah I'm sho', saw her as plain as day. She was headed this way with a mission in her eyes." Sarah said hoping it wasn't her mind playing tricks on her.

"Well, they should'a been here by now. Go look out the window."

"Why me? You go look!"

"Okay, we go together." The girls took each other by the hand and went to see if they could see anyone. "Ya see anythang?" Gina asked.

"Naw…, you?" Sarah replied, feeling Gina tremble in her hands.

"No."

Just then, a head popped up from beneath the tiny window carved into the top of the door. The girls jumped back yelling and running to the far end of the lean-to.

"Sorry, didn't mean to scare ya. I was walkin' in the woods and came cross this place. But, I didn't know anyone was here. It looked abandoned," The voice of the woman walking said.

"Who are ya?" Gina asked.

"The names Sadie," The woman replied, moving her face around the tiny window to get a better look at whom she was talking to. "Can I come in for a spell? I been walking a while." Sadie asked, wiping sweat from her forehead.

"No one comes out here. I been coming here fo' years and nevea seen another soul. You say you didn't even know this place was here, and ya lived not too far."

Gina whispered to Sarah.

"No shit...what ya tellin' me fo', this yo' place ain't it?" Sarah replied.

"Hello." Sadie called.

"Ummm.... Just a minute we comin'." Sarah got up and went to let the woman in. When she opened the door, she was taken aback as the woman was standing so close.

"Thank ya, woo..., like I say I been walkin' for a while. I thank I'm lost. Well now, y'all look like y'all done seen a ghost or somethin'. I didn't mean to give y'all a fright," Sadie said, as she sat in the closest seat to the door. "I don't 'spect ya got anythin' cold to drank? I sho' could use one." She asked fanning herself with her hand.

"Yeah, I'll get it fo' ya. Ain't cold though and it ain't water. It's all we got." Replied Gina, as she handed over the bottle.

"Careful now, it's a kick'a," said Sarah.

The woman tipped the bottle to her lips and drank until there was none left. The girls watched, wide eyed with their mouths dropped open, as she gulped to the last drop without taking a breath or choking on it.

"Damn Miss, ya was thirsty wasn'tcha. I ain't nevea seen no woman drank like that befo'. At least not off moonshine that strong." said Sarah, remembering how it burned her throat and chest sending her to her knees.

"'Scuse me, I reckon when ya as thirsty as I was, then nothin' gone come 'tween you and a drank. I owe you ladies a bottle, seems I done finished this one. What two young gals like y'all doin' way out here anyway?" Sadie asked leaning back in her chair and wiping sweat from her armpits.

"Umm..., we just gettin' away is all," Gina said "But, we should be gettin' back...I'm sho' our folks is lookin' fo' us, seein' it's gettin' late and all." Gina was moving to the door and eyeing Sarah to do the same.

"Well now, I ain't meant to spoil what evea y'all got goin' on out here. Y'all don't have to leave on-a-count'a me. Stay and I'll go." Sadie was eyeing Sarah as she spoke.

All the ladies stood waiting for the other to make the first move. Gina took special notice as Sadie watched Sarah. "Sadie, is it? Why don't we all head back into town."

"Yeah, that sho' would be nice. I don't 'spose ya know of a place I could stay for a day or two." Sadie asked still eyeing Sarah.

"No Ma'am, but if ya come wit' us I'm sho' we can talk someone into puttin' ya up for a day or two." Sarah replied, realizing the woman had been watching her and getting the strangest feeling.

Gina was leading the way, while Sadie walked slowly behind. The women walked for a while before Gina broke the silence. "Sadie, I have to ask what ya doin' out here, if ya ain't from 'round here?"

"Well, I was travel'n wit' a friend when he put me out the car—after an argument of course. I started walking and next thang I saw ya lean-to, and thought I would hold up here 'til mornin'."

"But, why not stay on the road?" Sarah asked. "Seems it would have been the safest route for not knowin' the area."

"Boy, you girls sho' ask loads of questions." Sadie replied, now annoyed by all the suspicious questioning.

"Look lady, we didn't mean anythin' by it. Just wonderin' why a woman would be way out here is all. Most older folks that live here don't come way out here. Let-a-lone a stranger." Gina replied.

"Yeah, we ain't meant nothin'. And, 'sides I know what ya mean I don't like too many questions either. Gina, leave her be now." Sarah intervened.

Sadie stopped cold in her tracks and watched Gina for a moment, annoyed by the tone in her voice. "Look if it's too much trouble, I'll gon' back to the lean-to and wait 'til mornin'. I'm sho' the ol' fool that left me here will be lookin' out this way for me anyway."

"No, we cain't do that. We cain't leave no woman out here like that. You come wit' us and he'll find ya in town. I'm sho' he's there lookin' fo' ya now." Sarah said taking her by the hand and continuing. Together the two women walked back into town, leaving Gina to trail behind.

There was something about Sadie that peeked Sarah's curiosity. She was feeling a connection to her—one she had never felt for any other human being—not even her mama.

The women made it back to town. Gina led the way into the house and without a word went up the stairs to get Savannah. Sarah took the woman into the parlor.

"Have a seat Sadie, want a cold drink?" Sarah asked as she took two glasses from behind the bar and grabbed the water jug from the counter.

"Sho' I'll have what you have'n. This sho' don't look like a roomin' house." Sadie replied as her eyes scanned the room.

"That's 'cause it ain't." At that moment, Savannah walked in.

"Well now..., I been told we got company. I'm Savannah. Who might you be?" She asked with her hand out.

"Glad to meet ya, I'm Sadie. The girls say you might be able to put me up for a day or two. My man done up and left me 'longside the road. I got money, I can pay." Sadie said with a gentle smile.

"Well now, Sadie, this ain't no roomin' house. I don't take in people off the street."

"Ya took me in and I come off the street." Sarah interrupted.

"Chil', that's different, now gon' upstairs this grown folks business."

Sadie watched Sarah as her eyes squinted and her face twisted. She grabbed the jug sitting in the middle of the table and poured herself a glass as Sarah's gaze with Savannah hardened.

"Grown folks business," Sarah said slowly. "The shit that go on in here...and the shit I'm doin', and now ya say this grown folks business. I'm grown-a-nuff to be making you money. But, not grown-a-nuff for your conversation. I'm payin' my keep Savannah, and I say she stay. She need help and I told her she can stay as my guest." Sarah was cold.

"Look-a-here gal, I don't know what don' got into ya since ya been here. But, I won't have that tone in here, not from you or anyone else. This woman got to go 'sides—Oh hell this is crazy—I don't have to explain nothin' to you or to her."

Savannah turned to show Sadie the way out. When Sadie stood from her seat, she called to Savannah. "Wait," she said, watching Savannah for a moment—something eerie behind her eyes.

As they stood in silence, Savannah felt scrutinized by the intense stare Sadie had on her, suddenly she was flooded with feelings of guilt and pity.

How could I put this woman out on the streets with night falling?

However, she ignored all her gut feelings, and aloud Sadie to stay for the night. She had to promise to stay upstairs in one of the empty rooms and not be seen by any of the others in the house.

"Sarah, can I have a moment wit'cha?" Savannah asked

"Yeah, Van, what is it? I was getting our guest some thangs to make her comfortable through the night." Sarah said sticking her head out of the closet.

"Well, nevea mind that fo' now, 'sides she wit' Gina."

Sarah knew where this conversation was going and wasn't in the mood to talk about it. "Look Van, I know whatcha thankin' and I'm just fine. I just got a bit upset when ya told me I was a chil'. I didn't mean to talk out of turn, it's just when Sadie come up and I heard her story. It reminded me of my own. Ya know wit' Papa leavin' me alone and all…ya know wit' nobody. 'Sides she real pretty ain't she. Maybe we can get her to stay. Ya need one mo' girl anyway now that Eva done gon' back to her mama."

Sarah didn't want Sadie to go. She had to figure out first why she felt such a strong connection to her. She felt as if she had known her, her whole life. Sadie's presence made her feel strong, independent, and fearless.

"I understand chil'. But, ya know she can't stay. You're doing the right thang by her tonight. In the morning she has got to go—even if I have to put her on a train myself." Savannah stood to walk out, to her surprise, Sadie was standing on the other side of the door. Savannah jumped back, astounded, knocking over the hand mirror that belonged to Sarah's mama. When it hit to the floor, it shattered.

"Oh my God, no," shouted Sarah, "what have ya done? My mama's mirror. It's all I had left of her. Look it's no good anymo'!" Sarah's heart was broken.

At that moment, Sadie pushed pass Savannah running over to help Sarah to her feet.

"Now..., now, she ain't mean to break it. I'm sho' she knows it brings her seven years bad luck..." Sadie said, with a sinister smirk on her face and eyeing Savannah as she spoke. "...'Sides I'm pretty sho' we can fix it. A little glue and some luck. Now it won't be as good as new, but ya still be able to look at that pretty face of yours—just be mo' of ya."

Sadie helped to pick up the pieces of mirror and placed them back on the vanity. Savannah noticed the air in the room had grown cold and with the look on Sadie's face, thought it might have been a mistake in letting her stay the night.

"Sarah, I'm sorry 'bout the mirror, I know how much it meant to ya." Savannah said. With no response from Sarah and only the frigid gaze from Sadie, she walked out closing the door slowly behind her.

Event 039.00

The train was nearing the station and Toby's heart was racing. He had tried to put out of his mind the fact that Sarah may not have wanted to see him. But, that wasn't going to keep him from trying.

As the train pulled into the station, he began to gather his things. For a moment, Tobias watched Grady staring out the window, wondering if he was waiting for someone to notice him. Slowly and what seemed wearily, Grady rose from his seat and walked off the train without a glance or a word toward his traveling companion.

Toby noticed when he departed he wasn't carrying any baggage, but he did leave a small tote on the seat. Picking it up he rushed out to find him.

"Hey man, wait up you forgot your bag." Toby yelled after him waving it in the air.

"Oh young blood, thanks. I don't know where my mind is. Strange being back here and not have anyone to greet cha." Grady was sad and sullen.

"Say man listen, if ya want to you can come wit' me I'm goin' to meet a friend in town. Ya hungry, maybe we can get a bite. But after that you on your own. 'Cause I ain't got no place to offer you to putcha head for the night." Toby felt sorry for Grady and thought, if the only thing he could do was help him get a hot meal, then he'd done his part.

Grady took him up on the offer and they headed towards the soda shop. They walked in silence as people on the streets seemed not to be able to take their eyes off Grady. Toby figured it had everything to do with his shabby and unkept appearance. The two men walked into the soda shop and took a seat in the back.

"Say man, order what evea ya like. I ain't really hungry myself and don't worry it's on me." Toby watched as Grady scanned over the menu and made his selection when the server came to take their orders.

"So, whatcha gonna do after ya leave here? There ain't really no roomin' house here in town. You gotta go up the road a bit to ol' lady Bea's place. But, since her death I ain't sho' they still takin' in boarders ya know." Toby was only making conversation to break the silence.

"That's all right I got friends on the edge of town. I'm sho' they'll put me up for the night. In fact, I *know* they'll be glad to put me up." Grady replied, with a crooked smile.

"That's great man...well here comes ya food and I got to get outta here. It was nice to meetchu." Toby was standing to walk out when he saw Charlie walking by in a daze and appearing lost. Toby felt he looked like he hadn't slept since he left for school.

"Charlie..., a Charles," Toby called running after him. "What's up wit'cha man, didn't you hear me callin'? Say man, you all right?" He asked concerned.

Charlie stood in a state of confusion for a moment then turned to Toby, staring through him before saying. "Hey man..., I'm sho' glad to see you. When ya get back?"

"Man, I just got back. What the hell you been smokin'? You got hold to some bad shit, huh. I told you that shit wasn't any good. You need to put it down. You look awful...all ashy and dry. And deciding to go bald was a bad idea too," Toby grabbed his friend and gave him a hug. "Damn man! When the last time you had a bath. You smell like a bucket-a-chittlin's," Laughing he pushed Charlie away. "I was just at the soda shop, we can go back, grab some drinks, and talk. 'Sides there is this ol' dude there I want ya to meet. He used to live here, he moved away, and now he's back. Anyway, I bought him a plate and I forgot to leave the money."

"Yeah man, that be nice..., it some strange shit goin' on here and I need to tell somebody befo' I go crazy. Although, it might be too late and I ain't had no stuff since ya left. But, believe me if'n I did now sho' would be the time." Charlie was looking over Toby's shoulder at the figure in the distance. "So... who...who's the ol' dude anyway?"

"Some ol' man named, Grady. Say he use to have a farm here and now he back to start ovea."

Charlie stopped in his tracks and pulled Toby by the arm into the walk of one of the buildings that had been closed for the past few days.

"Did you say Grady? Grady Lambert?" Charlie whispered.

"I nevea asked his last name, but yeah, he told me his name was Grady. Why?" Toby's eyes were fixed on Charlie.

"Man I tell ya, you sho' know how to pick the folks ya hang out wit'. That ol' man you feedin' in there... that's Sarah's ol' man. What the hell he doin' back here?" He thought about the images he had been shown by the strange woman—his heart was in his throat looking for an exit—with fear looming over his face, he leaned out to see if the figure was still following him.

"Like I said, he back to start ovea, that's all he told me. I didn't have twenty questions with the man. I was just makin' conversation to break the silence. And, 'sides he did most of the talkin'. He nevea said nothin' about Sarah. All he said is, he had family here and they would be glad to see him. As a matter of fact..." Toby realized this was the same man he'd heard horrible stories about. How he beat and raped Sarah, then left her there to whore herself out. All his rage came forth and he took off back to the soda shop. Leaving Charlie behind to wonder what just happened.

As Toby entered the shop, he found Grady had eatin' and gone.

"Where is the ol' man that was just here?" Toby asked a woman sitting at the counter.

"Grady? He slipped out the back way..." she responded watching the waitress, "po' thang, she don't know he gone yet. Tain't my business to tell her neitha."

"Damn!" Toby replied pounding his fist on the counter top. Charlie came running in behind him. Just then, Toby remembered Grady saying he was going to the house on edge of town for the night. "Sarah!" Toby whispered to himself. He knew he had to get there before him.

"A man, don't get involved in that. Leave that hoe be. Somethin' ain't right wit' that family. It ain't just so happen he back." Charlie pleaded with his friend, thinking of the images he had seen.

"Charlie I didn't come back for you to feed me more lines about devils and shit, if ya got something to say, then say it. Give me one just one good reason not to save her from him—and that life?"

Charlie opened his mouth to speak when he saw the woman in the window. "I...I don't have one." Charlie replied, with his heart heavy.

"I've got to reach Sarah befo' he do. Don't get in my way Charlie or ya gonna get hurt." Toby pushed passed him running out the door and up the road to the edge of town.

Man I'm already hurt, I just pray you don't... Charlie's thought was interrupted when the server asked if he needed help. "Nothin' you or anybody can give me to help me now." He replied as he walked out.

Event 040.00

Sarah and Sadie where trying to glue the pieces of the mirror back together. Sarah sat and watched Sadie, as she hummed to herself while carefully and slowly placing the broken pieces back into place.

"Sarah." Sadie called. "Why ya workin' here?"

"It's a long story, but I got plans to get outta this place," with her head down sighing she continued. "Not sho' what they are just yet though."

Sarah took the now glued and shattered mess of a mirror from Sadie and watched herself in it, reminiscing of times when she would watch her mama behind her braiding her hair.

Sadie took note of Sarah's sadness, picked up a comb and began to scratch Sarah's scalp. After a moment, Sarah got up, went over to the nightstand and pulled out a small white pouch. She found two glasses and poured herself and Sadie some whiskey. Sarah poured the contents of the white pouch onto the vanity table. Made lines like Gina had showed her and inhaled long and hard.

She turned to Sadie holding her hand and offered

her a snort of the white powder. Sadie took the steel rod and placed it at the edge of one of the lines. Sarah watched as the powder slowly disappeared. She could feel the room spinning.

Sarah was growing more and more captivated by Sadie.

"Sarah, do you know who you are?" Sadie asked.

"What?" She replied.

"Do you know who you are?" Sadie repeated.

"What kinda fool question is that, of course I know who I am."

"Tell me." Sadie stood to her feet, turning Sarah to face the mirror that sat on the vanity. She wasn't sure of what it was Sadie was asking or what she wanted to know.

Night was falling and the lighting in the room was dimming. She grabbed a match and lit the lamp that sat on the corner of the table. Then, turning back to the mirror.

"I'm not sho' 'bout whatcha askin' or whatcha wanna know. Ain't really much to tell. My mama was killed when her car broke down, my papa left and sent me to work here."

"No, tell me who *you* are, not what's happened to you." Sadie said again as she picked up the steel rod.

Sarah began to understand what it was she being asked. As she took a moment to think about it, her heart sadden.

"I don't know who I am, so far I've only been what others want me to be. I was my mama's daughter; I was my papa's punching bag and whore, now I'm...," The tears rolled down her face as she spoke. She reached for the steel rod saying no more. When Sarah lifted her head she noticed Sadie was no longer sitting next to her. She hadn't noticed her get up and walk over to the bed.

She watched and allowed the cocaine to take effect as Sadie pulled back the top covers and moved the pillows to the center of the bed. She motioned for Sarah to come to her. Getting up slowly she walked over and lay on the bed, Sadie joined her.

"Relax, the time has come..."

"What? What did you—"

"Hush now, the time has come." The room grew cold and turned a crimson red.

Sarah could hear the chanting of whispering voices. But, when she opened her eyes to see who was there, she saw no one. Her head heavy and spinning she lay back once more and closed her eyes.

"The time has come for you to claim what is rightfully yours." Sarah opened her eyes again and saw Sadie standing over her with Charlie.

"What's goin' on, Charlie whatcha doin' here?" Sarah was now afraid and wanting to get up. As she tried, Sadie lay her back down. Dizzy and weak Sarah was unable to fight back. She could feel her body—two shakes away from convulsing—tremble out of control. The voices began to chant in a low whisper, with Sadie leading them.

"No worries chil', the time has come for you to claim what is yours," Sadie whispered into her ear, "the Acumen have been waiting for you to return home."

Sarah could feel herself mouth the words, *"Return home?"*

Charlie was given a sign and slowly he climbed into bed with her....

"Sarah..., Sarah. What's goin' on in there? Open this door!" It was Savannah and a group of the other women.

"I'm..., I'm comin'." Sarah replied dazed, wondering what just happened. If anything happened at all.

What the hell is happening to me?

"What's goin' in here, girl? You all right? I been trying to get in here all afternoon. I thought you had gone out. 'Til Lue told me ya were still here. What ya been doin in here all day? Why wouldn't you open the door?"

"Whatcha talkin' 'bout I did go out. I been with Gina all day, we brought Sadie back with us."

"Sarah, whatcha talking 'bout, I ain't seen you all day." Gina replied, passing by the other women.

"Yes you did, at the lean-to in the middle of the woods. That's where we met Sadie. Where is she anyway?" Sarah protested holding her head—it felt like something was trying to pound its way out.

"Sarah what's wrong with you? You got the fev'a or somethin' you don't look so good," Savannah asked feeling her forehead. "And there ain't no Sadie here chil'..."

Bewildered Sarah said nothing.

"Okay everybody out, I'll tend to her from here, gon' now..., out," Savannah was shoveling women out like the nights trash. "Gina, you too. Gon' now, I'll letchu back in later."

"I told Van there was somethin' wrong wit' that gal." Lue said as she headed out.

"Shut up you ol' fool woman. There ain't nothin' wrong her but she just need some good rest." Gina said taking one last look back as she closed the door.

Not knowing what to do, Savannah led Sarah back to the bed and went to get cold cloths for her head. When she came back, Sarah was at the window in a daze. She stood and watched her for a moment, she felt Sarah hadn't even noticed she was gone and had come back.

"Sarah honey, come and sit down. I brought ya some water and cold cloths fo' ya head. What's goin on wit'chu gal? Please talk to me befo' you go outta yo' mind and take us all wit'cha."

"I swear, Savannah, I was out with Gina today. Out in the woods at an old lean-to, that's where we met Sadie. You and me argued about puttin' her up for the night. I got mad 'cause you called me a child. You saw her, you said she could stay the night. You put her in the room down the hall at the top of the stairs." Sarah was confused and wasn't sure if Savannah believed anything she was saying.

"Sarah, I done toldcha, ain't nobody been here all day...and you've been here from what the others say. Your tired chil' and ya need to rest. It may have all been just a dream. Ya told me that Gina had given you some stuff. Did you take any more of it?" Savannah was scanning the room for the powder.

"No." Sarah hoped she hadn't seen the little white bag on the vanity table.

"Was I really dreamin', I was really here all day?" Savannah nodded, puzzled by her questions. "It all seemed so real."

Savannah took her in her arms and held her tight. She could feel Sarah shaking in her bosom. "Sometimes our minds play nasty tricks on us, make us believe thangs others think is crazy."

As Sarah lay in Savannah's arms, she knew what she'd experienced wasn't a dream, she knew something had happened to her.

Nevertheless, how could she tell anyone? The longer she lay in thought, the more she felt it was just a dream.

They all can't be wrong about not seeing me leave here. I did have more dope. Maybe that's it, the effects for the dope and booze. I really have to stop doing that shit.

Right then she made herself a vow not to take any more of what Gina had to offer.

"Now chil', you rest I have to check on the others and let them know you okay."

"Thanks, can ya ask Gina to come in?"

"Sho' suga."

As Savannah approached Gina's room to inform her of Sarah's request, she heard whispers coming from inside. Unable to make out what was being said, she knocked on the door.

"Come in."

"Gina, Sarah's askin' for ya." Savannah watched the others as they stood to their feet—quick like a match had been stricken beneath them.

"How she doin'? she gon' be all right?" Gina asked.

"Yeah, she gon' be just fine. And Gina...I don't want that shit in this house anymore. I find out ya passin' it 'round like candy again, that's the end a ya, ya hear? I don't care how much money you bring in. Now you wanna snort your life away, that's fine, it's yo' life. But, don't take others down wit'cha." Savannah said to her in whisper, while holding on to her arm before allowing her to pass.

"I only give her a taste. The is rest on her." Gina replied as she pulled from her grip.

Gina walked slowly into Sarah's room—she did have some feelings of guilt about Sarah's behavior. "Hey missy, you all right ya gave us all a scare ya know."

"Yeah, I guess. Gina why you say you wasn't in the woods wit' me. You and me was at the lean-to."

"Really Sarah...I ain't seen ya all day, and I ain't got no idea what lean-to ya takin' 'bout."

"Sho' you do. Yo' lean-to out in the openin' of the woods." Sarah was eyeing her hoping to get a glimpse that she wasn't going crazy.

"Damn girl...how much of that shit you taking. I got a place, it ain't at the openin' of the woods. My place is small, but it ain't hardly no lean-to. And 'sides there ain't nothin' out there at the edge of them woods." Gina said offended at the thought of living in a lean-to.

"All right, what about Sadie? I know ya remember her, you was just as scared as me when we first saw her."

"Girl for the last time, I ain't seen nobody all day 'til I get here and everyone was tryna get in here. Hey...

what was ya doin' in here anyway? There was a foul smell coming outta here, filled the whole house and the air comin' from under ya door was cold as ice and there was a bright red light. Shoot girl, we all thought there was a fire or something in here. We almost called the sheriff, but Lue noticed there was no smoke." Gina asked looking around.

Sarah stopped with her inquisition and thought of the events that she knew wasn't a manifestation of her imagination and decided not to continue hounding the issue.

"I don't know. Maybe Van is right...all of it was a dream," *A bad demented dream.* "Look, that's the last time I do anymore coke, I think it's time to lay off the whiskey too. It's got me losin' my mind. I'm doin' shit I ain't really doin' and seein' shit that I cain't explain."

"You might be right. Maybe it's time I did the same" Gina replied laughing and taking a sip of Sarah's water, then cringing at the taste. "Damn, this shit liable to kill somebody!"

They both laughed and spent the rest of the day talking, until it was time to get ready for the evening guests.

Event 041.00

Grady had gone back to the old farm to see if there was anything he could salvage. "Damn the luck, I see that fool gal don' found all my moonshine." He said aloud to no one. He was rummaging through the house looking for anything he could take into town and sell.

He'd all but given up hope of finding anything of value when he came across a half bottle of moonshine. It had fallen becoming lodged between the stove and wall. "Yes!" Grady shouted pushing the stove over and gripping the bottle as if he'd found gold. Suddenly, he heard voices in the back room.

"Who's there?" He called out, walking slowly in the direction of the voices. "Sarah, that chu gal?" Grady was sure she'd gone, but he had no idea who else could have been there. As he approached the door the voices were coming from, he stopped dead in his tracks. He saw a flicker of red light emanating from under the doorway. He stood for a moment watching it and listening for the voices to start again.

"I asked who's in there, come on out and show yo'self." Grady's heart was pounding so hard and loud he thought for sure he would drop dead from fear. Placing his hand on the doorknob, he pulled back quickly because the door was opening slowly and creakily on its own. For a moment, he stood and waited for someone to emerge.

After a while when no one did, he pushed it open to get a better look inside. He could see the figure of a woman standing in the shadows.

"Who are ya and whatcha doin' in my house." Grady asked, his voice shaking.

"Such a foolish old man, you're about to find out." The figure replied.

"Look, this ain't no time fo' foolin' come out of there so's I can see ya." The figure moved slowly out of the shadow.

"Whatcho name woman?" Grady was squinting trying to get a better look—he knew he wasn't seeing what he thought he was. "Who you be woman?"

"Nevermind all that. You've been a bad man Grady and now it is time for him to collect."

"Wait…." Grady replied in fear.

"Silence old man, we've been beseeched and the time has come." The air grew cold and stale, from behind her back rose a demon like figure.

"Have mercy, please…."

"Underling, you failed, just as her fool mother did. We allowed you to the chance. Now it is too late." The demon replied.

"We have been watching and waiting."

In the dim light Grady found a sharp object next to him on the table, he picked it up, lunging towards the demon and stabbed him as hard as he could in the chest. He didn't move.

Grady watched as the sharp object backed out slowly from his chest. His eyes widened, the sweat began beading up on his forehead. Grady's body trembling as the demon soared through the air, backhanding him to the floor. Grady yelled out in pain.

"This will be your fate, Underling." He placed his hands over Grady's eyes and revealed to him his parallel world of pain and torcher—he screamed out for it to be over—but all that would be in vain.

"Your time has come, Grady Lambert." He heard the voice of the woman that was no longer there say. Leaving Grady—afraid—on the floor replaying over in his mind what just happened.

His body ached and his heart quivered with fear, leaving him lightheaded and weak. He searched franticly for his bottle of booze. Finding what was left he chugged it down without stopping to breathe. He lay there in pain trying to convince himself it was all just a dream.

"Oh dear God, what have I done?" He said aloud, holding the bottle and trying to find the strength to get up.

Event 042.00

Toby had searched the town high and low for Grady. Unable to find him he made up his mind to go over to Charlie's to get some rest and think of a way to get Sarah back.

On his way he passed his parents' house, the window was open. From the road he could see his parents at the dinner table with guests. He wanted to go in and tell them he was back and wasn't going back to school without Sarah at his side. He knew what the news would do to them, so with his head down and a deep sigh, he headed on towards Charlie's house.

At first glance it appeared there was no one home—the house seemed eerily empty—slowly he walked up the path to the front door. Before knocking he tried to see in through the window—there was no sign of movement inside. Not putting much thought into it he knocked on the door—no one answered. He knocked again, still no answer.

Wondering where Charlie went after they left the soda shop, Toby sat down on the stoop and waited.

He was going over in his mind what he was going to say to his parents, more importantly, what he was going to say to Sarah.

Getting up to take another look in the window he said aloud. "Where is that fool?" That's when the door opened slowly and there was a foul stench in the air. Covering his nose Toby tried to peer through the crack without getting too close. He didn't like the feeling he had. He felt a shiver crawl up his back making the fine hairs on his body stand on end.

"Charlie...man, thatchu? This shit ain't funny. Charlie?" He called. There was no answer. Moving toward the door he held his hand out to open it.

"Tob, what ya standin' out here fo' lookin like you gonna rob the place." Stunned, Tobias jumped back with eyes wide open.

"Oh shit man, you scared the hell outta me. Ya door opened by itself and where the hell you been?"

"I was...hey where I been don't matter. Did ya find old man Grady?" Charlie changed the subject afraid of what would happen if he said anything about what's been going on with him the last few days. "I bet he kicked yo ass when he found out 'bout you and his no good daughter."

"Man, everything ain't no joke, when you gonna grow up and stop being a wise guy?" Toby had had enough of Charlie and his snide remarks about Sarah. "And, 'sides what's goin' on wit'chu, you look like death. You sho' you feel all right?" The wind blew and Toby got a nose full of the foul stench emanating from inside the house. "Man, what is that damn smell? Smell like somebody died in there. What is goin' on?" Toby was watching the house when he asked the question.

"A man, whatcha say we stay out in the barn? See we got a real bad problem with a family of possum in the walls, I...I...think one of'em might have died. Got the whole house foul. I fixed up the loft and we be just fine out there." Charlie was leading Toby away from the front door as he spoke.

"In the barn! Man, I been on a train for hours and I'm tired and need to get cleaned up. I ain't sleepin' in no cold ass barn."

"Look man, you ain't sleepin in that house either! Now ya can sleep where I tell ya or ya can carry yo' ass over to yo' house and explain to yo' folks why ya back here."

Toby was in no mood to fight about anything else tonight. For a moment, he stood watching Charlie walk towards the barn shouting for him to come or go.

He took one last look at the house and thought he could see someone standing in the window, but when he wiped his eyes to get a better look, the figure was gone.

Something ain't right. Funk or no funk, Charlie hates sleepin' outside, a possum problem my ass.

Picking up is bag he ran over to the barn to make up—yet again—with his friend.

As Toby was nearing the barn, he could hear the sound of a woman's voice coming from inside. He hadn't seen anyone come into the yard. Climbing the old, half-put together ladder, he stuck his head into the opening and saw Charlie talking to a woman standing in a dark corner. Charlie appeared scared and shaken. When the two noticed they weren't alone their conversation ceased.

"Hey man, I see ya changed ya mind," Charlie said nervously. "Well come on up and meet my...my ummm..."

"So you're, Toby? Charlie don' told me all about-cha." The woman said stepping out of the shadow. Taken aback at how much the woman at first glance appeared to look much like Sarah. He stood for a moment motionless and couldn't find the words he was looking for. Clearing his throat, he said. "Ma'am."

"Well ya gonna stand there all night like a stuck pig with ya mouth hanging open or ya comin' on up?"

"Excuse me, Ma'am, it's just ya look so much like a friend of mine." Toby lost his balance and fell from the ladder, hitting the ground beneath him with a loud thud. He lay there for a second feeling his face turn flush, he kept his eyes closed, hoping what just happened didn't really happen. Feeling the pain began to surge through his body, he heard Charlie call out to him.

"Tob, ya all right?"

"Yeah man...just fine." Toby replied with a groan. Standing to his feet embarrassed and hurt, he ascended the ladder once more this time making it to the top.

"Man, that was a nasty fall," Charlie said with a smirk, "here you gonna sleep ovea here." Toby followed him to a spot in the corner of the loft.

"Ya sho' ya all right, that *was* a nasty fall ya took." The woman asked as she watched the boys get themselves together.

"I'm fine, Miss, just took the wind outta me. By the way, ya didn't tell me ya name and how ya know Charles."

"Well now, I'm just and old friend of the family is all. I just come to let Charlie know he'll see his ma and pa again tomorrow evening. Well...I 'spose I'll leave ya boys be. I gots to be gettin' back." The woman was talking as she was going down the ladder, never telling Toby who she was. "Night now. Charlie, see ya again real soon."

"Man, who was that?" Toby asked.

"Man, it's like she said just a friend of the families."

"I didn't know ya folks was gone, where they at."

"A man, why all the questions? I thought you was tired and wanted to get some rest." Charlie said not wanting to tell him the real reason the woman had shown up.

"Yo' business is yo' business man, I get it. 'Sides I need help gettin' Sarah back. Whatcha think I ought to say to her. I been going over and over it in my mind, but I cain't come up with the right words."

"Look man, ya my cousin and best friend I don't want to see ya get hurt. Please man, I'm beggin' ya, leave while ya still can. Ya asked me to keep an eye on her and well," Charlie took a long deep breath looking for the right words. "She ain't no damn good. Ya know she a hoe and ya know what she do."

"I know all that. I was there rememba, that's why I'm here to get her out."

"There ain't no out for her, Toby, she cain't nevea get out...ya hearin' me good. *NEVEA*. Look-a-here blood, I love ya like nobody's business. If ya ain't ne-vea listened to me befo' do it now. Leave while you still can. Without her." Toby had a quick flashback of his father telling him the same thing.

Charlie wanted to tell him everything—about the woman, Sarah and the strange night. Not to men-tion the events of this morning when he had gone to look for Grady. Inconspicuously, Charlie rotated his shoulder. It was still aching from where he been stabbed by Grady.

He wanted to grab Tobias by the shoulders and shake him until he would agree to go back to New York without her, so he did the only thing he thought would work.

"Look...there is somethin' I need to tell ya. I'm only doin' this so you will see Sarah for what she really is. I...I...," He paused searching his mind for the right words. "Aww man, there ain't no easy way to say it...I fucked her...twice." Saying those words hurt him more than when he was a child and mistakenly shot himself in the foot with a dart gun.

He knew his words would hurt Toby just as bad.

Toby's eyes rose to meet Charlie's—who was star-ing at him, silently praying he wouldn't get punched in the face.

Toby wasn't sure if he had heard him correctly. With his head cocked to the side and eyes squinted he asked in a calm voice. "What...the...fuck you say nigga?"

"You heard me...man, don't make me say it again."

"Naw man, I ain't heard shit. Now what the fuck ya say?"

"Fine have it cho way. I...fucked...Sarah. It was the night of my birthday and Uncle Busta took me over there and I—"

Toby didn't allow him to finish his sentence. He reached out with all his might and punched Charlie in the face. The two men rolled around on the floor exchanging blows and shouting profanities at each other. Charlie allowed Toby to get the best of the ordeal. The fight quickly ended when the two rolled off the top of the loft.

Angry, hurt, and tired they lay in their fallen spaces and said nothing.

Toby couldn't comprehend what he'd just heard, he lay there feeling betrayed. Heartbroken he said. "I cain't stay here, I got to get out. Ya know man, I know ya don't won't me with her, but the choice is mine. Outta all people...I nevea thought *you* would do me like that. I gotta...I gotta go. I cain't stay here wit'chu." As Toby left, Charlie called out to him.

"Toby, ya don't understand man. It ain't what ya think. I cain't explain...I wish I could. Toby, please don't go over to that house, bad things are gonna happen. People are gon' die there tonight!" Charlie's voice trailed off as he realized, he had said too much.

"Man, now ya really gon' off the deep end. Ya need to get off that shit. It's fuckin' wit'cha mind. Ya don' said some way out shit in the past, but now ya gone too far. I'm out and if I see ya 'round her or me again somebody gon' die all right! Get off that shit, man!" He yelled from the barn door.

Once outside he took a moment to think about what Charlie had said.

Does he really dislike Sarah that much he would come up with such a fool story to keep me from her?

Toby noticed Charlie wasn't the same person he had left behind only weeks ago.

With his heart torn and feeling alone, he walked back to town for a drink, with Sarah heavy on his mind.

Charlie watched as Toby headed up the road.

"Underling, when will you learn?" A voice came from behind. "What did you tell that boy? No one can stand in our way. You never could keep your fool mouth shut, just like yo daddy, always flapping your gums."

Charlie turned to see a figure standing behind him. "I ain't told him nothin'. Really I ain't said a thang." He pleaded with tears filling the wells of his eyes.

"Yeah, well you won't be saying much of anything anymore." She held out her hand and with the twist of her wrist, Charlie felt his throat set ablaze.

He tried to yell, but nothing came out. With that, he was left alone on the ground, clutching his throat and trying to catch his breath.

Event 043.00

The girls spent most of the early evening talking. Between conversations, Sarah's thoughts would drift back to the events of the morning. She knew deep in her sole she wasn't going crazy and she knew it had nothing to do with the amount of powder she had snorted.

A few times, she wanted to grab Gina by the shoulders shake her and scream for her to confess all she knew.

"Girl, you sho' you all right? You've been acting strange all evening." Gina asked as she was heading for the door.

"No, I'm not sho' about much of anything right now. I just don't feel like myself, silly I know. But, something's changing in me, Gina." Sarah replied watching herself in the mirror.

Even if no one believed what she was saying, she knew she was different. She's known it since that dreaded day her papa took away her innocence.

At that moment, she laughed a sultry laugh, finding the irony in her thought—for the first time in her life—she was feeling like the cat's meow. She was looking different, and talking different. In a strange way, she was enjoying the feeling of the new her. She was confident, feeling as if nothing in the world could ever hurt her again. At the same time she was afraid of it all.

"Well, when you figure it out, you let me know all right. I wanna be on the good side of it." Gina replied jokingly. "I need to get myself ready. I got me a new dress...I'm sho' gonna knock the socks off some of them ol' jealous bitches 'round here tonight," Gina continued, with a wink. "So, I'll see ya later, okay."

"Yeah, see ya later." Sarah replied, not paying much attention.

Sarah was left alone thinking and talking aloud to herself. "I know I'm not crazy. I know them things really happened." Pacing back and forth, she wondered what happened to Sadie. She knew she was probably the only one that would be able to explain what was going on. *"Charlie..."* She thought. *"He was here too, that rotten little bastard. I bet his ass knows what the hell is going on. Well no use in worrin' over it now. I got to get ready for tonight. Tonight, they all gone see."*

Suddenly, Sarah felt an intense pain in her stomach. It felt as if someone had stabbed her in the gut and twisted the blade. She bent over in agony. Sweat began pouring from her forehead. Her heart pounding so loudly, it was all she could hear as it echoed in her head. Her blood boiled in her veins and set her body on fire and she fell to her knees.

The pain was too powerful, rendering her cries

soundless. Her eyes were blurred by the tears that filled them.

As she lay curled up on the floor she heard a voice whisper to her. "Tonight."

"Tonight…what's…what's tonight?" She asked through the pain.

"You take your place where you belong?"

"Where I belong…what is my place? Make this pain stop." She groaned.

The room once more grew cold and turned a crimson red. She could feel a hand on her head.

"The time is near. Tonight."

Savannah thought about going to check on Sarah, but she thought she would give her some more time to herself. Instead, she went to see Gina and ask how things were.

"Gina, mind if I come in for a moment." Savannah asked sticking her head in the door.

"Naw, come on in." Gina replied pulling a dressing gown from the rack.

"I won't keep ya, just come to see if Sarah toldcha anything 'bout what's goin' on. I know it's been rough for her since she got here."

"No, she ain't really said nothin' 'bout anythin'. I ask and she always find a way to change the subject or get me to talk 'bout myself, funny, she good at that."

"All right then, I'll just have to keep a close eye on her tonight. Now 'bout you miss thang." Savannah pulled out a chair to sit in. "This shit you been pas-sin' 'round like candy. I want it to stop. I want ya to get yo'self off that mess. Now I know it help with these ol' fools, but it's getting foke in trouble."

"Look Miss Van, I know what you tryna say and I got a handle on it. It was Sarah who couldn't handle it. 'Sides what I do outside these walls is my doin'."

"That's just it, Gina, ya ain't outside these walls when ya doin' it."

Rolling her eyes and letting out a big sigh, she replied. "Fine, I understand nomo' powder in ya house. I can still have a drank cain't I?"

"Look, no need in ya bein' snide. We all need some-thing to keep a smile on our faces. Lord knows it ain't the men comin' in here doin' it."

Heavy hearted and wishing she knew how to make things better. Savannah got up to walk out when Gina stopped her.

"Miss Van, why ya do it, if it make ya so unhappy?"

With her head down and a single tear welling in her eye, "It's all I know." She replied and closed the door.

Event 044.00

Grady made up his mind he needed to get out of the house. "If they wanted me dead they would have done it." He said aloud.

He tried to put the matter out of his mind, but the pain he felt rushing through his body was a constant reminder. He made his way out the door, down the front path to the road. Standing still for a moment—to listen and scan the area—he headed into town, looking over his shoulder with every step.

Along the way, he passed the area where the sheriff had informed him of his wife's body. For a moment, he stood and wished she were still with him. "I miss ya and one day Hawkins gonna pay for what he done to ya." He said and continued on.

He thought about Sarah and wondered if she was still at the house in town. That thought fast faded, as he remembered he didn't have any whiskey. He made a quick detour in the direction he knew he could score a free bottle or two.

Soon, Grady found himself standing in front of the house that held Sarah.

For a moment he thought, *how could I have done all those nasty things to ya. How could I have left you in a place like this?*

As the thoughts ran through his mind he was growing angry with himself, but then, fear set in from what he'd been told by the woman, he quickly scarfed down the one bottle he was able to get. The liquor rushed through his blood stream allowing all the remorse felt only moments ago to cease.

A pair of men coming up the alley interrupted his thoughts.

"Hey man, cain't gets no action standing there lookin' at a closed doe." One of the men said as they passed him.

"Sho' ya right. Sho' ya right," Grady replied with a laugh. "Don't know where my mind was."

"Should be on all the pussy behind this doe." The other man said, while he nudged his friend, then they both disappeared inside.

Grady stood outside the door allowing the booze to give him the courage he needed to get what he wanted.

He noticed someone peeking out from behind the curtain.

"Oh hell, what is he doin' here? I thought that fool said he was leaving town?" Savannah said.

"Who?" asked Lue.

"Grady."

"Sarah's pa?"

"Yeah...what other Grady you know?" Savannah closed the curtain. "Shit, I don't know what he want, but I got to get him outta here fo' Sarah sees him. Go up and keep her there 'til I say it's ok."

"Me! Why me? You know me and that gal ain't on the best of terms. Send someone else." Lue replied with her hands on her hips.

"Oh damn, Lue be the bigger woman...oh neveamind, no time for all that now...Gina!" Savannah rushed passed Lue to find Gina. Lue pulled back the curtain to find Grady reaching for the doorknob. Her heart jumped into her throat.

Meanwhile, Toby was walking up the road going over in his mind what he was going to say to Sarah. Every word he came up with sounded ridiculous. Therefore, he figured it would be best to wing it when he arrived.

His mind fell back to Charlie. He knew how Charlie felt about Sarah, but he never expected him to go so far. He wondered if it was true or was he just trying to make him mad enough to say forget it all.

Nevertheless, whatever the reason he knew how he felt and no one or anything was going to stand in his way. As he was approaching town he heard his name being called.

"Toby...," The voice called out.

Turning to see who was there he saw no one.

"Toby...."

"Charlie, I ain't in no mood fo' you tonight, come out and tell me why you said them things back at the barn." Tobias was squinting trying to get a better look in the dark. "Charlie?" He called again. "Fo'getchu man. When you grow the fuck up...come see me." He yelled out to a friend that wasn't there.

Then he heard it again. "Toby, stay away." With that, there was a large gust of wind. With a chill running though his body, he folded his arms and tucked his neck into his shoulders. "Oh damn, now I'm hearing thangs." He walked fast to his destination. He figured there was no need in worrying about what Charlie was up to—at this point he had bigger fish to fry.

When he reached the edge of town he went into the saloon to have a drink before going over to talk with Sarah, still unsure of what he was going to say. Watching out the window he thought he had caught a glimpse of Grady across the way. Clearing his eyes to get a better look, he saw it was him.

He jumped from his table—leaving a wade of cash behind him. He ran out into the street. Just when he was about to call out to him, a woman opened the door to let Grady in. "Damn!" He yelled. "It's too late now, he'll nevea let her go." Standing there, he searched his mind franticly looking for a strategy to free her. "I gotta make my move."

"Make yo' move. Who ya talkin' to standin' here in the street. Ya libel to get run over."

"No one just thinkin' out loud." Toby had forgotten he stopped in the middle of the road.

"Well, I saw ya come out of the saloon, wanna go back in for a drink. It's on me." asked the woman.

"No not now, I have to get inside that house."

"Then just walk up and go in. Ya cain't get nothing standin' out here talkin' to yo'self. I was on my way inside too. You lookin' fo' someone special?"

"Yeah, I am. You know Sarah?" Toby asked.

"Of course I know her. Strange little thang, she scares me. Whatcha want wit'da?"

"Nothin' I can explain in a short time."

"Too bad. Ya sho' ya wouldn't rather have that drank?" The woman asked again.

"I'm sho'."

"Suite yo'self, then" she replied, leading Toby inside taking him into the kitchen past the parlor and other guests.

Lue managed to take Grady up to her room without Sarah seeing him, there they waited for Savannah.

"So ol' friend Whatcha doin back here? Thought fo' sho' you would be gone fo' good." Lue asked nervously.

"Well, wasn't shit fo' me there, so I figure I come back here and start over. Where is Savannah?"

"Oh she...ummm...she 'round, she be in in a minute. Want a drank?"

"Sho' do. Some of that fine whiskey y'all give out."

"Comin' right up. Now you just stay right there and I'll be right back." Lue closed the door behind her. Quickly she walked to Savannah's room. "Van, you in there? Van?" She called out. With no response she went to get the drink she had promised Grady.

From the stairs she could see Toby sitting in the kitchen with a worried look on his face. "Oh my God, this shit ain't gone be good. Why the hell they both here? I told Van that gal was trouble. I said it…I said that gal is trouble, Van. And something bad is in the air." She complained to herself, as she continued on to the parlor. She noticed Savannah standing at the window.

"Where is he? I don't see him out there." Savannah asked to no one.

"He up in my room." Lue replied.

"Oh Lue…," She said, her heart picking up the pace, "up in yo' room! What the hell he doin' up there? Why you ain't keep him outside 'til I come back."

"He was openin' the doe, what was I supposed to do? Tell'em he cain't come in!"

"Yes. Ya should've done that!"

"Look now…that would have started a fight and then all hell would have broken lose. 'sides he up there askin' fo you anyway."

"All right, gimme the drink I'll take it."

"Oh yeah…speaking of hell breaking loose… her boyfriend here too, he out in the kitchen." Lue replied sucking her teeth and leaning against the wall with her hands on her hips.

"O'Lawd, what else can happen tonight?"

"We should have got her outta here when I said." Lue remarked with wide eyes looking for Grady to come down the stairs. "I told you that gal was bad news. I sa—"

"Lue…not now wit' all that. Keep the boy in the kitchen as long as ya can."

"I got money to make. I ain't nobodies babysitter."

"Ya won't be makin' nothin' if this goes wrong. Now get."

Gina was running from the stairs out of breath, "Miss Van, somethin' wrong wit' Sarah. I been up there tryna get in her room, but she won't come to the door. And I cain't get it open either."

"Damn! Not again, this chil'…. Look Gina, I need ya to do somethin' for me, take this drink to the man in Lue's room and keep him there 'til I can get to him." Savannah shoved the drink in her hand and started to run up the stairs.

"Who this man?" Gina called after her.

"Just go. And hurry!"

With the drink in hand and shrugging her shoulders, Gina went up to Lue's room. When she opened the door, she saw a naked man standing next to the bed.

"Well, Well now. Ol' girl still puttin' on the ritz. Savannah send ya up to me?" Grady was standing eyeing Gina like a piece of meat.

"Look-a-here ol' fool, I'm just suppose to bring this drank up to ya is all. So don't get no ideas in ya head."

"Where Savannah and why it taken her so long to get to me? I ain't come here for no drank, but…ummm…I'll take it."

"No one comes here for the drinks fool. But, they are good. I'ma keep ya company 'til Miss Van can get to ya." Gina took a hard swig from the bottle she had brought with her, while Grady chugged the glass he was given.

When he tried to pull her to the bed, she thought it would be a good idea to break out her little black pouch.

"Hey, what ya say you and me have a bit of this

here? Get ya ready for Miss Van when she get here."
She thought about what she was told about passing
her coke out—but in this case, she didn't think Savannah would mind.

"What's in that bag?" Grady asked trying to reach
for it and stealing a kiss at the same time.

"Ya gotta be good or I won't share what's in this
here bag." Gina said waving it in the air.

"Oh gal, I'ma be good, I'ma be reeaal good. You got
no idea how good." Grady said with a smile. "Sayy…
why don't we make it extra special and invite that
sweet thang Sarah over here to join us."

"Sarah? Now whatcha want wit' her? I'm right here
and I'm all you need. Ya know ol' man, I nevea did
catch yo name." Gina asked.

"Grady," he replied taking a swig from the bottle,
he took from the table while Gina readied the coke.

"Grady…, Oh my Lor…" Gina stopped speaking
and let out a nervous chuckle.

"I'm what, gal?" Right then Savannah walked in.

"Grady, I heard ya was here. Gina honey, you're
wanted in the parlor." Savannah led her to the door
and whispered to her to try to get Sarah out of the
house.

Savannah turned to Grady who was still standing
there naked as a jaybird. The two just stood there
eyeing each other. She was hoping he would do what
all the men came to do and leave.

"Grady, whatchu doin back here? I told you not to
ever come here again."

"I can come and go as I please woman, now who in
the hell gonna give me what I come fo'? I been stan-

din' here ass to the wind fo' to long now." All the run around he was getting was starting to annoy him.

"Well now...we all tied up this evenin', but I'm sho' I can find ya a gal. Just you wait right here."

"I'm done waitin'! There be only one gal I want, seein' how long I been waitin', bring her to me...now!"

"Grady..., now you know I cain't do that." Savannah was trying to think of a way out of the situation. "Now look Grady, she done had a rough go of it since you left her here. Thangs ain't been right and sides she ain't feelin' well tonight. Let me get ya one of my other girls on the house. You can have a choice of two of'em"

Grady moved in closer to her, his face was twisted and his eyes squinted. He grabbed Savannah by the arm, twisting it, pulling her to the ground. "Now ya listen to me bitch, get me what I want and it won't be no trouble tonight." He said in a low and slow whisper.

Not sure what to do next, Savannah stood to her feet and walked out.

Event 045.00

Sarah could hear people moving about outside her door. Still unable to scream out for help, she lay on the floor hoping someone would break the door down. The pain was getting worse by the minute she kept trying to yell out, but it was no use. The room turned a crimson red, "Waait...his time is near...Waait," she could see a figure standing above her. "The time has come. Tonight you claim what is rightfully yours." said the woman.

Sarah was unable to speak aloud, but she somehow knew the woman could hear her thoughts. "Sadie?"

"I have been with you, Sarah."

"Stop this pain. It hurts so badly." Sarah asked, still curled up on the floor in the fetal position.

"Nothing I can do about that, it will stop when the time comes."

"What's happening to me?" Sarah asked watching Sadie stand above her.

"Nothing more than what is rightfully yours."

"What are you talking about?" She replied, puzzled

by what Sadie said.

"The time has come, Sarah." Sadie placed her hand over Sarah's eyes.

Sarah was taken back to the day she was born.

"See child this life was never meant for you. You have always been one of us. We've always known you would continue where your birth mother failed, but you had to come to us. Anna, Grady and your mother. They failed the ways of the Acumen. Old lady Bea's death was no accident—it was your wish that sealed her fate and yours. The promise you made long ago was the promise we had hoped for and tonight, your time has come."

"I cain't get in. The doe must be jammed. she was really upset when I left and she had a strange look in her eyes." Gina said.

"Keep trin' she might be in trouble." Savannah said walking back to the room where Grady was.

"What that fool ass gal doin' in there now?" Lue stated as she was coming up the stairs with Toby.

"What chu bring him up here fo'? This ain't the time." Gina said wide eyed.

At that moment, the door creaked open. Everyone stopped what they were doing and waited. There was cold air coming from the room and the fading of a crimson light.

"Sarah?" Gina called, "You all right?"

Toby ran passed them to see what was going on. Opening the door slowly, sticking his head in and then blinking his eyes to get them to adjust to the dim lighting. He walked in slow, calling out to her. "Sarah, ya in here?" There was no answer. Gina and the rest walked in behind him.

"She ain't here." Gina said.

"You mean to tell me all this time we been lookin' fo' her ass and she ain't even here." Replied Lue.

"Where can she be?" asked Toby.

"I'll go tell Savannah." Gina offered. She was on her way out to inform Savannah of the news when she saw her coming from the room where Grady was.

"What the hell is going on out here?" She asked.

"We cain't find her. She ain't in her room."

"Whatchu talking 'bout? Where is she?" Savannah replied peeking into the room.

Lue caught a glimpse of Sarah walking towards the room where Grady was. She couldn't believe what she was seeing, trying to find words to let the others know, but all she could do was point.

Sarah had a sinister look on her face, with her head held down and eyes peering up at them through her long hair, she turned to the room and walked in without a word to anyone.

"Sarah nooo!" Savannah called out. The group ran to the door as it slammed in their faces. Pulling at the knob no one could get the door to open.

"Well, Well. I thought chu wasn't want'n to see ya ol' man. How ya been gal? This place sho' gotchu lookin' fine." Grady was under the covers watching Sarah and lickin' his lips.

"Hello, Pa...I hear ya lookin fo' me." Sarah said gazing through him. "I come to give ya what you're owed." Sarah removed her clothing and climbed into bed with her pa. She straddled his body and began to rub his chest. He watched her and played with her breasts.

"Ya sho' learned how to treat a man gal, this gone be good."

"Shut the fuck up I done heard enough from you. It's my turn now." Sarah said with a smile. She leaned down to give him a kiss on the lips, moving to his chest, down to his stomach and last, his manhood. She stopped peered up at him without saying a word. She waited for him to notice.

Grady lay on his back, his body eager with anticipation his manhood growing larger, he noticed Sarah had stopped.

"What the fuck gal get back to work!" He shouted, grabbing her head and pushing it into his body.

Looking back at him one more time, "You asked for it." Allowing all her anger and rage to come forth, Sarah bit down as hard as she could. Grady cried out in agony as he saw blood dripping from her mouth.

"What the fuck, you bitch!" He screamed. The pain seething up his body rendered him immobile. He noticed Sarah still had his appendage in her mouth, as she peered up at him—watching him—he was afraid to move because he thought she would bit it off.

Sarah sat up slowly allowing the blood to run free from her lips. Again, she cried out in pain from the stabbing in her stomach.

"Your time has come, Papa." She said and grabbing the limp appendage in her hand, she gripped it tightly and ripped it from his body.

She sat atop of him watching as he gazed down at his broken body. The pain was too intense for him to continue screaming. Blood oozed from the now empty space between his legs.

The room was growing cold and dark. Grady could see Sarah was no longer on top of him, but at the foot of the bed. She held out her hand and dropped Grady's appendage to the floor.

There was frantic banging at the door and voices crying out to get in.

"Sarah, let me in. What's goin' on in there? Sarah!" Savannah yelled. "Somebody go get the sheriff."

"What's the matter Grady, did I take away somethin' that belongs to you? You took away my life. Tonight I take away yours. I told you, you would pay and the time has come." Sarah raised her hands, let out a scream and held her head back. She could hear the ripping of flesh and the cracking of bones—she felt like her body was set ablaze as large black wings appeared ripping free from her flesh and spanning the length of the room. Blood stained tears ran from her eyes, as her screams pierced the ears of everyone in the house that wronged her and sent them to their knees.

The longer she screamed people's ears and eyes began to bleed. Heads expanded exploding onto others standing around them.

Savannah was silenced when she saw the head of her best friend explode in front of her.

"What the hell is happening?" Toby asked still trying to get in the door.

"I think it's Sarah." Savannah said in shock.

"Sarah? What the hell, how? Sarah...Sarah open the door!" Toby yelled. He then noticed smoke coming up from the staircase. He ran to see what was happening. "The house is on fire, the people can't get out. If I can get in the room we can get Sarah and jump out the window." When he turned to look at Gina, he noticed her standing in the corner with blood tears staining her face and she was holding her ears.

"Oh dear God, what have we done?" Savannah said falling to her knees.

Grady watched in horror—trying to climb from the bed—he was tossed back on and a table was shoved in front of the door to block the unwanted intruders. Wild wind whipped around the room throwing things in every direction.

As Sarah eyed Grady, she held her head to the side

saying, "You better hope the devil doesn't know your dead. See you in hell, Grady." Reaching out her hand, she grabbed him by the throat twisting—he was no longer able to scream. She then reached for his legs and with brute strength, she tore him in two—dropping each half at her side and wiping his blood from her face.

She watched as his lifeless, broken body lay at her feet. That's when the pain hit her again. She let out a yell so loud it broke out all the windows in the house. Allowing flames to engulf all those that were not already dead.

Outside Sarah could hear Toby calling to her. She let out another loud cry from the pain surging rampant in her gut. And then, on bended knees she gave birth to the child she had been shown in her vision. She reached down picking up the baby and looking into her raven colored eyes.

"The time has come. We have been waiting for you." She heard Sadie say. "Sarah, bring her home."

At that moment the door opened and Toby was the first to enter. He stood in bewilderment as he saw Sarah standing there with a red misty glow around her, a massive wingspan, a baby in her arms and Grady split in two beside her.

"Leave this town, Toby and never return." Sarah said in a loud, yet sultry voice as she held her screaming baby in her arms.

"Sarah," he called stunned by the images in front of him. Another look at the baby, then into the eyes of the creature standing in front of him he asked. "Sarah, is she mine?"

"Leave or you will perish with the others."

"The stories..., they were true.... Did you know?" He asked.

"I'm sorry." She replied.

Toby bewildered and weak feel to his knees. Unexpectedly, he felt someone pulling him across the floor—everything around him was blurry—he could hear the sounds of burning and cracking wood from the flames. He could hear the faint sounds of people yelling out in pain and he could feel the light touches of people reaching for him as he passed them by.

It was another scene from the movie that played out in his mind as his father told him the story of Sarah and her family. Only this time he was a part of it.

Once outside able to focus and catch his breath—he saw it was Savannah who had rescued him from the flames and laid him next to Gina.

Looking back up at the house, he saw Sarah and Charlie standing in the blazing flames watching them through one of the windows.

"I toldcha no good could come from her." He heard Charlie say.

Holding her underling tight to her bosom, she spread her enormous wings and after whispering a silent good-bye to Toby,

Sarah...Rose.